IMPOSTURE

Hunters become the hunted in this gripping murder mystery

RAY CLARK

Published by The Book Folks

London, 2021

ISBN 978-1-913516-94-9

www.thebookfolks.com

"Virtue owns a more eternal foe than force or fraud: old custom, legal crime, and bloody faith the foulest birth of time."

Percy Bysshe Shelley

Part One

Chapter One

Sunday 30th November (01:15 a.m.)

Detective Sergeant Sean Reilly brought the pool car to a halt on Main Street in Burley in Wharfedale, parking in front of the patrol car that some PC had left across the width of the road, as if he'd been drunk.

Jumping out, Detective Inspector Stewart Gardener caught sight of the street lamp and the iron railings at the edge of the kerb, both bent over at precarious angles. A large section of grass had been ripped up into clumps, leaving evidence in the form of tread pattern. In the distance, he noticed branches and bricks and, possibly car parts, strewn across the road, not to mention damage to a brick wall.

Both men flashed their warrant cards and introduced themselves.

The young officer tipped his helmet. "PC Roberts, sir, Ilkley." He was early twenties and carried more weight than he ought to have, sporting a double chin and puffy eyes.

"What do we know?" Gardener asked Roberts, glancing at an old gentleman standing next to the constable.

"This is Edward," said Roberts, "Edward Makepeace. He lives in the village. He was out for a late-night walk when he spotted the damage, and the body."

Gardener nodded. The man was small and waif-like: timid, slim, and no more than five feet tall. He wore a thick black quilted jacket over a grey pinstriped suit with a white shirt, black tie and a black bowler hat. "How are you?" asked Gardener, tipping his hat.

"Oh, well," said Makepeace, tipping his hat. "You know what it's like when you get to my age."

Gardener didn't but felt sure he would one day. "Would you like to tell us what you found, please, Mr Makepeace?"

He repeated the story the PC had mentioned, but in more detail. On leaving the village everything had been fine. When he returned from his walk he saw what the officers could see now.

"This is how you found her, Edward?" asked Reilly.

"Yes, sir."

"You haven't touched anything?"

"No. I got a little closer and asked if she was okay, but even with my poor eyesight I could see that she wasn't."

"When did you make the call, Mr Makepeace?" asked Gardener.

Edward glanced at his watch. "About an hour ago."

Gardener made a quick calculation. Edward left home at around a quarter to midnight. Perhaps he hadn't walked far so all the carnage in front of them probably happened before twelve fifteen, leaving a thirty-minute window. A lot had been crammed in during that half hour.

"Do you recognise her?"

"I've seen her and her husband about the village, but I'm afraid I don't know their names."

"Have you managed to ascertain who she is?" Gardener asked Roberts.

"No, sir," he replied. "I haven't been here much longer than you. I checked to see if she was alive, found she wasn't, called it in myself, and then started to question Edward."

Gardener knelt down beside the body of a woman, late forties to early fifties, adequately dressed for the time of year. She had long blonde hair in a fashionable bob, with a slim figure, well-manicured nails and a smooth complexion. In life, he felt she would have been quite pretty.

The SIO still checked for a pulse but found none. She was cold to the touch. Her left arm was trapped underneath her body, but the right extended outwards, clutching a mobile phone. A dark blue handbag lay a few feet away.

Reilly joined Gardener, kneeling down alongside the body.

"I wonder what this is all about, Sean?"

Reilly peered down the street to the damaged wall, before staring at the ruined railings behind them. "If she's been hit by a car down there, she's a long way from the scene of the accident."

Gardener followed the direction of his partner's eyes. "It seems unlikely she was hit over there" – he pointed, then glanced back at Reilly – "and landed over here."

"No," said Reilly, "and judging by her face, and the state of the body, both of which look untouched, I don't think she's been dragged over here by the vehicle."

"So what *has* happened to her?" asked Gardener, standing up. He then turned to the old gent. "Can I ask why you were out so late, Mr Makepeace?"

"I'm afraid I can't sleep; quite common when you get to my age," replied Edward. "My wife died recently and I find it impossible to settle. I miss her terribly. Going for a walk helps clear my mind."

Gardener nodded, accepting his explanation. He knew what Edward was going through. He asked Roberts to take a full statement.

He turned to his partner. "I think we need to go over there and see if that scene tells us anything."

Chapter Two

Gardener noticed branches strewn across the road. Mixed in with those were pieces of plastic in various colours, and rubble and bricks from the wall of the nearest cottage, one section of which had virtually been demolished.

Reilly had a torch with him despite visibility being good, and a nearby street light allowing them a clear view.

Gardener studied the road and the deep, black tyre marks.

"What do you think?" he asked his partner.

"Something big judging by the width of the tyres and the mess that wall is in."

Gardener glanced above his head; a number of broken branches hung loosely, which could drop at any minute.

Reilly shone his torch on a section of the wall that still remained intact. Deep gouges and scratches – if that's what you could call them – decorated the surface.

"Conditions are good," said Gardener. "Why would a vehicle suddenly go out of control here?"

"Could be any number of reasons, boss. Drunk driving comes to mind first."

"An argument, maybe? One of them grabs the wheel… they lose control," offered Gardener.

"Not sure I buy that one. I'd wager someone was over the limit here. This accident probably sobered him or her up which is why they've done a runner."

"Unless the driver took a call on the mobile."

"Texting, more like," said Reilly.

Gardener peered at the wall. It was Yorkshire stone, five bricks high but at the moment, a large middle section around fifteen feet long was missing, and only two bricks high. "I'd say the vehicle was not only big but must have been going at some speed. Look at the damage: bricks everywhere, broken branches."

Reilly shone his torch into the garden behind the wall, glancing at more mess. "Especially for the bricks to have travelled that far. Which might rule out texting."

The sergeant moved the torch to his right, giving him a wider view of the area, before shining it further down Main Street.

Realising there was little either of them could do, they scurried back to the body.

Staring down, Reilly said, "Let's assume she wasn't hit by the vehicle, she's still dead, so how did that happen?"

"Good question, Sean," replied Gardener. "More than anything we need identification."

Reilly approached the handbag, slipped on a pair of latex gloves, picked up the bag, and glanced inside. He withdrew a purse, opened it and removed a credit card. "Ann Marie Hunter."

He placed the handbag back on the ground and approached the body, examining her neck and head very carefully, stopping rather quickly.

"She's got a hell of a lump on the back of her head. She's bumped into something she shouldn't have done."

"Someone, you mean."

Reilly nodded. "There's a lot more to this than meets the eye. She hasn't been hit by a vehicle."

"Maybe she was a witness to an accident," suggested Gardener, "and someone's tried to silence her."

Reilly stood up, glancing around. His eyes suddenly stopped and focused on something behind Gardener.

"You might just be right."

Chapter Three

Reilly shone the torch toward a green enamel electric box about twelve feet away from his partner, across a grass verge, located next to a fence leading into a field. The beam picked up a pair of feet.

Gardener scurried toward the box. The only noise he registered in the dead of night was the buzzing of the damaged street light, which created an eerie atmosphere.

At that point, a car on Ilkley Road approached the roundabout and Gardener could quite clearly see from the signal that the driver wanted to enter the village via Main Street.

"Can you stop him? Send him back the other way," Gardener asked PC Roberts, who quickly ran off.

The second body that no one had noticed was mostly in the shadow behind the electric box, as if someone wanted it hidden. Either that or they were drunk and had passed out, which he seriously doubted.

As Reilly shone the torch, Gardener noticed a pair of legs, dressed in trousers that almost certainly belonged to a suit. Peering further in, he caught sight of a sensible pair of walking boots, both of which were soiled with mud and grass stains to name but two. He wore a thick camel hair coat and his clothes spoke of money so it was very unlikely he was intoxicated, or here of his own accord.

Had they found what Ann Marie Hunter had been a witness to?

The gap between the electric box and the fence was narrow. Gardener took the torch from Reilly, leaned in closer, casting the beam further. One arm was by the victim's side, the other draped across his stomach. The left hand had a wedding ring and bore scratches but from what, Gardener had no idea. A hat covered the man's face.

Gardener pointed the torch at the man's chest. He could see no movement, indicating he wasn't breathing.

"Hello," said Gardener, feeling stupid. "Are you okay?"

No response.

Gardener pulled a pair of latex gloves from his pocket, slipped his hands into them and carefully removed the hat. He detected no breathing and asked if Reilly might have a small mirror in the car. He then checked for a pulse but found none. The sergeant returned within minutes, clutching the remains of a broken wing mirror, which he mentioned was from the boot of their own vehicle. He held it over the mouth of the male victim – to no avail. He was definitely deceased.

Gardener stood up and glanced at his partner. He removed his own hat and scratched his head. "I can't make any sense of this."

"Without CCTV we're not likely to." Reilly glanced around. "And there doesn't seem to be much of that."

"I have a really bad feeling about it all," continued Gardener. "We have a heavy car travelling at some speed, that smashes into a brick wall back there. It appears to have bounced off the wall and still continued at high speed before finishing up here. Look at the clumps of overturned soil and the damage to the railings and the street lamp. Why did it stop here?" He glanced quickly at both bodies. "It doesn't look like either of these have actually *been* hit."

"I don't think we can rule him out as not being hit yet, boss," said Reilly, staring at the body behind the electric box. "I've seen some strange things over the years. I once saw a bloke hit by a car and he flew into the air, landed some distance away, but when the ambulance got to him there wasn't a scratch – he hadn't even lost a drop of blood. Happens that way sometimes."

Gardener knelt back down and rummaged through the suit pockets of the male victim retrieving a leather wallet. Pulling out a credit card, he read it, rolled his eyes, and then passed it to Reilly.

"David Hunter. The plot thickens."

Gardener grabbed his mobile and punched in a series of numbers. "Time to call this in, Sean. We need everyone here."

Chapter Four

The scene in the village switched in an instant, in the shape of four police cars, four vans and two trucks. Gardener left Reilly with PC Roberts and Edward Makepeace, while he met with Scenes of Crime Officers and issued some tasks; he wanted an inner and outer cordon put into place immediately, with marquees constructed. Burley was sealed off in record time, resembling something out of *The Quatermass Experiment*.

Gardener raised his head, took it all in. A quiet country village locked down, the scene of mysterious murders. Floating between here and the roundabout to the main A65 were a number of SOCOs, all in white paper suits. There were cars all over the place with flashing blue lights, headlights still burning; resembling an abandoned film set.

A bunch of spectators had finally gathered at either end of the crime scene tape, as they always did. Where had they been when he'd needed them? And where the hell had they come from? The amount of people that had gathered due to noise from the scene and the bright lights was now around twenty, and growing. What was the betting that no one had seen or heard anything?

Reilly had checked the statement Roberts had taken from Edward Makepeace and then asked the young PC to take the old man home. Gardener dragged his team to one side at the edge of the inner cordon: Colin Sharp, Paul Benson, Patrick Edwards and Dave Rawson were huddled together. He was also pleased to see the two newer recruits in the shape of Julie Longstaff and Sarah Gates.

Reilly explained what they had so far pieced together.

"Have you *any* idea what happened?" asked Colin Sharp. "Did Mr Makepeace actually see anything?"

"No," replied Gardener. He explained what Edward was doing out and how he had discovered the scene.

"So we don't know if anyone was actually *hit* by the car?" asked Sarah Gates.

"No," replied Reilly. "It doesn't look that way, but looks can be deceiving."

"For what it's worth," said Gardener, "we certainly don't think Ann Marie Hunter was hit by anything other than a large blunt object."

"She has a hell of a lump on the back of her head," added Reilly.

As his sergeant made that comment, Gardener saw the Home Office pathologist, George Fitzgerald, pull up. After he'd exited the car, the SIO spent a few minutes bringing him up to speed before rejoining his team.

"This will be really awkward; an RTC without witnesses always is. I've called the Collision Investigation Unit. They are the experts in fatal RTCs so we'll let them do their job, and hopefully they can help and point us in the right direction.

"From what they're saying, they're going to run a 360-degree camera over the entire scene. That should produce a 3D computer image of the whole area. Then we can 'float' through on the computer. Fingers crossed we'll find something to go on."

Gardener stared around the village, peering at the nearest houses. "If there's a question of whether or not someone could see something from their location, the lab will be able to print the whole scene with a 3D printer. But, as you know, without a car and witnesses – we'll be struggling."

"Is there any blood at the scene, that would help?" asked Sharp.

"I agree, Colin," replied Gardener. "Blood on the scene would be a great starter for ten with footmarks left. A blood pattern analysis expert might tell us the point of impact, possible speed of the vehicle, and where the body landed, etc. It would help to know if either of the two bodies has been moved. But so far, we haven't seen anything."

"But to be fair," added Reilly, "it is dark and we haven't had the time to comb the area."

Gardener agreed, and then said, "Hopefully, there will be something; fibres caught on twigs, or the wall, footprints on grass verges."

"Fitz should be able to help with the bodies," said Rawson. "A post-mortem will tell us a bit more."

Julie Longstaff glanced around. "Is there any CCTV in the village?"

"Not that we know of," said Reilly, "but while you were on your way we took the trouble to find out that there are a couple close to the area."

"Once we get that information we can pull the CCTV from every building in a set radius," said Gardener. "The parameters will have to be set by the density of the population. Burley is a remote village, so we'll have to go large, maybe a mile or so."

"And there's always ANPR cameras," said Benson. "They're almost everywhere now; installed in police cars, both marked and unmarked, so every time a car drives past one of us we get the number plate recorded with a photo of the occupants."

Gardener nodded. "Which would be great if we actually had a number plate. Nevertheless, I'll be tasking an action team to go through all ANPR cameras both before and after – especially after – looking for accident damage, and any vehicle that has a report attached to it: reported stolen, no keeper details known, involved in crime, etc. We'll be looking at cars registered from outside the area and after that, any other cars."

Gardener knew it had to be treated as a full-on murder crime scene. With more officers, a path, action teams, CCTV recovery teams, house-to-house teams, and search teams. He knew it would be expensive.

"What do you want us to do, boss?" asked Rawson.

"Split into teams of two and start questioning everyone. I know it's early and no one appreciates the job we have to do but an immediate house-to-house is vital, in case there are people visiting who don't live here. Two of you have a look at the point of impact with the wall – a paint sample would be great. Then we can contact car manufacturers. With a bit of luck we'll find something that might make this mountain worth climbing."

Chapter Five

The incident room had been set up late the previous day but it was Tuesday morning before the team were given the chance to convene to share information. Little had filtered in on the Monday as everyone had been out collecting it, including the SOCOs, the fingertip search team and the CIU – though Gardener realised it could be a short while before *they* came up with anything.

Gardener stood in front of three whiteboards. Reilly sat on a desk to his left. The rest of the team were dotted around with drinks and notebooks at the ready.

"Okay," said Gardener, "we know who the victims are but have any of you managed to find out anything about their lives: do they have family? Where do they live and work?"

Dave Rawson took the lead. "The neighbours speak pretty well of the Hunters; I say neighbours but the house they lived in is detached and set back from the main road."

"Yes," added Colin Sharp. "It's called Highway Cottage but they don't strictly have any neighbours, although their garden joins up with another. A Mrs Sheila Poskitt lives in the bungalow there. She reckoned they were friendly but quiet, a couple who kept to themselves. They were always there if you needed them but very rarely interfered with you."

"Sounds like the perfect couple," said Reilly, "but someone wanted them dead."

"What was the house like?" Gardener asked.

"Large," said Rawson, "with a double garage but only one car inside."

"Any idea what they did for a living?"

Sarah Gates jumped in. "One or two people indicated that David Hunter worked for a bank in Leeds."

"Does anyone know which one?"

"No," said Longstaff, "but judging by the place they lived in it didn't look like they had any money problems."

"Okay," said Gardener, "in that case, can you ladies have a look around the house, see if you can find any personal documents that will give us a lead? I'd particularly like any computers that you find, and also a phone for David Hunter."

The girls nodded.

"We had a phone for Ann Marie, didn't we?" asked Paul Benson. "Did that reveal anything?"

"No," said Gardener. "All we found were a number of texts from what we take to be friends. So perhaps you and Patrick can go through it and identify everyone who has called or sent a text, and follow up on anything that's amiss?"

Patrick Edwards nodded, taking notes.

Gardener took a sip of water. "The big question here is, does anyone have anything on the collision, or possible accident?"

"We've drawn a blank on that, sir," said Julie Longstaff. Gardener had transferred Longstaff from the station in Bramfield because she had a very valuable knowledge of computers. She was around six feet in height with shoulder length blonde hair and brown eyes. At twenty-five, Longstaff was single, dedicated and would, in his opinion, work well with Sarah Gates; both were an asset to the team as Bob Anderson and Frank Thornton were both on compassionate leave.

"We picked up something," said Colin Sharp, meaning he and Dave Rawson.

Rawson took over. "We found a couple who came out of The Malt public house sometime around eleven thirty. They reckoned they saw a stationary vehicle nestled between two overhanging elms in the park, off the Main Street. It was opposite a row of two-storey cottages, in the vicinity of the church of St. Mary's."

"Interesting," said Gardener.

"Don't suppose they got the number plate?" Reilly asked.

"No," replied Sharp. "They didn't really hang around, and they live in the opposite direction."

"But they mentioned that the engine was running and four people were inside," said Rawson. "They saw that as they left the pub and drew a little closer to the vehicle."

"Four people?" questioned Reilly.

"Yes," said Sharp, "with the engine running."

"Which suggests they were waiting there for a reason," said Gardener.

"Did you get any more info?" Reilly asked.

"It was a 4x4," said Sharp, "but they couldn't say what make. Neither husband nor wife have ever owned a car in their life so they have no idea about cars."

"And it was white," added Rawson.

"That's a start," said Gardener. "Given that there was quite a large pile of debris on the road, do we have a paint sample?"

"Yes," said Edwards. "The fingertip search also gave us the remains of one or two more parts to go with it; broken bits of plastic. No idea what they are but a couple of them have numbers on."

Gardener thought about that for a moment. It was something. "In that case, send off what you can for forensic analysis. That should give us the manufacturer, and with a bit of luck the make and model. From there, we can start to look at how common the vehicle is, how old.

"If we get all of that information we can have you looking at dealerships and probably auctions. Let's see who bought one. You can also search the DVLA database for the make, model and colour and see if we can then narrow it down to postcodes."

"The main focus might well be on scrapyards," said Reilly. "Backstreet garages. Depending on how bad the damage is, are they going to get rid of it or try to repair it?"

"You might ask the paint manufacturer – if you find them – about individual sales. That should keep the two of you busy for a while."

Gardener glanced at the file in front of him, opened it and leafed his way through the contents. "Fitz has managed to carry out post-mortems in record time on both David and Ann Marie Hunter. Depending on how you look at it, there isn't much good news."

"Why?" asked Sharp. "What does he say?"

"That Ann Marie died as a result of a blow to the head, which was serious enough to cause a brain haemorrhage."

"Was she hit by the car?" asked Sarah Gates.

"Not according to the report."

"So who hit her and what with?" asked Longstaff. "We never noticed any weapons at the scene."

"We don't know at the moment," said Reilly. "Whatever it was, they'll have taken it with them."

"Best guess on what happened," said Gardener, "is that there may have been an altercation between her husband and the people in the car, to which she was a witness, and she was silenced. The chances are, her husband was hit, and perhaps she saw it, or heard it, and tackled those responsible when they were trying to hide him. When we found her she was clutching her phone."

"Major mistake by whoever hit her," said Sharp, "leaving the phone."

"Could be any number of reasons for that," said Reilly. "Maybe she didn't die instantly; maybe whoever hit her cleared off pretty sharpish and she tried to phone for help afterwards."

"Or she was trying to reach her husband," added Gardener, glancing at the report again, "whose injuries *were* consistent with being hit by a vehicle. Most of his bones were broken, organs ruptured, and he had a lot of internal bleeding."

"But there wasn't a mark on him from what we saw," added Sharp.

"No," said Gardener, "but somebody wanted him dead, and did a good enough number to make sure that was the case. What we need to know is who, and why?"

Chapter Six

As Gardener and the team filed out of the room, he was approached by a desk sergeant whose name he wasn't sure of, but he knew she manned the desk well and did a great job of seeing messages were delivered to the right people.

"Mr Gardener, Mr Reilly? There's someone here to see you." Gardener was saved any embarrassment as he glanced at her name badge – Brenda Long.

"His name is Roger Hunter, brother of David."

That pleased Gardener; a family member. As yet they'd had very little information on the Hunters so it was a welcome intervention.

"Can you give us five minutes, please, and then maybe show him up to the fourth floor? We'll meet him outside the lift."

It was in fact Reilly who met the man, guiding him into a suite normally reserved for high-level meetings. The room was long and angular with a panoramic window affording a view of the city; thick pile carpets, easy chairs and low tables spoke of ease and relaxation.

"Have a seat, Mr Hunter," said Gardener, staring at a short squat man with a solid frame; around five feet eight, with thinning ginger hair. He had large biceps, a muscular chest and strong hands, which suggested he worked out regularly. Brick Shithouse was the term that came to mind.

"Would you like a coffee?" asked Reilly.

"No, thank you," said Roger, "never drink it, but tea would be nice."

Reilly made the arrangements and whilst he was waiting, the man pulled out a packet of pistachio nuts from an inside pocket, which he dropped on the table after opening.

"I came as soon as I could but I neither live nor work around here."

Reilly returned with the drinks and took a seat.

"I'm pleased you did, Mr Hunter, you may be able to help us with our investigation."

"I was hoping you could help me. I'm at a loss as to what's happened. I've spoken to David's neighbour, Sheila Poskitt, and she said something about a car crash, but his car's in the garage without a scratch on it."

"There *was* an incident with a vehicle," replied Gardener, "but it wasn't his car. At the moment, we're still trying to work out what happened ourselves."

To help Roger Hunter understand, Gardener took him through what he so far knew, which wasn't a great deal.

"So you think *David* was hit by a vehicle, but not Ann Marie?"

"That's what the post-mortem suggested," replied Gardener, "but we have a lot more ground to cover. Aside from yourself, is there any other family?"

"Sorry, no, they were never blessed with children."

"Where did your brother and sister-in-law work?" Reilly asked Roger Hunter. "At the moment we only know from the neighbours that Roger worked for a bank, but we don't know which one."

"Trans Global on Merrion Street."

"What did he do?"

"Strangely enough I'm not really sure. Finance director comes to mind."

Gardener didn't bother asking what that entailed. Now that he had the name and address of the bank he would find out from the horse's mouth.

"When did you last see your brother?" Reilly asked.

"We're not very close-knit. We phone each other perhaps once a month but I think the last time I actually saw him was perhaps a year ago."

"What do you do, Roger?" asked Reilly.

Roger Hunter smiled, but it was pained. "Government work, very boring, but necessary."

"What does that mean?" asked Reilly.

"If I told you I'd have to kill you, Mr Reilly."

All three men laughed, especially Gardener, thinking how much easier said than done it would be with his partner.

"It was worth a try," said Reilly.

"One of the things we'd like to try and find out is why they were both out around midnight. Are you aware of any family problems?"

"None that I can think of but I'm sure that neither of them told me everything."

"Any financial problems?"

"It's highly unlikely, given David's position, and their status in life. He had a good pension, a good salary, and a number of sound investments. House was paid for, new car every three years."

"How long had he worked for the bank?" Gardener asked.

"Pretty much all his life, since the eighties."

"Obviously a trusted employee," said Reilly.

"You'd think so," said Roger Hunter, taking a mouthful of tea before reaching for the pistachio nuts. "People who can't be trusted don't get to work for a bank in the first place."

"Would you say they had a sound marriage?"

"It was certainly very good; not perfect, but then, whose is?"

Good point, thought Gardener. Though Roger was David's brother he probably wouldn't gain much ground with his line of questioning if they never saw much of each other, but he had picked up some useful information.

"I'm going out on a limb here, Mr Hunter," said Gardener, "but you wouldn't be aware of any enemies your brother might have had; perhaps someone who may want to do him some harm?"

Roger Hunter was taken aback by the question. "Do him any harm? I don't think so. I know he worked for a bank so I don't doubt he picked up one or two enemies, the current economic climate being what it is, but I don't think anyone would go so far as to kill him."

"You'd be surprised," added Reilly. "Where are you staying, Roger?"

"If it's okay with you two I thought I might stay at the house. Unless it's a crime scene."

"We don't think it is, but we'd like access to the house during the day today. We'd like to take their computer, and we would also like to see if David's phone is in the house. We can check through paperwork, and providing there is nothing to suggest the house itself is a crime scene, you can take possession."

Roger Hunter nodded. "It sounds like you have your work cut out so I won't bother you any further. But I do have one more question. Have you any idea when the bodies will be released, and when I might be able to bury my brother and his wife?"

Gardener figured that question would eventually come into play. "If you leave me your contact details I will do everything I can to make sure it's sooner rather than later."

Chapter Seven

Alan Braithwaite strolled past The Malt as the church bell chimed the first of its ten rings. A bitingly cold wind snaked its way through the centre of the village, forcing him to pull his overcoat tighter around his body.

Another ten minutes should see the first signs of frostbite, thought Braithwaite, unless his Jack Russell terrier, Spike, managed to do his business early and therefore call it a day.

He seriously doubted that. The dog was out every morning come rain or shine. The scheduled walk took them to the end of the village and the roundabout before Spike would even consider turning back; might make a difference if he had a lead but he didn't like putting the dog on one, preferring to allow it the freedom to roam.

Traffic in the village was quiet. He hadn't yet seen a vehicle, or another human being.

What he *had* seen were a number of police posters pinned to street lights and telegraph poles, appealing for witnesses to the hit and run: had anyone seen anything suspicious; cars they didn't recognise? That was a tough one. It was a village, there were people driving in and out all day that the residents had never seen.

Braithwaite walked around the left-hand bend leading out of the village, Spike happily trotting along in front of him, stopping every two or three feet to have a sniff at something – though his owner could never see what. The wall belonging to the Frost family was badly damaged where a vehicle had hit it – only now, two orange and white cones connected by police tape still cordoned off the path.

As the roundabout came into view, so too did the damaged railings; they were covered with flowers, and standing in front of them was a fellow neighbour, Wendy Higgins, with her brown Labrador, Pouch. Wendy was a widower, having lost her husband three years ago to a sudden heart attack. The man hadn't lingered. Here one minute, gone the next.

"Good morning, Alan," said Wendy as she spotted him.

Braithwaite noticed she'd lost weight recently and hoped she was okay but didn't like to mention it. Women can be funny about things like that.

"Morning."

The two dogs met up, touched noses and then roamed across the grass verge toward the fence and the field.

"Not the best morning to be out."

"I wouldn't be if it wasn't for him," replied Braithwaite.

Wendy Higgins laughed. "Slaves, that's all we are. We care more about them than ourselves." She huddled into her coat a little and stared at the electric box. "Bad business, that."

What could he do but nod in agreement?

"I wonder what happened to them? How long were they laying there unnoticed?" asked Wendy Higgins.

"I've no idea, love, but I'm sure the police will get to the bottom of it."

"I keep wondering what they were doing out at that time of night." Wendy's gaze was distant. "You're not safe anywhere these days. You don't think it was one of those terror groups, do you?"

"I shouldn't think so. Burley is a small village. They usually target people in big cities; there's more of them to hit."

"What a dreadful world we live in. My doors are at locked at six every night, Alan. I don't trust anyone anymore." She glanced over at the dogs, both quite happy stretched out on the grass. "Have they found the vehicle yet, do you know?"

"There's been nothing in the papers or on the news. Plenty of posters appealing for help. A good spell in the army wouldn't hurt them. Never did me any harm… if I could just get *my* hands on them."

"Terrible, terrible business, but you shouldn't work yourself up, Alan. I mean this in the nicest possible way but I suspect your army days are well behind you," said Wendy. "Anyway, I shan't keep you any longer. I've walked Pouch and I think we're both ready for a hot drink and a few biscuits."

Both of them glanced over at their dogs but only Pouch was sitting on the grass verge in front of the electric box.

Braithwaite turned his head in all directions but he saw nothing of Spike.

"You didn't see him wander off, did you?" he asked Wendy.

"I'm afraid not."

"Spike!"

Pouch stared at both of them but if Spike was around he wasn't letting on.

"He can't be far away," said Wendy. "I'll help you look for him."

"I couldn't ask you to do that, love, it's bitterly cold."

"We've been out half an hour already, a few more minutes isn't going to make much difference."

"Spike!"

Pouch lifted himself to his feet and wandered closer. Wendy Higgins placed his lead back onto his collar, as if something bad had happened to Spike and she didn't want Pouch going the same way, wherever that was.

Braithwaite stared beyond the electric box at the overgrown field. "He can only be in there, surely."

"You go and have a look and I'll try around here."

Braithwaite nodded. He scurried to the fence, standing on the first rung, gaining some height. Peering into the field wasn't helping. The grass was way overgrown and even if Spike *was* in there he wouldn't see him.

But then he heard a growl.

He turned back, shouting to his friend.

Wendy and Pouch came over.

"I think he's in there. I've just heard him growling."

"Is he okay?"

Braithwaite yelled a couple more times with no luck. On the third shout, the dog barked. He climbed the fence, dropped into the field, where the grass reached up to his waist.

"Careful, Alan, you don't know what's in there."

"I know Spike is."

"Yes, but we don't know what else."

Braithwaite decided to risk it on the basis that Spike didn't sound hurt. He continued to call the dog's name, hoping it would carry on barking.

Within minutes he found the terrier sitting in front of an expensive brown leather attaché case. The steel locks were tarnished and the grainy exterior was ravaged, indicating it had been in the field for some time; nothing a decent clean wouldn't put right.

Braithwaite bent down to retrieve the case, wondering where it had come from? He couldn't open it because the latches would require the correct numbers. Apart from that it had a set of tumblers that needed keys. If they were anywhere around here he wasn't going to look for *them*, he'd freeze to death.

"Come on, let's get out of here," he said to Spike.

He found Wendy Higgins waiting for him when he reached the edge of the field.

"Everything okay?" she asked.

"Seems to be. I've just found this."

She gave it the once over. "Where?"

"In the middle of that lot." He glanced at Spike. "He was guarding it."

"Looks expensive," said Wendy, "is it locked?"

"Yes. Must be something important because it has numbered codes *and* keys, but I couldn't find them."

A dark expression crossed Wendy's features. "You don't think it has anything to do with the hit and run, do you?"

Alan Braithwaite stared at her. "It crossed my mind."

Wendy Higgins had her phone out, dialling 999.

Chapter Eight

Two further days passed without any useful information coming to light, and nothing positive from the discovery of the attaché case. Gardener and Reilly were sitting in the incident room sorting through witness statements amounting to very little, when Patrick Edwards and Paul Benson found them.

"How's it going with the statements, sir?" asked Edwards.

"Slowly, Patrick," replied Gardener. "The only positive we have is that three separate witnesses have confirmed the presence of the 4x4 in the village within the time range."

"They all say the same thing," added Reilly. "It was white. The engine was running. Four people were inside – although one couple said the occupants appeared to be arguing with each other."

"No one remembers a registration," said Gardener. "How have you two got on?"

"We've actually managed to pick up the tyre tread pattern," said Edwards.

"Both from the scene of the collision," offered Paul Benson, "and the grass verge where the vehicle hit the railings. There was enough of a print for the tech guys to come up with something."

"That sounds positive," said Reilly.

"Not as much as you think," replied Edwards. "We know it's a 4x4. The search narrowed the tyres down to possibly an Overfinch."

"A what?"

"A Range Rover," replied Benson. "From that we've discovered that they were fitted to thirty-five million vehicles worldwide. Only three million were sold in this country but it's still like looking for a needle in a haystack."

Gardener sighed. "But at least it's something. Do we know the make of the tyres?"

"Yes," replied Benson. "It was a Goodyear Wrangler, but they also fitted Michelin and Bridgestone to some of the vehicles so that might help to narrow it down again."

"What about the paint scrapings?" Gardener asked.

"It helped, but there are still over five hundred thousand to comb through, with no idea where it was bought. We don't have a registration, or even a partial one."

"Good luck with that one," said Reilly.

"Are there any registered in this area?" asked Gardener.

"No," replied Benson. "Not white ones anyway."

As Edwards and Benson were discussing their find, Gates and Longstaff entered the room. Both were laughing and chattering. Each of them held a bottle of coke in one hand and a Mars bar in the other.

Reilly jumped up. "Now we're talking, girls."

Both deviated away from Reilly. "No you don't," said Gates, "these are all ours."

"So much for team players," muttered Reilly, making his way to the coffee machine.

"It's not all bad," said Longstaff, dropping a couple of chunky KitKats on the table in front of him, creating a smile as wide as the Liffey.

"I take it all back."

"Please tell me some good news," said Gardener.

"I wish we could," replied Gates, taking a seat.

Longstaff joined her and took a sip of coke. "We've just come from the bank."

Reilly sat down, placing bottled water in front of Gardener, with a coffee for himself. "Knowing what we know about banks and how secretive they like to be, I guess it didn't go well."

"Actually," said Gates, "it depends on how you look at it."

"Go on," said Gardener.

"Cyber crime is all over this one," said Longstaff.

"Cyber crime?"

Gates nodded. "They've been at it for a few days. It appears that there are some irregularities in bank procedure."

"Yes," said Longstaff. "Brian Jennings, the manager, isn't quite sure what's happened but it involved David Hunter. There wasn't a lot more they could – or would – tell us."

"I'd look at that as positive," said Paul Benson.

Gardener shook his head. "If cyber crime are involved there must be a whole side to this story that we know nothing about."

"Which means we're going to need your help, sir," said Longstaff. "We'll need you to contact them and see if you can get them to cooperate."

Chapter Nine

Four days after the attaché case had been discovered – seven following the hit and run – two cyber crime team officers from Bradford walked into Millgarth police station in Leeds and asked to speak to DI Gardener. They were shown into his office.

"Grab a seat," said Reilly.

The Bradford Two introduced themselves as DI Steve Winter and his partner, DS Shona Pearson. Winter was a thin, fresh-faced youth with a head of spikey black hair and wire-rimmed glasses. If he turned sideways on, Gardener would have trouble seeing him. Shona Pearson was a pretty woman, also slim, late twenties, with olive skin and almond eyes.

Gardener stood and, shaking hands with them, he introduced Reilly, who took an order for drinks and swiftly returned with them.

"I have to say," started Gardener, "that when one of my officers informed me that cyber crime were already involved in a murder case we were investigating, it more than piqued my curiosity."

"And ours," replied Winter, "but from what we've learned about the case, we figured it wouldn't be long before something serious happened."

"Would you mind telling us your involvement, Mr Gardener?" Shona Pearson asked.

Between them, he and Reilly explained the strange events of the hit and run. The Bradford Two listened without interruption and then came straight to the point.

"How much do you know about computers, sir?" Pearson asked Gardener.

"A little," he replied, "but I'm certainly no expert."

"Mr Reilly?" she inquired.

"Less than him."

"Do you know anything about Bitcoins, Mr Gardener?" asked Steve Winter.

"No," said Gardener. "I'm afraid you have the edge on me there. I've heard the term but I've managed to stay away from it."

Shona Pearson continued, "I'm not being disrespectful here when I say that we'll try to make it as simple as we can."

"It's a modern bank account," elaborated Winter. "A 'wallet' is basically the Bitcoin equivalent of a bank account. It allows you to receive Bitcoins, store them, and then send them to others.

"It's digital currency. There are two types. Virtual Currency; unregulated digital money, which is usually issued and controlled by its developers, used and accepted among the members of a specific virtual community.

"And then there's Cryptocurrency; a digital token that relies on cryptography for chaining together digital signatures of token transfers, peer-to-peer networking and decentralisation."

Reilly stared blankly at Winter. "Jesus Christ. You're not talking my language here, son. I have enough trouble with normal bank accounts."

Winter smiled, and continued, "Essentially, every hacker loves dealing in Bitcoins because they think they are completely untraceable. But that's not true. With every Bitcoin transaction, anyone with an ounce of skill can see the entire chain block.

"A Bitcoin wallet is similar to a numbered Swiss bank account in old money. We might not know who sits behind the account, but we know the account number.

"So, people with Bitcoin wallets will pay money in and out of their account for all sorts of things, some of them illegal – like buying ransomware on the dark net; some of them legitimate – like renting server space in Canada.

"What we have to do in cyber crime is something called cluster analysis. We look at what Bitcoin wallets are being used to feed scam money into, and then establish if any of the wallets have been used for legal purposes. If so, it's very likely they used some kind of traceable identification linked to the legal transaction. That way we find the black hat hackers."

The meeting grew very quiet with everyone glancing around the table, opening and closing files.

Finally, Gardener said, "Are you saying that you think David and Ann Marie Hunter were involved in something illegal?"

"That they were ripping the bank off?" added Reilly.

Shona Pearson leaned forward. "Actually, that's not what we think, sir. To be perfectly honest, *we* think it was the Hunters who were being blackmailed."

"Blackmailed?" questioned Reilly. "Any idea who, or why?"

"We're not sure, yet," replied Pearson. "This case is still in its infancy for us."

Winter continued. "The online crooks infected computers of the Trans Global Bank with a brand-new Trojan system nicknamed *Octopus*, giving them direct access to the company's network and online banking passwords–"

Gardener interrupted him. "What's Octopus?"

"Never mind that," added Reilly, "you might need to explain how a Trojan works, for me."

Winter nodded. "An attacker who has compromised an account holder's PC can control every aspect of what the victim sees or does not see, because that bad guy can then intercept, delete, modify or re-route all communications to and from the infected PC. If a bank's system of authenticating a transaction depends solely on the customer's PC being infection-free, then that system is trivially vulnerable to compromise in the face of today's more stealthy banking Trojans.

"I find it hard to believe that there are still banks using nothing more than passwords for online authentication on commercial accounts. Then again, some of the techniques being folded into today's banking Trojan's can defeat many of the most advanced client-side authentication mechanisms in use today.

"Banks often complain that commercial account takeover victims might have spotted thefts had the customer merely reconciled its accounts at day's end. But several new malware strains allow attackers to manipulate the balance displayed when the victim logs in to his or her account.

"Perhaps the most elegant fraud techniques being built into Trojans involve an approach known as 'session riding', where the fraudster in control of a victim's PC simply waits until the user logs in, and then silently hijacks that session to move money out of the account.

"With the Trans Global Bank, it was a new strain of malware that we dubbed Octopus. It's very active and appears to have tentacles wandering off all over the place, looking into everything. It hijacks customers' online banking sessions in real time using their session ID tokens. We've also discovered that Octopus keeps online banking sessions open after customers think they have 'logged off', enabling criminals to extract money and commit fraud unnoticed."

Reilly smiled and sipped his coffee. "I think I'll stick to standard practice from now on."

"That makes two of us," said Gardener, staring at his phone, wondering why youngsters today ran their entire lives on them.

"Anyway," said Winter, "a week later, the thieves made their move by sending a series of unauthorised wire transfers to money mules, individuals who were hired to help launder the funds and relay them to crooks overseas.

"The first three wires totalled more than £350,000. When David Hunter went to log in to his company's accounts fifteen minutes prior to the first fraudulent transfers going out, he found the account was locked. The site said the account was overdue for security updates.

"He asked Brian Jennings, the bank manager, for assistance, and was told he needed to deal with the bank's back office customer service. They were alerted but could not provide an answer for what was going on. They said they would look into it. Within seven days, the thieves sent out fifteen more wires totalling nearly £2.5 million. The bank was unable to reverse any of those fraudulent wires."

How crime had moved on from the standard wage heist of the olden days, thought Gardener. "I spoke to David Hunter's brother, Roger, recently. When we met, I asked if David and Ann Marie had any financial problems that he knew about."

"He said they didn't," added Reilly, "but this tells me there was obviously something amiss. Do these thieves have names?"

Winter reached into a briefcase and pulled out some more paperwork. "They do but when you hear them you'll probably laugh, like we did."

Shona Pearson took over. "These are what we've uncovered. We have a Jack Heaton, an Edna Hart."

"She sounds like your average librarian," said Gardener. "Conrad Morse."

Reilly laughed. "Christ, it gets worse."

"And finally, Alfie Price?" said Winter.

"These names can't be real," asked Reilly.

"Now you know why I said that," added Winter. "Totally bogus, but it's no less than we expected. What we did manage to uncover is that the scam appeared to have been engineered by an outfit called DPA, and at the moment that is literally all we know about them – apart from the four bogus names."

"I love Conrad Morse," said Reilly. "Where the hell did he find that one?"

Winter continued, "The first time anything happened, access was gained through head office in London. The bank's clientele comprises mainly of footballers but there were other sportsmen and women, as well as musicians, actors and TV personalities – all with lots of money.

"On that occasion, DPA were simply snooping, but they deliberately left a trail informing head office in London that something was going on, but *they* wouldn't be able to figure out what. No money had been taken but a pathway led to the branch in Leeds."

"These guys must be good," said Gardener, "if they're confident enough to leave a trail without concern of being found."

"Oh, they are," said Shona Pearson.

"Head office contacted Brian Jennings," said Winter. "Naturally, he knew nothing about it, and he *could* prove exactly where he was when it had happened. He was attending a lunch in the Queen's Hotel in the city centre. Despite being annoyed about it, head office realised they could do very little other than beef up security, but it was supposed to be the best, considering the money that they had paid.

"Three days later, DPA broke into the system again, this time at the Leeds branch. On that occasion they really disrupted things by moving around lots of money and contacting customers about possible losses. The bank discovered that £350,000 could not be accounted for. The login had come from head office.

"Brian Jennings called in David Hunter before consulting head office. Despite his obvious embarrassment, Hunter couldn't offer an explanation. The manager of head office, Bill Patterson, came under suspicion and had been suspended with full pay until the matter was resolved. Hunter had been told to be on his guard for anything else suspicious and, at the same time, maintain the utmost secrecy. He couldn't tell anyone."

Winter continued, "Two days prior to the death of the Hunters, DPA visited both mainframes on the same night using David's log in, and the infamous Octopus Trojan software. That's when the 'anything else suspicious' came into play. Three million pounds disappeared without trace. As far as Brian Jennings could ascertain, it had David Hunter's footprints all over it. What he simply couldn't understand was why.

"We've spoken to Jennings. Hunter had no answers, which caused him some serious concerns. He asked Jennings not to call the police immediately. Firstly, he was not guilty, and secondly, he said he wanted a chance to see if he could find out who *was* responsible. Against his better wishes, Jennings offered Hunter four hours to provide a solution. After that, head office and the police would be informed. All the money had been transferred into Bitcoin accounts."

"So what happened, then?" Gardener asked.

"We don't know."

"You don't know?" questioned Reilly.

"Other than the four names you have, do you know anything else about this company?" Gardener asked.

"No," replied Winter. "Whoever they are, they're absolute specialists. Other than what they wanted us to see, they have left no trace of themselves whatsoever. They floated in and out like cyber ghosts. I can't tell you who they are, where they started, or even where they are located. Nothing. Absolutely nothing."

Gardener shook his head, wondering what on earth *he* was supposed to do about it all.

Chapter Ten

"DPA?" repeated Dave Rawson. "What the hell does that stand for?"

"We don't actually know, yet," replied Gardener.

It was early evening and the team were in the incident room, following a long and demanding – not to mention, unproductive – day. After Gardener and Reilly had spoken to Winter and Pearson, the pair of them had driven to Burley in Wharfedale to speak to Roger Hunter.

David Hunter's brother was as amazed as anyone at the revelations of blackmail and cyber crime. They questioned him about any phone calls he'd had with his brother recently, and how he felt about the tone of the conversation. Roger said they were fine and he couldn't detect any problems David might have been having.

He went on to explain the only unusual snippet he could recall was talk of a foreign holiday, because they were homebirds who rarely travelled abroad, unlike Roger who seemed to be somewhere other than the UK most of the time.

He'd never heard of DPA, or the four names they had, nor could he think of anyone with a white 4x4 in the village; but then he didn't live there. As they were leaving, Gardener could see something was bothering him. When questioned, Hunter had said that for some reason he couldn't think of, the name Alfie Price rang a bell.

"Didn't cyber give you anything to go on?" asked Colin Sharp, sipping a coffee.

"Other than the four bogus names," said Reilly, "no. They mentioned a lot of technical shite about Trojans and Bitcoins and God knows what else."

"What about a website?" asked Julie Longstaff, smiling at Reilly's terminology.

"They don't appear to have one," said Gardener.

"Rubbish," said Longstaff, and then quickly apologised because the comment wasn't aimed at her superior officer. "Everyone – especially an outfit of their calibre – has a website these days. It'll just be very well hidden."

"If you're offering a service, what's the point in hiding it?" asked Rawson.

"Depends what the service is," said Longstaff.

"Maybe we should google it, Julie," said Sarah Gates.

"Good idea," said Gardener, figuring that if cyber couldn't find anything he doubted they would, but he knew they were both quite experienced in IT.

"And other than the four names, we have nothing else to go on?" asked Paul Benson.

"We don't even have four names," said Reilly. "At least not names we can check."

"We'll check them out anyway, sir," said Gates.

"I've just had a thought," said Rawson. "We probably have four false names, but it might not necessarily be four different people. Could be one."

"Good point, Dave," said Gardener, "but until we know more there's not a lot we can do. So there's another task, continue checking out those four names, see if they *do* lead us somewhere."

"This stuff about the Bitcoins," said Patrick Edwards, "did they give you any references, or account numbers?"

Now Gardener actually thought about it, neither Winter nor Pearson did mention anything. Whether or not they didn't know, he wasn't sure, but he would follow it up because they had mentioned something.

Reilly glanced at Gates and Longstaff. "Anything?"

"Not really," said Longstaff, glancing up from her phone. "All I can see at the moment is a load of stuff about data protection, and a company who make top end microphones, who are actually called DPA."

"Well that's probably a task for you two ladies tomorrow," said Gardener. "Stay here, in the IT room, and see if you can figure anything out. It's possible that a fresh set of eyes and minds on the job might uncover something."

Gates nodded but didn't actually take her eyes from the screen.

"Until then," continued Gardener, "we're going to need more people like Alan Braithwaite who might be lucky enough to stumble across a piece of evidence. That reminds me, we recovered David Hunter's computer and his mobile from the house but we haven't heard anything from IT. There must be something on those."

Gardener turned around and made notes on the whiteboards of the actions he had mentioned.

"Did anyone follow up with Edward Makepeace to see if he has remembered anything else about the night in question?"

Longstaff raised her hand. "We did but he had nothing new to add."

"It's not surprising," said Reilly. "We still don't have anything concrete from the witness statements either. Problem is, it was the wrong time of night – or morning – for people to be out."

"That's true, Sean," said Gardener, "but there's always someone who can't sleep. They get out of bed, head for the toilet and then stand for a few minutes staring out of the window. Surely there must be one witness to all of this carnage. It's not as if a 4x4 hitting a wall at some speed doesn't cause a noise."

"You'd think not, boss, but we've had appeals out in newspapers and on TV and still no one's come forward."

Gardener sighed. "Okay, for want of nothing better to do, let's try again. House-to-house calls just in case someone remembers something. And let's check every single house within a short radius of the crash site again for CCTV, although you'd have thought we'd have heard something by now if they have."

"What about the people who live at the house with the damaged wall?" Reilly asked. "Do we have a statement from them?"

"No," said Rawson. "Neighbour told us they're in the south of France. They have a holiday place there. It's warmer."

"Okay for some," said Reilly.

"But we've left word for them to contact us," said Sharp.

Another note on the whiteboard before Gardener turned to Benson and Edwards. "So, what about the car in question? Are you lads any further on in your quest?"

"We've compiled a list of all the dealers in the Yorkshire area: north, south, east and west," said Benson. "We've contacted about half of them and asked for a list of all white Overfinches sold in the last three years. Problem is, at the moment we don't even know how old this thing is. But once we have that list we can start contacting people and hope we strike it lucky."

"If that doesn't produce anything," said Gardener, "get on to the company and ask for a list of every white Overfinch sold in the UK in the last five years. In fact, do it anyway, let's cover all bases. I don't suppose we've had one reported stolen?"

"Not yet," replied Edwards.

"Nothing from the breakers, garages or repair shops?" asked Reilly.

"There's plenty of them in the area; we haven't managed to speak to anywhere near all of them, but so far, nothing," Edwards replied.

Benson added, "The Overfinch is a bit of a specialist vehicle so the breakers don't really see them."

"Have we managed to go through the traffic cameras within a ten-mile radius of Burley?" asked Gardener. "Just in case this thing was picked up on camera somewhere. A large white Overfinch with a smashed-up front end would stick out."

"We contacted traffic," said Benson, "and asked them if they would go through what they have. They said they'd get back to us if they find anything."

"I wouldn't hold your breath with that one," said Reilly. "You know what traffic are like."

"A law unto themselves," added Gardener. "Perhaps you should have a word with them, Sean."

"Christ!" said Rawson, "they'll never speak to us again if you let him loose."

"Once is all we need," replied Gardener, updating the board again, before turning and concluding the meeting. "Okay, plenty to keep us going. I know it looks hopeless but keep pressing on. Old-fashioned legwork will be the key to success with this one. I think we should also pay the bank another visit. I don't know when cyber last spoke to them but there may have been a development since."

He added that to the board. "Okay everyone, grab yourselves some sleep and let's start all over again in the morning."

Chapter Eleven

In his entire career, Gardener could not remember a case so lacking in information. Ten days in and still they had little or nothing to go on.

Another phone call from the Bradford Two, requesting Gardener and Reilly's assistance at the cyber unit changed all that.

An hour later they were sitting in a hi-tech office in the Bradford police station, manned by a CIU officer called Neil Farrah. He was bulky and slovenly, dressed casually in a pair of dark coloured chinos, white shirt and a black sports jacket – no tie. His hair was dark and wild and he had a week's worth of growth on his chin. Farrah's skin texture suggested he never saw daylight, which was backed up by the fact that the rumour mill at Bradford reckoned no one saw him arrive or leave, leaving them to assume he lived in the office.

"Do you know anything about 3D mapping?" Farrah asked Gardener.

"Not a lot," replied Gardener, taking a seat. "We've never had to use it."

Farrah asked them both to move their chairs so they could see the screen. Without even asking he brought them both a drink, one of which was bottled water for Gardener. Despite appearances, Gardener liked him.

"Clever stuff, this," said Farrah, taking his seat, with a hi-energy drink. "We stood a camera in the centre of the scene, letting it slowly rotate on the stand. It continuously takes photos of every inch of the scene but it doesn't do it in the style of a film.

"We then moved the tripod to all four corners of that scene and did the same again. The program mashes all the pictures together and builds up a full 3D image. It's accurate to within millimetres of objects and street furniture, such as phone boxes, etc."

"And electric boxes?" asked Reilly.

"Oh yes, we got that. Once it's completely mapped, you can then do a virtual walk through of the crime scene from your desk, adding or taking things away as you see fit to try different hypotheses on what actually happened."

"It all sounds very interesting, Mr Farrah," said Gardener.

"We're currently trialling a new system from a company called White Tile, which does a similar kind of thing but in real time using wearable tech in the form of glasses. The OIC can walk through a live scene, recording everything as they go, and virtually tag the evidence as they process the scene. It has a few bugs but may be the way we go in the future."

Farrah continued, tapping more keys. A 3D map of Burley in Wharfedale appeared on the monitor, with a four-wheel drive vehicle parked at one side of the road, which Gardener took to be the park. Farrah hit another button. As he set things in motion, he talked his way through it.

"They started their journey from the parkland area on Main Street, opposite the row of two-storey cottages. Any further back, they wouldn't have been able to see the intended target. Judging by all the information we've fed in, the vehicle was moving slowly to start with and then somewhere around here" – Farrah pointed to the map of Main Street on the screen – "it picked up speed. Serious speed.

"From the damage done to the wall we estimate possibly sixty mph. It came to a stop at the railings, but not before removing a speed sign in the process. We're obviously not sure what happened then but from what you've said we know a witness by the name of Edward Makepeace happened upon the scene."

Farrah glanced at Gardener. "How have you got on with him, has he been able to tell you anything more?"

"I'm afraid not," said Gardener. "All of this happened during his walk."

"Where did he walk to and from, did he tell you?"

"Around the village," said Reilly. "Came out of his house, left the village at one end, walked along the A65 and then came back in at the other end, and saw the mess."

"So if the damaged vehicle didn't pass him, it must have gone towards Leeds and not Skipton."

"If it did," Gardener replied, "we don't have anything to back that up on the traffic cameras."

"Yet," added Reilly.

"We rely heavily on witness statements and CCTV. There is very little CCTV in the village – or the area – and because of the time it happened, no witnesses. That end of the village doesn't have any houses."

"Must have caused a hell of a racket," said Reilly, "somebody must have *heard* it."

"We've spoken to everybody," continued Gardener. "One or two did hear a loud bang, but no one went to see what was going on. Most of them were dazed from being woken up, and when nothing else occurred they went back to sleep, thinking they'd dreamed it."

"If only they had," said Farrah. "We had a team filming the road using a digital pressure scanner. It actually managed to pick up the tyre tread pattern when the vehicle was only inching along, which we passed on to one of your lads."

Gardener remembered Patrick Edwards sharing that little nugget, which was quite useful. "I don't suppose you've identified the vehicle in the hit and run, have you?"

"Funny you should ask about the registration plate," said Farrah, tapping buttons all over the place at an incredible speed. "I think I can finally help you with that one."

That comment alone, if it was true, lifted Gardener's spirits. "How have you done that?"

"The 3D mapping discovered a CCTV camera, bloody well hidden from the naked eye."

"Where?"

"The people who live at the house with the damaged wall."

"How did we miss that?" Reilly asked, of no one in particular.

Gardener watched the scene unfold on the screen again, with the white 4x4 travelling at speed before crashing into the wall and then swerving away. He was still wondering what had caused the collision. The computer suddenly beeped a few times and zeroed in on an object placed on the trunk of a tree, hidden by branches.

"There it is," said Farrah.

Gardener and Reilly leaned in closer.

"If those people are still away, how the hell did you get into the CCTV?" asked Reilly.

"Do you really want to know?" asked Farrah.

"I don't think so," replied Gardener.

The computer switched images and then zoomed in on the white 4x4, and the rear registration plate as it sped away.

Chapter Twelve

As quickly as the information was digesting, Gardener's phone rang. He listened to a message before glancing at Reilly.

"That was Winter in cyber, he's found something interesting."

"I wouldn't have banked on this much good luck when I woke up this morning," said Reilly. "Let's head to his office."

"Thank you, Mr Farrah," said Gardener, "I really appreciate what you've done for us."

"Keep me posted," he said.

Gardener and Reilly left Farrah's office. On the way to his new destination, Gardener phoned Edwards and gave him the registration of the vehicle. Five minutes later and one floor down they were sitting with Winter and Pearson. Gardener denied the offer of a drink but Reilly's eyes widened when it was offered with mince pies.

Once seated, Winter went on to summarise what they had so far picked up. "We've been really busy in the last few days, digging into David Hunter's computer, his phone records and the information we found in the attaché case. We're pretty sure now that he *was* being blackmailed because of the evidence we've found to support it. He was clever enough to recognise what was going on. He'd managed to start a trace; made a note of the Bitcoin wallet the blackmail money was moving to."

That had answered one of Gardener's questions so he remained silent for the time being.

"Are you saying that you have real names for these people now?" asked Reilly.

Shona Pearson nodded and raised her eyes. "We think so. It's taken since we spoke to you last to get past all the firewalls and secret codes embedded in some of their programming. What we've come up with is, James Henshaw, Zoe Harrison, Michael Foreman, and Anthony Palmer."

"And why do you think they're real?" asked Gardener.

"We managed to unearth them through the cryptocurrency transactions," said Winter, "and David Hunter's computer – although that took some cracking."

"Stands to reason, he worked for a bank," said Reilly.

Winter nodded. "We continued to dig into the initials DPA. We're still not sure what it stands for, or whether or not they have a website yet, but what we did find – at least we believed we did – was that they operated from a business premises in Leeds called V-Tech."

"Leeds?" questioned Gardener.

"However," said Shona Pearson, "when we checked, it didn't exist. It was a bunch of derelict buildings on a waste piece of land at the end of a small side street. So they are still managing to cover their tracks – every step of the way."

"What about home addresses?" Gardener asked. "Were you able to get anything on those?"

Shona Pearson passed him a printout of all the information they had so far uncovered. Whether or not the addresses were real was another matter.

"Thank you for this, you must have been working around the clock." Gardener had to think quickly. "We obviously have two cases here, with two specialist teams. The cyber crime is certainly all yours and I suspect you still have a long way to go before you uncover all of that stuff.

"The hit and run, and the murders of David and Ann Marie Hunter are ours. To save us all running round, we need to put a SPOC in place: one from your team in my incident room, and one from ours in yours."

Winter nodded. "Would you like to do that, Shona?"

"Yes, I'm up for it, be interesting see how you guys work."

Glancing at the time it was midday. Gardener was on the phone immediately requesting a callout for every member of his team back in the incident room within the hour for a briefing and fresh tasks.

Chapter Thirteen

Another two days passed before the team assembled again to give Gardener the results of his previous actions, following Farrah's and Winter's revelations. Finally having a registration meant he wanted to know more about the vehicle: where had it been bought; what they actually knew about it and where was it now.

As far as people were concerned, he wanted everyone who lived near the DPA team questioned as to their whereabouts. Were the addresses real, or a dead end like the business premises? Were the cyber crime scammers at home, or had they too disappeared like the vehicle? Had they left the country? Airports needed checking. He wanted his team all over it because it was very late in the day to gather information from an old crime scene. Everyone knew the first twenty-four hours were the most important.

Although they had finally started to move, he still didn't feel like they were any further on. Once his team was assembled, Gardener told them that he and Reilly had visited the address of James Henshaw the previous afternoon.

"Don't tell me," said Rawson, "it was false, probably a care home or something."

"No, believe it or not," said Gardener. "But James wasn't home."

"Who was?" asked Rawson. "And where was *he*?"

"That's where it all gets complicated," said Reilly.

"Don't tell me," said Sharp, "he doesn't exist."

"Oh, he does," said Reilly.

Gardener took over. "We forced DCI Briggs to get us a warrant and we searched the house, took everything we could lay our hands on – which wasn't much: the family computer and Rosie's mobile. His wife, Rosie, said he was in Brussels on a business trip. We interrogated her, she wasn't very happy. Judging by what she said, she's as much in the dark about her husband's activities as anyone else. He's a very successful businessman going by their standard of living but she doesn't seem to know half and a quarter of what he's up to."

"And she certainly doesn't believe he was involved in any of this," added Reilly.

"Was he in Brussels?" Sharp asked.

"Not that we found. We checked the details she had: where he was staying, where he'd left from, and when. Nothing matched up. He is most definitely not at the hotel, and he was not on the flight he was supposed to be on."

"Bet that pleased her," said Rawson.

"She wasn't in the best of moods when we left," said Reilly.

"Have you any idea where he is?" asked Benson.

"No," said Reilly. "Here's another good one, the wife confirmed they had a Range Rover Overfinch that had been involved in an accident, which was being repaired in a garage in Skipton. We took the details, paid the garage a visit, they'd never seen it."

"Did she say anything about the accident, what she believed it to be?" asked Julie Longstaff.

"She only knows what her husband told her," said Gardener, "that someone hit him at a junction in Leeds, but she wasn't sure where."

"And you have no idea where the vehicle really is?" asked Gates.

"No."

"I wouldn't like to be in his shoes when he finally shows his face," said Sharp.

"Do you get the impression she's in on it?" asked Rawson.

"We don't think so," said Gardener. "Her reactions were pretty genuine."

"Especially when she found out he wasn't in Brussels," said Reilly.

"So if his car was smashed up and he went out to work every day, how did he get there?" asked Colin Sharp.

"According to Rosie he was out of the door pretty early every morning, almost always before anyone else in the house had risen. She said he was regularly picked up by the others, they took it in turns."

"So they all had cars," said Rawson. "Don't suppose she knows the models, does she, or a registration?"

Gardener shook his head. "Afraid not."

Rawson sighed. "Might have helped if she had."

"What about the registration of the Overfinch?" asked Longstaff.

"J1 AME," said Gardener, glancing at Patrick Edwards. "What have you found, Patrick?"

"It's registered to Hammer Studios in Buckinghamshire, sir."

"Hammer Studios?" repeated Reilly. "Didn't think they were still around."

"To a company or an individual?" Gardener asked.

"A Mr Lee, C. Lee."

"Mr C. Lee of Hammer Studios, out at Bray?" said Rawson. "That's inventive."

Gardener shook his head. He'd seen enough films – courtesy of his father – to know what that could possibly mean. Christopher Lee was one of the biggest stars of his day.

Edwards continued. "Me and Paul discussed the plate, trying to work it out – what it might stand for."

Benson took over. "J, A & E might stand for Jack, Alfie – or Anthony, as the case may be – and Edna."

"But we're not sure about the M," said Edwards, "unless it was Morse and not Conrad."

"Further digging revealed the car had its first service at a dealership in Slough. We contacted them. It didn't get us very far, other than verification but it was worth a call."

"Did you find out who paid the bill?" asked Gardener. "And how they paid? Was there any footage of the individual in the dealership?"

"We're just waiting for that, sir," said Benson. "They got a bit cagey and read us the spiel about data protection and all that."

"So we read them the riot act," said Edwards, "and we asked Mr Briggs to give them a call and send us what we needed."

"But we don't have it yet?" Gardener asked.

Benson shook his head. "No."

"Give them another call, keep on the case."

"We banged it on the ANPR but so far, no pings."

"We need to read traffic the riot act as well, see what they can find on the CCTV cameras," said Reilly, "but if we haven't seen anything on ANPR, maybe they removed the number plates after the accident. But even that should have stood out."

"What about James' home PC?" asked Sharp.

"We scoured it," said Longstaff. "Been at it all night, the only thing on it was family home movie footage."

"So there's obviously a business computer somewhere else," said Gates, "the important one that does all the damage."

"I know I wanted all the airports checking," said Gardener, "and I realise it was a tall order, and I doubt you'll have managed all that in two days, but do we have anything at all on James Henshaw?"

"If he left the country he didn't use his own name, or any of the others we know them by."

"What we need here are some good photos of them all so that we can go back to the airports," said Gardener, glancing at the whiteboard. "So far we only have one of James Henshaw courtesy of his wife. What about phones, internet, or bank accounts? Did his computer reveal any of that?"

"Nothing we can put to good use," said Gates.

"What about the other three?" Gardener asked.

"Michael Foreman lives in Skipton," said Rawson, "or did until he disappeared."

"He's disappeared as well?" Gardener asked.

"According to his neighbours he's not been seen for a while."

"When was the last time?"

"No one can remember. It doesn't seem the sort of a place where people mix. New apartment block, I don't think anyone really knows anyone else. Anyway, I've left a message for the caretaker to call us, see if he can shed any light on it."

"I think we'll find they've all disappeared, boss," said Reilly.

Sharp took over. "Edna Hart, real name Zoe Harrison, has a Wharfe apartment on the River Aire. It's pretty much the same type of place, very upmarket. I'd be surprised if anyone actually knew their neighbour. We did speak to the apartment either side, but they said they'd only spoken to her a couple of times and even then it was only pleasantries. No one knew what car she drove."

"And she's not home, either?"

"Nope. Neither is Alfie Price, real name Anthony Palmer, who lives in Burley."

"Burley?"

"That's the address we have," said Sharp.

Same village as where the Hunters lived, thought Gardener. Perhaps it might be worth running the name past Roger Hunter. "I know we'll need warrants to search the places but have you looked through windows, or letter boxes, to see if there is any sign of life?"

Rawson nodded. "Here's the big one. We did find the caretaker in Zoe Harrison's block. After some gentle persuasion he let us have a quick look round. The place appeared to have been cleared, of everything – incriminating or otherwise."

"It's empty?" asked Gardener.

"Apart from mail piling up on the mat, yes, almost as if she's moved," said Sharp. "The only problem is, we have no idea where. There aren't enough hours in the day at the moment."

Gardener nodded. He knew they were right, and he may now need further operational support officers to help with the legwork. What he'd really like was Anderson and Thornton back with him.

"I feel like we're back at square one," said Reilly. "Like we're in one of those bastard computer games where if you make a mistake you're transported back to level one so you have to start all over again."

Chapter Fourteen

"Anthony Palmer?" said Roger Hunter. "Yes, I know *of* him. Why has he sprung up?"

Gardener and Reilly had taken the opportunity to leave the office for a while. Their first stop in Burley was a three-bedroom detached bungalow in Manor Park, the home of Anthony Palmer. There was no answer, as expected. But his house wasn't totally empty from what they could see through the windows. The garage was closed and locked so he couldn't check on a car. Gardener wondered why his place had not been cleared.

After a scout around the building they dropped in on Roger Hunter to see if he knew the man who lived so close, and who appeared to be involved in the death of his brother.

Gardener explained to Roger Hunter what he had been told.

Roger Hunter stood up. "Please, let me make you a drink and I'll explain something that might help you considerably."

Roger returned with mugs of tea, placed them on a small table in a sparsely decorated living room and took his seat.

"I can't believe what's happening here. How does he come to be involved in the hit and run? He's family, for God's sake."

"Family?" repeated Reilly.

Gardener was suddenly reminded of the rule of thumb with a murder inquiry; any suspicious deaths and you always start with the family.

"My brother and his wife were Anthony's only real family. He was Ann Marie's nephew. Anthony's parents died when he was in his late teens. He has no brothers or sisters.

"Prior to their death, his parents were music hall entertainers. They travelled all over the UK with a variety of theatre companies. They died tragically when their car was in a collision with a coach on the M62 returning to Leeds from Liverpool."

"When was that?" asked Reilly.

"About fifteen years ago, I think, in December. Anthony was originally born in Leeds but until the time he was six, the family moved around: two years in Bristol, and another two in Milton Keynes before a stint in Liverpool. They moved back to Leeds and found a house in Wellington Hill when Anthony was nine."

"So you think he was late teens when his parents died. Can you remember how old?" asked Gardener.

"Possibly sixteen, maybe a little older."

"At that age, did he really need anyone to look after him?" asked Reilly.

"Because of all the moving around, his parents were the only people he had ever been close to. Anthony prefers his own company. Having said that, although he's a bit of a loner, he will adapt and fit in if needed. But the only people he relied on were his parents and after they had died, he had no one, until Ann Marie stepped in. This is what beats me. Why and how has he come to be mixed up in all this crap?"

"We will get an answer for you, Mr Hunter," said Gardener. "Trust me."

"Can you tell us anything more about him, Roger?" Reilly asked.

"I can but it's all second-hand. I only met him once or twice, so anything I tell you is what my brother told me."

"We'll settle for that for now," said Reilly, notebook at the ready.

"It was David who told me that Anthony is a real oddball," continued Roger. "Everything in his life has to be in order. He has a routine and does not like to deviate from it. He wakes up at the same time every day, eats at the same time, exercises and showers at the same time. Nothing is left to chance. He does not like chance.

"All holidays are planned to the last second: when he will go, what he is going to do whilst there, when he will return, and what he will do on his return. Anthony is not a people person. If the circumstances require it, he'll talk the hind leg off a donkey. But according to David – not Ann Marie – Anthony has a dark side to him."

"We can see that," said Gardener.

"He has little or no compassion," said Roger. "He will ruin anyone financially without turning a hair; an attitude that seemed to develop following the death of his parents. But I certainly wouldn't have thought he would bite the hand that feeds him."

"Something must have happened between them all," said Reilly.

"But what could be so bad that it would cause this?" asked Roger Hunter.

"You said just now, that he will ruin anyone financially without turning a hair," said Gardener, "do you have any evidence to back that up?"

"I don't have anything specific I can quote. All I can tell you is that he was very good with computers, but I suspect you know that already. In fact, David reckoned Anthony was better than anyone he had ever seen."

Gardener could see now why they were in the dark about the DPA's activities. If Anthony Palmer – not to mention the rest of them – were as good as they were claiming, Gardener's team would have a mountain to climb.

Roger sipped his tea before continuing, all the while with the expression of a haunted man, as if he should have seen what was coming, and the results of Anthony's actions were a legacy he would rather not face.

"Anthony's long-standing ambition had been to start up his own IT company. The death of his parents not only devastated him, it left him bloody penniless, because the money they had set up in a trust fund collapsed due to a loophole in the policy. That was probably his introduction to how life can let you down."

"Might even account for how he's turned and what's led him up this path," said Reilly.

"I imagine it had something to do with it," replied Roger, "but I'm sure there's more to it. Anyway, Anthony eventually attended college and studied IT. From there he went to university."

"Do you know which one?"

"No, probably here in Leeds, but I'm sure David or Ann Marie would be able to tell you."

Roger stopped suddenly, and then corrected himself: "Had they been here."

Gardener allowed Roger Hunter a moment's silence and was quite relieved when he took up the story again.

"I think Anthony knew enough about computers to realise their potential and the havoc he could wreak with them. I remember David telling me that he'd discovered Anthony had been developing and selling cures for viruses, which is why I said what I did about ruining people financially, because that's what computer viruses do, don't they?"

Gardener couldn't do anything but agree. At least he was learning more about one of the potential monsters responsible for the deaths of two people. He could only term him as a monster because it appears that he wantonly set out to destroy them. But he needed to know why, and at the moment he wasn't hearing anything to point him in the right direction. What had happened to cause such an act of violence?

Roger Hunter finished his tea. "I'm afraid I can't tell you any more than that, gentlemen. As I said, it's all second-hand. I only met him on a couple of occasions, family gatherings, so to speak. But even then I got the impression that he couldn't really be trusted – something in his eyes. I wish you the best of luck with him if he is your man. He's as slippery as an eel."

"We're beginning to realise that."

Roger Hunter sighed, his gaze distant. "I'd love to know what went on to cause such a rift. And why didn't my brother say something?"

"Don't beat yourself up about it, Roger," said Reilly. "All sorts of weird things happen within families, secrets buried for years."

Gardener rose to leave. "Thank you for your time, Mr Hunter, at least you've given us something positive to work with."

Chapter Fifteen

Two days later Gardener was more than pleased to hear from Winter, especially when he said they'd had a breakthrough, and Shona Pearson was on her way round. The second phone call he'd taken was from the caretaker of Michael Foreman's apartment block. Gardener asked if the man would check his apartment and when he returned to the phone, he confirmed it was totally empty, aside from mail.

Gardener had rallied his team to the incident room when Shona walked through the door with a Manila folder in her right hand.

Gardener offered her a drink. She accepted. Reilly brought it. She placed the folder on the table and took the coffee. "God, I need this," she said, taking a sip.

"Tough day?" Gardener asked.

"Tough night. In fact, they all roll into one now. Can't remember the last time I saw my home."

"We've pulled a few of them in our time," said Reilly, with most of the team nodding in agreement.

Gardener hoped it would all be worth it. "Your boss sounded excited."

Shona Pearson put the coffee cup on the table, grabbed the Manila folder and opened it up. She produced four A4 photographs, spreading them out in front of Gardener.

"Are these who I think?"

"We're pretty certain," replied Pearson. She pointed to each photo in turn and supplied a name. "Anthony Palmer, James Henshaw, Zoe Harrison and Michael Foreman."

Gardener thought they were all young, but then most people who specialised in IT were. It was what they had grown up with.

"How recent?"

"Not that recent, sometime around the university years."

"Which university did they go to?" Longstaff asked, as she and the other members of the team gathered around the table.

"Leeds."

"All of them?" asked Gardener.

"Yes, all of them. We managed to track down one of their tutors, which wasn't too hard; he's still there. His name is Dave Walsh."

"Did he remember them?" Reilly asked.

"Said he'd never forget them. Walsh spent a lot of time with them because they were brilliant. Perhaps the brightest students he'd ever taught."

"Christ," said Reilly, "that's all we need."

"According to Walsh," continued Pearson, "prior to their death, Anthony Palmer's parents had encouraged him to continue with his education once he'd left school. Eventually he realised they were right and respected their wishes. He enrolled himself into Leeds and settled into an IT degree.

"Here's where it gets interesting. Toward the end of the course, Palmer found himself competing for the top place with three other students, who had all started the same week; four students in total, with no idea the others existed when they started, and what effect they were all going to have on each other's life."

"I think I know where this is going," said Colin Sharp, chomping on a Scottish shortbread.

"You're probably right," said Pearson. "The tutors agreed that all four were exceptional. It would be hard to separate them when it came to the final exams. Palmer came second to a girl called Zoe Harrison."

"Who came third and fourth?" asked Gates.

"Not sure."

"Did they know each other at university?" Gardener asked.

"According to Walsh, and one or two of the other tutors, no, they didn't. I suspect they were aware of each other."

"You'd have to be," said Longstaff, "with marks like they had."

Shona Pearson nodded. "Although they were aware of each other, they didn't socialise. Apparently they moved in different circles."

"Well, something brought them all together," said Reilly.

Gardener pinned the photos onto the whiteboard. "So what we need to find out is, how and when did they all meet up outside of university?"

"And what set them on the road to breaking the law?" asked Colin Sharp.

"And whatever that something was," said Gates, "did it happen to all four of them as a team, or just one of them?"

"Good point," said Reilly. "Did one of them recruit the others after something had happened?"

Gardener shook his head. "I can't imagine David Hunter willingly having anything to do with this... event, or whatever it was. He didn't seem the type from what we've heard."

"But that's just it, boss," said Reilly, "we don't really know him, not yet. Maybe something did happen way back in the past, and either one or all of them has never forgiven him."

"We certainly need to find out," said Gardener. "There's no telling where this will end."

"We've also emailed the photos over to the station," said Pearson. "We thought maybe you could print off some copies for your own use."

"Thank you," said Gardener, his mind whirring.

Before he could actually issue any tasks, Shona Pearson produced more paper from the folder.

"What we also have here from David Hunter's phone is Anthony Palmer's mobile number."

"Have you tried it?"

"Yes, straight to voicemail," said Pearson. "From that we managed to get numbers for the other three."

An air of excitement prevailed.

"Don't suppose any of them answered?" asked Reilly.

"No, but they are still active numbers, because they all go to voicemail."

"I suspect you've already tried to trace them?" Gardener asked.

Shona Pearson smiled. "Yes, but they're not stupid. All of their phones are switched off most of the time. And when I say most, I mean probably twenty-three and a half hours a day."

"Meaning they only switch them on to collect messages and then switch them straight off again," said Gates.

"People as clever as these won't allow anyone to trace them through their phones," said Longstaff. "What about the mobile providers, can they give us anything?"

"Well that's the strange one," said Pearson, "we can't actually find out who they are at the moment. Everything seems to re-route all over the place. When we try to put a trace on we just get blocked."

"They must have a provider," offered Gardener.

"Unless they've figured out how to get all their calls for free," said Reilly.

Gardener nodded. "Probably have." He glanced at Gates and Longstaff. "Would you ladies like to have a go at that one?"

They agreed in unison.

"Okay," said Gardener, "we have no idea where this lot is; are they still here in the UK, or abroad somewhere? Let's have copies of the photos and the rest of you back at the airports with digital ID. Run everything they have through photo recognition, especially the new passport system in customs, and double-check everything through CCTV. One of them must have made a mistake somewhere. No one can be that good."

"Let's hope not, for our sakes," said Reilly.

Chapter Sixteen

Following a phone call from Roger Hunter, Gardener and Reilly were back at Highway Cottage in Burley. Despite the fact that he had been living in his brother's house for something close to three weeks, it didn't appear to *be* lived in at all. Gardener had the impression that Roger Hunter was merely a caretaker.

"How are you?" asked Gardener, sipping tea.

"I've been better."

"I'm sorry for what you've been put through. Losing family is never easy."

"You sound like you have previous experience."

"Like you wouldn't believe," replied Gardener.

"Do you have any other family, Roger?" asked Reilly.

"No. I'm a loner. Always have been. I've had one or two relationships but I could never commit to them. I operate better alone."

Gardener brought up the phone call that summoned them over.

Roger glanced at the coffee table between them. On the top were a couple of diaries. Underneath them was a large white envelope.

"I couldn't stop thinking about what you'd told me, about Anthony Palmer. I'm struggling to believe he would do that to my brother, and Ann Marie."

"You can't choose your family, Roger," said Reilly.

Roger grabbed a handful of pistachio nuts. After chewing he washed them down with some tea before picking up one of the diaries.

"David was always the secretive one of the two of us. When we were kids he used to hide things from me."

"What sort of things?" Gardener asked.

"Stupid stuff. Things that he'd think I'd want. I remember him hiding a bloody abacus in a bag, inside a case, under the wardrobe. God knows why, I didn't want it. I didn't know how to use it. But that was what he did. If there was something he wanted, or something he couldn't understand, he wouldn't ask anyone for help about it, he'd fester. He'd hide the bloody things away until he could come up with a solution."

"What have you found?" Gardener asked, sitting back in his chair.

"This," said Roger, holding a diary aloft.

"Where was it?" asked Reilly.

"In the bathroom cupboard behind a false panel. You wouldn't have known it was there unless you were a bit anal like me. If things don't look right, they're usually not. I noticed a slight slant on this panel so I moved it. Found these."

"What's in them?" asked Gardener, reaching out for the book.

"A couple of things." Roger opened the diary at a particular page and then passed it over to Gardener. Reilly moved closer.

"It seems that my brother had arranged to meet with Anthony Palmer. From what I can gather, David had told Anthony about the mess he had found himself in, despite the fact that none of it was his doing.

"He was convinced that he was being conned by a hacker who had used the fact that he was employed by a private bank with some extremely large accounts. They had used his identity to break in and shift money around – to their advantage.

"David basically knew nothing about how it had happened. He wanted Anthony's help to sort things out.

Little did he know that he was being conned by a member of his own family."

Gardener was skimming pages. Some of what Roger had said was there. A lot of other pages were gibberish, which Gardener guessed might have been something connected to the cryptocurrencies.

Roger picked up the other diary and leafed through till he found what he wanted. "This one also makes me wonder if, at the last minute, David had managed to find out who was behind the scam and was perhaps arranging to meet someone else in an effort to expose them."

"Do you not think he might have picked a better time and place, Roger?" asked Reilly.

"Possibly so," said Roger, "but judging by what has happened, it would appear that David played right into Anthony's hands. Somehow or other, and I don't know how because there's nothing in here, Anthony and his crew found out and decided to do something about it. I'm not saying they wanted to remove him altogether. Maybe what they had planned all went wrong. But what better time than midnight in a sleepy little village."

"There's a lot of ifs and buts there, Mr Hunter," said Gardener, "but you put forward a very good theory."

"I doubt anything would be impossible with this lot," said Reilly. "Looking at how good they are with computers, it would be easy for them to drop some spyware into your brother's computer and follow his every move."

"Stands to reason that they would know where he was going and when," said Roger.

"Trouble is," said Reilly, "we've been through his computer, we didn't find anything."

"Maybe this lot are clever enough to plant a program that self-destructs when it's done its business," answered Roger.

"Maybe so," said Gardener, "but it still doesn't answer what started all of this in the first place."

Roger picked up a third diary. "What you're looking for might be in here. When Anthony left university he had a series of menial jobs before jumping onto the IT ladder. He eventually approached David for a loan. Anthony was devastated – as were Ann Marie and David – when the bank refused him, despite his being able to show them potential figures, and a reasonably solid business plan put together by David. One excuse was the state of the economy; they were not up for putting money into small businesses. He should try a small bank, not the prestigious one that employed a member of his family."

"That must have gone down well," said Reilly, leafing through one of the diaries.

"According to all the notes I've found, Anthony never forgave them."

Gardener thought about it. "I can see why he would carry a grudge, but killing someone is a whole different ball game. That suggests it was more than a refusal of a loan."

"I'm inclined to agree," said Roger, "but that's where you come in. I'm just pleased I could share something with you."

"We appreciate that, Mr Hunter," said Gardener. "Can we take these, please?"

Roger Hunter nodded.

Gardener was about to stand up before asking, "Was there something else?" he asked, staring at the A4 envelope.

Roger glanced at it. His expression suddenly took on one of those light-bulb moments when something suddenly comes flooding back to you.

"Do I detect you discovered something else?" Gardener asked.

"You asked me about someone called Alfie Price recently. With everything that's happened, my brother, the hit and run, not being able to get any closure, it went completely out of my mind. I believe Alfie Price is Anthony Palmer."

"Go on," said Gardener, aware of the information, but the man obviously knew something he didn't.

Roger opened the envelope and took out some photographs. Gardener could see that they were old. As Roger flicked his way through them he stared at one in particular before passing it over to Gardener. The picture appeared to be a ventriloquist's dummy: the face porcelain, hard and shiny. Short black hair, big red lips, parted slightly with a twisted, lopsided grin. He wore a black suit with a white shirt and red tie. The most disturbing aspect however, were the eyes, as if somehow they were human, and had the ability to stare into your soul and read what you were thinking.

"That's pretty creepy," said Reilly, "what the hell is it?"

"It's the start of a really strange story," said Roger. "I remember something about this because Ann Marie told me when she found out. That, gentlemen, is Alfie Price."

Roger paused, then continued, "It's a clown doll, toy and ghost all rolled into one. It belonged to Anthony's parents, Jennifer and Richard Palmer. Apparently it was named after the two legends of the horror genre – Vincent Price and Alfred Hitchcock."

"That's interesting," said Gardener. He told Roger about the vehicle used in the hit and run being registered to Hammer Studios in the name of C. Lee.

"That's just the type of damaged mind you're dealing with here. Anyway, Richard came across the doll toy in a junk shop in Toxteth near Liverpool. Being entertainers and fans of creepy memorabilia, he bought it for £25.

"Shortly after taking Alfie home, they began experiencing bizarre occurrences. A number of times, Alfie suddenly vanished from where they left him, only to reappear in unexpected places. Richard once found the clown doll with both arms pointing straight at him. He later set up a tape recorder nearby. He captured a deep, raspy type of voice uttering the words 'You belong to me!' But the room was always empty."

"Christ," said Reilly.

"Richard researched the doll," said Roger Hunter. "He believed it to be possessed by the spirit of a child, but the identity of the ghost remained a mystery. Whether he found out more and never said, or he simply couldn't find anything, I don't know.

"But the strangest thing ever, was that once the authorities untangled the wreckage of their car, Alfie Price was found in the boot."

"Why was that so strange?" Gardener asked.

"Because the doll had disappeared eleven years previously – either that or it had been made to disappear, by Richard."

"Why would he do that?"

"Because Anthony actually suffers from coulrophobia: he is absolutely terrified of clowns – totally and utterly petrified."

"We can have these, as well, can we?" Gardener asked.

"Yes, of course. They're no use to me."

"Well thank you for your time and patience, Mr Hunter. All of this will be a great help to us."

"Then maybe you can help me, now, please?"

"Go on," said Gardener.

"Now we seem to have moved ahead, and you guys have a reason for all of this, can I please bury my brother and his wife? Life has to go on and I cannot stay here forever. I have to have some normality back."

Gardener nodded and tipped his hat. It was a reasonable request.

Chapter Seventeen

The time was shortly before midnight. The building, Millgarth police station in Leeds; the location, the incident room. Two men sat amidst a mountain of information, both on paper and on whiteboards. The atmosphere in the room was downbeat but the relationship between the two was, as always, rock solid.

Reilly sat down and placed a cup of tea in front of Gardener. A coffee and a Mars bar was his choice of pick-me-up.

Gardener stared at the whiteboards and shook his head. Three weeks had passed since the hit and run and whilst it would be fair to say that they had unearthed a number of clues as to what might have happened, and why – not to mention the identities of those involved – they were in fact no nearer to making an arrest than they had been on the night itself.

The team had retired for the day, having offered reports and information, most of which led to nothing, leaving the two at the top to try and salvage a plan of action as to where to go next.

"I thought we might have had something from the airports," sighed Gardener, unable to believe that even the smallest piece of evidence didn't appear to exist.

"It's not surprising," said Reilly, sipping his coffee. "We know how clever these people are. They obviously have more false IDs than we know about, so popping in and out of the country should be quite easy for them."

"They must have false passports as well."

"Wouldn't be too difficult, would it?"

"But there wasn't even anything on the digital software," said Gardener. "None of the photos were recognised."

"Which leaves another possibility."

"That they haven't left the country at all?" Gardener observed.

Reilly unwrapped his chocolate bar but paused before biting. "Which could make finding them even harder. They could be anywhere in the UK. We have no idea what mode of transport they are using."

Gardener sifted through the paperwork. "Did the mobile numbers lead us anywhere?"

"I don't think so. Longstaff and Gates spoke to all the providers they knew about. None of those numbers for the DPA team have ever existed."

"And those two are certainly tech savvy. If they can't find them then I'll wager no one else can."

"How is that possible?" Reilly asked. "Surely there must be a record of their phones and the calls they've made somewhere."

"There will be," said Gardener. "But this DPA lot know how to cover their tracks. Look at that thing they infected the bank with, that Trojan called Octopus. If they can concoct something like that, then hiding phone numbers will be a walk in the park."

Reilly nodded in acceptance, finally taking a bite of the Mars bar.

Gardener's mood was part defeat but mostly annoyance. Robbie Crater had slipped the net, making that a cold case. He certainly didn't want another. "I can't believe we've drawn a complete blank."

"It's not a complete blank, boss. We know a lot more than we did three weeks ago. We know who they are, where they live – or lived, some of what they've been up to. But we just can't find *them*, at the moment."

Gardener shook his head and ran his hands through his hair. "The trouble is, we know so much but so little. We know they exist but proof of their existence is only in cyberspace."

"Apart from James Henshaw and Anthony Palmer," offered Reilly.

Gardener nodded. "We've found out what they've been up to, and where they are supposed to have operated from. Is it possible for four people to completely disappear?"

"You wouldn't have thought so, in this day and age, but people do it all the time."

"They do, but there's usually a trace of some kind. All online presence has ceased. Their phone numbers have ceased to exist. Two homes have been cleared of everything – incriminating or otherwise. And they have all disappeared from planet Earth. How is that possible?"

"Maybe not all," said Reilly. "Palmer's house isn't empty. Maybe we only need to find him."

The silence said it all. Gardener and Reilly rose in unison and headed for the door, turning out the lights as they left.

Part Two

Chapter Eighteen

Three months after the hit and run.

The plane touched down and taxied to the terminal. Despite being in first class the procedure was still the same but within seconds of the aircraft hitting the tarmac, a succession of clicks on seat belts signalled the impatience of the passengers waiting to leave.

Two of them stood up, reaching overhead, when a stewardess reminded them to sit back down and fasten their seat belts.

Anthony wondered why; why did you have to keep your seat belt fastened when the plane was trundling along at ten miles per hour on its way to a safe destination to dock? What the hell did they think would happen?

Nevertheless, he cooperated.

When it finally stopped almost everyone was standing. Somehow they always managed to beat him. One passenger was even at the door to leave, case in hand.

Within seconds of departing they were rushing down empty corridors to the carousel. The conversations around him were of frustrating and unnecessary business trips and holidays from hell – although how anyone could have a bad holiday in the Bahamas was beyond Anthony.

The queue at the passport booth was relatively short but judging by the jobsworths inside the glass cabins it was set to grow longer. *Why did they make you feel so uncomfortable? Was it a trait of the job when you attended the interview?* Give us your most aggressive stare; see if you can cause someone to wither without uttering a word.

Anthony moved forward, presenting his passport. The woman took it. She had short black hair clinging to her scalp, a severe expression, and an attitude that said, whatever it is you're thinking of saying – don't! He was reminded of Zoe.

"How long have you been away, sir?" she asked.

"A few weeks," replied Anthony.

"Business or pleasure?"

"Both."

What the hell was she doing? wondered Anthony. All she had to do was check the picture and let him through.

"No personal baggage?"

"No, it's not worth the aggro these days, might as well put it all in the suitcase."

She handed the passport back. "Have a safe journey, sir."

Anthony was surprised. He'd have laid odds he'd end up being dragged to one side, left to wait for hours before being strip-searched in a private room.

What an imagination, thought Anthony. That's what comes of working with those three.

Talking of which, as Anthony descended the staircase to the carousel he switched on his phone. He had a few minutes to spare because the belt was still empty and stationary.

The crowds had already gathered. *Where the hell had they come from?*

Glancing at his phone, he realised a problem of sorts. With no signal, the phone hadn't connected to anywhere. Maybe it would when he was outside.

Anthony wanted a meeting as soon as possible. He had done a lot of thinking while he was away. He needed to make changes, take control of his life, maybe even go it alone – or retire altogether.

Two years ago he would never have thought that. Not even one year ago, or six months.

But everything changed three months ago. They'd gone a step too far.

That was down to Zoe. He didn't think for one second if the other two – or himself – had been driving, that they would have killed David; and deliberately, in his opinion.

Yes, thought Anthony, it was time to move on.

He spotted his suitcase and moved forward through the complaining throng, who were moaning about not having seen theirs.

He grabbed it, dropped it onto the floor, extended the handle and headed for the "nothing to declare" aisle.

With customs cleared he entered the terminal to see a number of people holding placards. He didn't spot anyone he knew so he continued to the exit for the car parks, threading his way through even more people, all intent on blocking his way.

To his right he heard convoluted conversations. To his left he could hear music. Not the usual piped crap they always played – music you couldn't put a name to in a million years; it had more of a brass band or circus feel to it.

He was about ten feet from the door when he heard a loud scream that made him jump.

Anthony turned to see what it was.

Three seconds later he fainted.

Chapter Nineteen

Anthony woke up with a crowd round him. Initially he didn't recognise anyone and he hadn't a clue where he was. People were prodding and poking him, asking him what had happened. Was he okay? Thin people; fat people; old people; young people. You name it, he had them in front of him.

A multitude of colours and strange sounds suddenly exploded in his mind and Anthony remembered exactly what had happened.

He raised himself from the floor and rose to his feet almost in one movement, his head all over the place, glancing in every direction. "Where is he? Where is he?"

"Who are you talking about, son?" an old man asked.

"The clown. The clown," shouted Anthony, "the fucking clown. Where is he?"

"I'm not sure," said a woman with large glasses and wild red hair.

"He's around here somewhere," replied a teenager dressed like a tramp. "Do you want us to get him?"

"I fucking don't," said Anthony, picking up his case, trying to make a run for it. As he was about to move, a doctor appeared, with a nurse.

Anthony was going nowhere until he'd had a thorough examination. He argued but it made no difference. The pair of them marched him off into a side room, which turned out to be a staff restroom-cum-canteen. It was clean, quiet, pleasant smelling, and warm. Sweet tea was brought to him and he sat there for quite some time answering questions.

The doctor said he had coulrophobia.

Anthony knew exactly what it was. He didn't need to be told; thirty fucking years he had been frightened stiff of clowns – he didn't need a quack to analyse it.

They had left him with a second cup of sweet tea, and some time to compose himself; they said they would call back once he'd had time to calm down.

Fat chance. The tea had done nothing to help and Anthony once again relived the episode of what should have been a birthday treat.

As his parents were music hall entertainers they loved anything connected to the world of showbiz, including the circus, which is where they decided to take him for his seventh birthday.

The circus came to Liverpool once a year and occupied a site close to the Albert Dock, which it shared with a travelling fair.

The highlight of the evening was The Big Top, which Anthony's parents left till last. Before going into the tent, Anthony spotted the hall of mirrors and asked if he could have a wander round.

His mother joined him but they parted company quite early. The hall of mirrors was a strange place, which reminded him of the ghost train. The entrance was a darkened narrow corridor with wooden boards underfoot, and weirdly painted walls.

The music was new to Anthony, and was also befitting of something weird, designed – in his opinion – to frighten children, not encourage them. He discovered later in life that it was a tune called "Superstitious Feeling" by the band, Harlequin. He really didn't like it and felt reluctant to go any further because he was alone.

With little choice, Anthony continued. As he turned a corner the hall itself opened out. A number of mirrors were randomly placed. Anthony stood in front of the first one, which broke all the tension. His reflection was a version of Anthony that was all fat and dumpy. He was about a foot tall and the same around. As he started to laugh, the figure in the mirror copied him and all his teeth resembled tent pegs at awkward angles, which made him laugh even more. As he held his belly and doubled up, the reflection in the mirror nearly disappeared through the floor.

Another mirror made him tall; others made him appear far away, as if in a tunnel, or very close up like a magnifying glass.

Anthony lost all track of time. The song started again. It was the beginning of verse two when everything went downhill.

> *The flashing of a light*
> *Slashes through the night*
> *Changing colours in the face*
>
> *You meet a stranger's eyes*
> *Gripping like a vice*
> *Noises shouting out a face*

Anthony came across a mirror that warped all of his features. He resembled an alien. It was hilarious and he was helpless.

The laughing however stopped, almost immediately, because the mirror also distorted the features of the clown standing directly behind him.

Anthony turned very quickly. He had absolutely no idea where the hell that thing with the large head, black soulless eyes, white face and massive red nose had come from.

Anthony pissed himself and then saw a multitude of colours but was unable to put them together: red, blue, yellow, white. He managed a quick glance at the elephant sized feet but the clown suddenly shrieked with laughter and threw his arms in the air.

Nothing else registered because Anthony fainted. He finally came round outside, surrounded by a number of people – including the clown, who now wore a very sad face. Anthony screamed so loud that almost everyone in the crowd ducked or jumped back. He started hyperventilating but St John Ambulance was on hand.

Once inside the safety of a tent with the clown out of sight he managed to calm down. That was when one of the medics suggested he might be suffering from something known as coulrophobia. Anthony wasn't sure what upset him most; the clown, or that he had actually wet himself. But the fear was so intense that he wet himself nearly every time he saw one.

The door opened, breaking his reverie. The nurse returned. She was young, early twenties, blonde, with a soft complexion and bright eyes.

"How are you?"

"I'm good, thank you," he lied. His nerves were still in tatters and all he wanted to do was leave.

"We were worried about you."

"I'm okay now, honestly. It's something I've learned to live with. Been terrified of them all my life."

"So was my mum; truth be known I think everyone's a little frightened of clowns."

Anthony stood up. "Well, thank you for everything, I really appreciate it. But I need to be going now."

"If you're sure."

"Yes, thank you."

Anthony picked up his case, heading for the door.

"Don't forget," persisted the nurse, "if you need to talk we can put you in touch with someone."

"Thank you."

Anthony left the room, walked about ten yards with his head glancing in every direction. He eventually stood near the toilets with his back to the wall for at least ten minutes before he thought it was safe to leave.

He grabbed his case and raced for the exit doors.

As he reached them and stepped outside into the winter sunshine he noticed a mobile roadshow presented by Radio Leeds. It was a charity event to raise awareness of oesophageal cancer.

He pushed himself onwards and walked past the outdoor unit when he heard a pop quiz the DJ was running between two contestants. He asked one of them to name the song from the burst of lyrics.

Anthony heard it and froze. His head spun, his legs turned to jelly and his stomach was ready to revolt.

There's trouble up ahead
My mind is flashing red
And evil's just around the bend

You're in a cold embrace
Lost without a trace
It's getting very near the end

His grip on the case relaxed and he had to use the roadshow stage to lean against.

"Oh please, God, not again."

It was the third verse from "Superstitious Feeling" by Harlequin.

Anthony really didn't know which way to turn. He'd already fainted because of the clown, and now here he was listening to the words of the world's unluckiest song – for him, anyway.

Every single time he heard the song, something bad happened.

He felt a tap on his shoulder and a voice asked if he was okay.

Anthony grabbed his case and simply replied that he was fine without even checking to see who it was.

He needed the car park. He had to leave the bloody airport before anything else happened.

Due to the confusion and the frustration, it took him nearly ten minutes to find which park he'd left his car in.

When he finally made it to the space, Anthony dropped his case, threw his hands in the air and shouted at the top of his voice.

"Will you please fuck off?"

Chapter Twenty

The driver of the Evoque edged his way up The Headrow in the centre of Leeds, sticking to the speed limit because he didn't want to draw attention to himself. He wasn't bothered about being seen, more about being caught.

In the back of the vehicle, handcuffed and trussed up underneath the parcel shelf, his passenger constantly moaned. The driver figured his prisoner was in a real bad place about now.

He increased the volume on the radio to cut out the moaning. He was fed up of hearing it.

The traffic lights changed to green. The bus in front of him moved off and he hung a left onto Albion Street.

The morning was clear and bright but cold because of the bitter wind skating its way across the city. Pedestrians huddled into winter clothing. One teenager held the flaps of her coat tightly together but flatly refused to let go of her mobile – or her burger; who the hell ate burgers at ten o'clock in the morning?

He passed Curry's PC World on his left and Waterstones on his right, before cruising down to the bottom, where Albion Street turned into a pedestrian precinct.

The passenger moaned again, shouting for help. The driver knew he was way beyond that. It was only a matter of time, but he wouldn't be around to see – or listen – to the results.

As the road bore round to the left, Butts Court appeared on the right. Fixed to the wall about twenty feet above were a pair of CCTV cameras.

He wasn't concerned about those. The vehicle wasn't registered to him. Whoever came to investigate the crime he was about to commit would draw quite a number of blanks. If and when they did make some headway, it would all be over.

His prisoner let out a banshee type scream, which ended with a question.

"For fuck's sake what have you given me?"

The driver didn't bother to reply. The man wouldn't have to bear it for much longer.

He pulled the Evoque to his left, stopped, selected reverse and backed his way up Butts Court. The other end of the street was a dead end; otherwise he would have driven straight in.

Glancing out of the back window he saw a hoodie coming toward the vehicle. He was unlikely to cause a problem. Most of them were in their own world, paying more attention to their phones.

The driver pulled up near the ramp that led to underground parking. He killed the engine, jumped out and walked around to the back of the vehicle.

He glanced around. Across the road he saw a truck tight up to a loading bay. Despite hearing voices and fork trucks whirring around he doubted anyone would give him a second glance.

He opened the tailgate. The man yelled and shielded his eyes and face from the sun. His passenger had deteriorated. His complexion was pale. A vein in his neck had inflamed. He had blisters around his mouth, which had also started to swell. Another few minutes, guessed the driver, and he wouldn't be able to speak at all. His eyes were swollen and his skin was turning red.

"What have you done to me?" The sentence had taken some effort because of the effect of the swelling of his lips.

The driver ignored him. He unlocked the handcuffs, dragged him out of the vehicle, across the pavement, dumping him into a corner between the wall and the metal fencing.

"Hey."

The driver turned to see the hoodie, dressed in baggy warehouse jeans and white trainers. How unlucky could he be; the only hoodie in the world who actually did notice the life around him?

"What are you doing?"

"What's it to you?"

"Is this a film?"

The driver wondered what the hell he was talking about until he glanced down at his own clothing: a white contamination suit with a white hood, and gloves.

"That looks fucking wicked," said the hoodie, peering around, "where's the rest of the cameras?"

His prisoner moaned, as if on cue.

The hoodie grabbed his phone and pointed it at them.

The driver wasn't having any of that and covered the distance to the hoodie in two strides. He grabbed the man's right hand with his left and squeezed.

The hoodie immediately buckled, dropped to the concrete, his face a ball of confusion. "The fuck are you doing?"

"Let go of the phone."

"Me hand, me hand, you're crushing me fucking hand."

"If you don't let go of the phone you won't have a hand to worry about."

The hoodie did as he was told, at which point he was moaning louder than the man who'd been trussed up in the back of the Evoque.

The driver grabbed the phone, switched it off and put it in his pocket.

The hoodie stood up, rubbing his hand. "Fucking maniac. Give me the phone back."

The driver figured action was needed before someone else came sniffing. Clenching his right fist he punched the hoodie hard and fast in his solar plexus, who ended up face down on the concrete, winded and almost vomiting. He brought his knees to his chest and struggled to catch his breath.

The driver picked him up and rolled him down the ramp to the underground car park. Someone would find him, but he'd be okay, unlike the other shape he'd dragged out of the vehicle.

It was time to go. The driver turned to face his passenger. He knelt closer.

"Have a nice life, what's left of it."

It was all the prisoner could do to raise his arms but they fell to the ground almost immediately.

The driver jumped back into the Evoque and started the vehicle, relieved that no one else had intervened.

He drove off Butts Court, turned right, back on to Short Street, passing the Q-Park on the left. At the bottom he turned right again, onto Upper Basinghall Street, passing another CCTV camera.

At the end of the street he rejoined The Headrow and the inner ring road, floating past the town hall on his right as he made his way back home.

Job done. One down, three to go.

Chapter Twenty-one

Where was his car?

Anthony glanced around, checking as many of the cars as he could see. There were plenty of BMWs, many of them 7-series. But none were his.

He stared at the airport terminal, working out his bearings. He spotted all the landmarks. He was definitely in the correct car park.

He was good with numbers, worked with computers and had a very good memory for where he left things.

The car simply wasn't there.

It wasn't as if the space was empty. There was simply another car in it – a white Mini.

Deflated and sighing, Anthony sat down on his suitcase, wondering if his day was ever going to improve.

The flight had been late. Once he'd landed he'd had to put up with that needle-faced bitch in passport control. As if that wasn't bad enough, the fucking clown more than made up for it. What in God's name was a clown doing at an airport? After his recovery and being held up by the medical staff, the world's unluckiest song made an appearance, setting his nerves on edge. No good ever came of anything when he heard that song.

And now his car was missing.

Anthony raised his head to the sky. "Please tell me, Lord, if you have anything else planned, let's fucking have it, now!"

Anthony thought about the car. It had obviously been stolen. But when? Why? Who had taken it?

All of those questions could probably be answered quite easily. The airport would have CCTV.

Why were bad things happening to him? Karma. That's why. He'd done some bad things himself recently. Maybe it was payback.

He stood up, glancing across the car park; not another soul in sight.

Anthony grabbed his phone from his pocket. Clicking the button at the side the screen prompted his password. Once he'd entered that, the phone informed him it was emergency calls only. There was no signal.

What did "emergency calls only" mean? Could he actually call anyone? He supposed he could always phone the police.

Anthony heard voices. When he glanced around it was a couple at the other end of the car park. He was always amazed by how sound travelled.

Another thought suddenly entered his mind. *Had* the car been stolen, or was he the victim of a prank? It was always possible. One of the other three could have done it, though he couldn't think why.

Then again, they may have taken his car for another reason. Perhaps the same reason that one of them could have played around with his phone service. They were all good enough with computers to do that. Anthony should know.

A chill wind crossed the car park, forcing Anthony to pull his jacket tighter. He wasn't in the Bahamas now.

If the other three *were* involved in the theft of his car and messing with his phone, they wouldn't appreciate the police becoming involved. Come to think of it, in light of what had happened three months ago, Anthony wouldn't appreciate the police digging into his life either. He had no idea where that could lead.

He paused, staring over at the terminal. It was only a ten-minute walk, no more.

He set off, passing a number of people along the way; one or two nodded but no one actually spoke.

As he neared the main building a taxi was dropping off. Once the driver had unloaded the suitcases he bade his fare goodbye and skipped around to the driver's door.

"Are you free, mate?" Anthony shouted.

The driver was dressed in jeans, a grey shirt and black leather jacket. With a weary expression, he turned to face Anthony.

"Where do you want to go?"

"Burley in Wharfedale."

"When?"

"How about now?"

"I'm not sure, I have another fare, maybe."

Anthony dragged a wad of notes from his pocket. He never went anywhere without a pocket full of money.

He peeled off one hundred pounds. "We go now. No questions asked. It'll take you ten minutes and it'll be the best tax-free cash you'll earn this week."

The driver didn't argue.

The journey took twenty minutes, conducted in silence.

When Anthony finally opened his front door, he struggled to push it more than six inches.

He glanced down.

"What the fuck?"

Chapter Twenty-two

Gardener glanced at the queue. There were three people in front of him, and at least another ten behind. The shop was bursting. At the speed the counter assistant was working, it probably wouldn't take long for him to be served. In the meantime he would have to put up with some brash piped music.

Chris had harped on about a new pair of football boots for the last week. Not simply any boots, they had to be specific – in colour and brand. By the time he'd finished his sermon, Gardener didn't need it writing down. His son had also dropped some heavy hints about the new Leeds Utd strip. Gardener dropped heavier ones, of the negative variety.

As he had time on his hands he was more than happy to buy the boots. He had no pending cases, unless you counted the disappearance of a certain Robbie Carter – though he doubted that man would reappear any time soon. The DPA case had all but died.

The music stopped for a second or two. He heard one or two random shouts outside on the pedestrian precinct of Bond Street, but paid little attention because the music soon started again. The queue moved forward two places because another checkout girl had joined her friend.

A commotion at the front door of the shop drew Gardener's attention once again. A plump, middle-aged redhead wearing a heavy winter coat and carrying an M&S carrier bag slipped inside. She barged straight up to the counter.

"Can I use your phone?"

One of the assistants glanced at the redhead as if she'd lost her marbles. "Don't *you* have one?"

"Do you think I'd be asking if I had?" She immediately turned her head toward the door and back to the counter again. "Hurry up, will you, it's an emergency."

"Excuse me but I do have customers." Despite the protest she handed the shop phone over.

Gardener leaned forward. "Excuse me, but do you have a problem?"

"Don't worry, you'll get served."

"That's not what I meant."

She put the phone to her ear. "I don't, but someone out there does. Who are you anyway?"

Gardener flashed his warrant card.

The woman dropped the phone back on the counter, grabbing Gardener's elbow. "Come with me. There's a man out here and I think he's been attacked. He's staggering all over the place."

"What makes you think he's been attacked?" Gardener asked, dropping the boots on the counter, allowing himself to be led outside.

"Wait till you see him."

Out in the open air a sharp wind whistled around his ears and crept down his neck. Gardener adjusted his hat slightly.

The redhead pointed to the area where Bond Street met Albion Street, a distance of about thirty yards. Gardener peered at the staggering man. He was stocky, balding, badly dressed in a sweatshirt and jeans – neither of which appeared to be clean. He had his hands to his face but judging by the amount of gesticulating he was in some pain.

"What's your name?" he asked the redhead, reaching for his mobile.

"Millie," she replied.

"Millie what?"

"Johnson, Millie Johnson."

"When did you first become aware of him?" Gardener noticed that most of the people milling around that section of shops were giving the man a wide berth. Mothers pulled children closer, before shooting off in a completely different direction. A number of gawking teenagers remained, all with phones in hand.

"A couple of minutes ago."

"Was he acting like this?"

"Yes," she replied, glancing around – though he couldn't figure out why.

"Where did you come from?"

"No idea."

"Did he say anything to you?"

"No. You don't think I was going to hang around, do you? You never know what's wrong with him – could be anything."

The man suddenly dropped to his knees and let out an ear-piercing scream, one that even Gardener heard.

"Mrs Johnson, you need to wait here. Please do not leave the shop. I'm going to see what I can do for him and then I'll come back and we'll resume this conversation."

Her eyes widened. "I don't know nothing."

He ducked back into the shop and ran to the counter, displaying his warrant card.

"I need a whistle."

"Not you as well. There are people in front of you, you know."

"A whistle, now," he demanded. "It's an emergency, don't make me ask again."

Something in his expression must have informed the girl that if she didn't comply immediately she'd spend the night behind bars. Reaching under the counter she drew out a white cardboard box. He grabbed a simple silver whistle, one used by referees.

"I'll be back," he said, taking it from her.

"Okay, Arnie," muttered the girl.

Gardener ran outside and covered the distance to the injured man in no time at all, blowing his whistle all the way. By the time he reached his destination he had everyone's attention.

The man was still on his knees but had now lowered his head to the ground, as if he was praying; maybe he was. He was very quiet.

Gardener blew the whistle once more and he realised he had absolute silence. He flashed the warrant card. "I am a police officer, I need to ask if everyone can please stay where they are."

Reaching for his mobile, Gardener glanced at the man on the pavement. "Excuse me, can you please tell me your name?"

There was no answer, aside from a deep, guttural moan followed by a hissing sound.

Gardener gloved up and pulled out a disposable mask from his pocket. He noticed the man's neck was red raw and blistered, swollen up much larger than normal. Judging by the movement of his stomach he was having trouble breathing. There was something seriously wrong with him. Gardener was already dialling for an ambulance.

He leaned in closer to the man, touching his shoulder. "Excuse me…"

The man immediately recoiled from Gardener's touch. He raised his head from the ground and wailed something unintelligible. Gardener could immediately see why. His eyes were as red as his skin, and his lips resembled boiled sausages. Gardener doubted they would be having a conversation.

Having made a connection on the phone, Gardener spoke to an operator, told them as much as he could about what was happening and where they were; who he was and the fact that he needed an ambulance as soon as humanly possible.

"Do you need any help, mate?" asked a teenager in a red jacket, with blue trousers, a shock of blond hair, lip studs and earrings. His phone was at the ready and he was snapping pictures of the man on the floor.

"Yes," said Gardener. "I need you to put that phone away and step back over to that shop window… now!" As his voice rose for the last word he was pointing in the direction he needed the idiot to go.

The teenager didn't need telling twice.

Gardener had walked into a scene from hell. It wasn't immediately evident what was wrong with the man, where he'd come from, or what had happened to him. Or whether or not someone had actually done something to him.

He doubted it was an acid attack. What really concerned him was that he didn't know what it *could* be, whether or not it was contagious; or if there was a lunatic around the next corner plying whatever substance he had to someone else's face.

He definitely needed to contain the situation, but how? The whole world and his brother had suddenly turned up. The crime scene was contaminated to buggery now.

Saving the man's life was a bigger concern. He was going to need backup.

Gardener glanced at the man. "Did someone do this to you?"

There was no reply but Gardener detected what he thought was a perceptible nod of the head.

Suddenly the man let out a scream that sounded like a chainsaw backfiring. Whatever was wrong with him it had affected his breathing. Gardener saw that his breathing was becoming even more erratic. The man fell to the ground with body tremors, as if he had gone into a seizure.

Gardener had absolutely no idea what to do. He'd been on the force all of his working life; he'd seen things that would turn people's stomachs without trying but he'd never witnessed anything like the man on the floor.

Hazchem and Special Ops ran through his mind. That would be a game changer.

As he raised his head he noticed a rather tall vehicle with flashing lights but it wasn't an ambulance. The council refuse wagon had pulled to a stop in front of the NCP Car Park. Four men with hi-vis jackets jumped out, two of them staring at him. The other two were peering down the ramp leading to the underground car park.

Gardener glanced at the injured man who was now writhing around on the ground. He really needed to think very quickly about what to do and how to contain everything.

He dialled the station, setting off immediately toward the bin wagon, blowing his whistle, as if he'd lost his mind.

"You lot, stay exactly where you are. Don't move."

"Who, me?" asked the desk sergeant on the other end of Gardener's mobile.

Gardener explained who he was, what he'd been caught up in, and requested immediate backup from anywhere close at hand – and very possibly his own team, as he knew instinctively where the incident was heading.

Putting the phone in his pocket he shouted at the bin men, flashing his warrant card. "I need you lot to come with me, now."

"Can't do that, guv, we're on council business." The man was at least twenty-stone, with a fat lumpy face that appeared to have been the sick joke of a bad pottery session. His eyes were bulbous and he had more hair sprouting from his nose than his head. But the biggest mistake he was making was pushing his luck.

Gardener's temper hit new heights, which meant he stared solely at the man with the big mouth and spoke very slowly.

"You see this badge? It means I can override any council orders you have. When I say I want you lot to come with me now – that is exactly what I mean. No argument."

He had all of their attention. "Follow me. I need you to create a cordon."

"What do you mean?"

"I need you to create a boundary. Don't let anyone inside. Now come on!"

Gardener ran back to the injured man who still face down on the ground, moaning and writhing.

He directed the bin men to form a square, standing in opposing corners. That was a task in itself because each and every one of them kept glancing at the man on the floor and then at Gardener, asking stupid questions.

He stared around at the shoppers, blowing his whistle again.

"Can I have your attention, please? Do not, I repeat, do not move from where you are now."

"Excuse me, guv," said lump head.

Gardener noticed he was holding a roll of red and white tape – from where he had no idea. "Thought you might need this. Wrap it round us all and create a proper boundary, like."

Gardener smiled; perhaps the man wasn't so bad after all. He quickly rolled the tape around the man's body before setting off for the next. Once he'd finished he blew the whistle again, addressing a crowd he would have preferred not to have been there.

"Please stay where you are and do not try to walk through the tape. I have called for an ambulance, and more police officers to deal with what's happening. We'll need to take a statement from every one of you."

He dropped to his knees and told the man to hang on – which was probably pointless – repeating that he had called for an ambulance. He then asked once again if he could do anything to help.

With a very serious effort the man raised his head. His face was now so red Gardener thought it had been set on fire. His milky white eyes signified that he might even have gone blind in the short time he'd been on the floor.

What in God's name had happened?

In the distance, Gardener heard the siren of the ambulance. He wondered if they might have a problem reaching him, unsure if the bin wagon was blocking their path.

He was suddenly shoved and a scream in his right ear distracted his attention. The man on the floor had reared upwards, gripping Gardener's shoulders.

He would never forget the expression of sheer terror carved into the injured man's features; wide eyes with deep crow's feet underneath them. His mouth was fully open but Gardener could see very little because his tongue had ballooned to twice its size, probably making breathing impossible.

Gardener's last thought was confirmed as he heard the death rattle somewhere at the back of his throat.

The man breathed his last and collapsed to the ground as the medics finally reached him.

Chapter Twenty-three

Welcome to hell, thought Gardener.

"Is he dead?" shouted lump head.

Gardener nodded to confirm.

He heard a retching sound behind him as one of the other bin men threw up. That was all he needed.

Gardener phoned the station again, explained what had happened and was quietly relieved when the desk sergeant told him his team had been despatched, as well as a number of operational support officers. They would now have to add the Home Office pathologist, Dr George Fitzgerald, to the list of attending officers. Against his better judgement he held back on Special Ops until Fitz had seen the victim.

Fortunately for him, as he disconnected the call, two uniformed constables appeared, introducing themselves as Carole Phillips and Mike Howlett.

"I see you've got your work cut out," said Howlett. He was young, not much older than Patrick Edwards, one of Gardener's own team, with short black hair and blue eyes.

Carole Phillips was blonde, short and well built. She was eyeing up the bin man who'd been sick. "What can we do to help?"

"Take the names and addresses of everyone you can see, please."

"Can we let them go after that?"

"Probably not," said Gardener. "I'll let you know." He briefly explained what had happened to the man on the floor.

"Is it a Hazchem scene?"

"I hope not," said Gardener. "If it is, we'll be here forever. For now, please get as many names and addresses as you can and see if anyone knows exactly where the man came from and which route he took to arrive here. If it is possible, try and find out what he touched on the way."

"Do we know who he is?" asked Phillips.

"I'm just going to see if I can find out."

Once again, for the benefit of the crowd, Gardener blew his whistle and told them to cooperate with the constables. He had no doubt that a lot of people – especially those furthest from the scene – would already have slipped away, wanting no part of it. He made a note to talk to whoever was responsible for the CCTV around the corner.

The two uniforms moved off and Gardener returned to the body on the precinct. Gloves still on he reached into all the pockets he could find; one on the sweatshirt and four in the jeans – all were empty.

Brilliant!

All four of the bin men were on their phones. No doubt they had pictures for Facebook and Instagram, though he suspected at least one of them was explaining the hold up, or their absence from work.

A number of officers appeared at the cordon, immediately setting up the scene. He could see a marquee was being dragged towards the area. Scene suits were being handed round. One of the officers had a log sheet, when another voice sounded from behind – one he recognised immediately.

"What do we have here, then?"

"A nightmare, Sean. That's what we have – a full blown nightmare."

Reilly suited up and stepped within the confines of the red and white tape.

"A full-blown Hazchem nightmare?" asked Reilly, after glancing at the body.

"Maybe."

"You haven't called it yet?"

"You know what will happen when I do."

"A big fuck-off tent for a start."

"We'd have the circus in town; government techs, military personnel with all manner of gadgets to sniff chemicals if airborne or if on contact surfaces."

"The body wouldn't be moved for ages," continued Reilly. "We wouldn't be allowed anywhere near until it was safe."

"All that lot," said Gardener, pointing to possible witnesses, "would have to go through decontamination procedures with statements taken from them afterwards."

"I don't think I'd want to be anywhere near when it all kicks off," added Reilly. "But if this bloke has something dangerous – and looking at him he hasn't died from a dose of the clap – we need to know about it, and we need to protect everyone including ourselves."

"You're not telling me anything I don't know, Sean, but my gut feeling tells me it isn't a Hazchem scene. Let's see what Fitz says."

"Do we know who he is?" Reilly asked, staring at the body.

"I've quickly checked his pockets, but feel free to delve a little deeper. There might be something on him somewhere."

"I knew I shouldn't have come. Why do I get all the best jobs?"

"I'm pretty sure with your track record and the places you've been you're immune to everything."

Reilly laughed and then nodded to something over Gardener's shoulder. "I'd better hurry up, then. Our man's here."

Gardener turned and spotted Fitz walking toward them wearing a black cape and suit, with a top hat, walking cane, and medical bag. He made his way through a crowd that resembled a set of film company extras. It was very eerie.

"Boss," shouted Reilly. "Might have something." Reilly had searched underneath the sweatshirt, found two driving licences in the pocket of a plain cotton shirt.

"Why two licences?" Gardener asked, taking them.

"Man's obviously a wrong 'un."

"So this could be payback?"

"More than likely," said Reilly.

"Chances are someone's given him something but we still can't rule out the fact that it might be contagious."

"But where the hell has he come from? Look how many buildings we have around here. Office buildings, rooms above shops, a car park over there. He could have been anywhere."

"The quicker we get the team onto it the better," replied Gardener. "If this has been done to him in the vicinity, surely we're going to find the evidence."

"In that case, we'd better call in a PolSA team. An area this size is going to need a fingertip search."

"Already done it, Sean."

Gardener stood and approached his team, who were all lurking at the edge of the outer cordon. All of them were present, awaiting his instructions, which for now, was a basic, house-to-house or shop-to-shop search and question. He wanted Albion Street and the surrounding streets blocking off completely, if they hadn't already been done, and he needed as many basic witness statements as possible in order that they could plan the follow-ups in an incident room, which he hoped would be later today.

"I thought you two might be involved," said Fitz, as he ducked underneath the red and white tape. "Anything sinister is bound to have your name on it."

The pathologist glanced at the man on the floor. "What's happened here?"

Reilly stood up and moved away. "We were hoping you could tell us."

Gardener briefed Fitz and allowed him to make an immediate inspection.

A flurry of activity a few yards away suggested the press were baying for blood. Fortunately for Gardener, the marquee was ready to block the scene completely. Gardener signalled to one of the constables to keep the press where they were for now. Not that he doubted they would already have pictures. There were enough two- or three-storey office blocks with a bird's-eye view.

Gardener waited while the marquee was fully erected and leaned in towards Fitz. "Anything? Whatever you say might very well depend on which call I make next."

Fitz returned his attention to the body. "Skin red and blistering. There's a lot of swelling to the body. Judging by the eyes, whatever it is has caused blindness. Was this how he was when you first saw him?"

"Not quite as bad. His eyes were very red but he wasn't blind. His tongue hadn't swelled up as much on first sight."

"Which means he's had respiratory tract problems. He'll have suffered nose and sinus pain, very probably a sore throat, shortness of breath. Was he coughing a lot?"

"No," said Gardener, "he couldn't even talk, though he did manage a scream."

"I wouldn't be surprised if we find fluid in his lungs." Fitz checked underneath the clothing for further signs. "I suspect he'll have had serious abdominal pain, but I can't see any sign of diarrhoea or vomiting. What were his movements like?"

"A bit erratic. His walking wasn't coordinated. When he was on the ground his body was trembling. I need to know if he's been exposed to something serious."

"Almost certainly," replied Fitz, "no doubt a nerve agent of some description."

Fitz stopped talking and leaned in much closer to the victim's neck.

Gardener suddenly wondered at the size of the Russian community in Leeds, especially at the mention of a nerve agent. The situation was growing worse.

Fitz had produced a scalpel and a magnifying glass from his case. He was peering very closely at the victim's neck.

"What have you seen, Herr Doktor?" asked Reilly.

"Too much of you two, for one day," replied Fitz. "Look closely here." He pointed to the victim's neck.

Gardener noticed a small red mark that had also swollen and blistered like the rest of the skin.

"I suspect he's been injected with something and left to suffer the consequences. The question – and biggest problem for you two – is where and when was it done?"

"And is whatever he has, contagious?"

"Well I won't know that until I investigate. But you know as well as I do, if you don't call it in and something happens to the population of Leeds there's bound to be hell to pay, and your badge will be on the line."

"Gut feeling, Fitz?" asked Reilly.

Fitz studied the body once more and finally sighed. He glanced at both detectives. "Off the record?"

"What else?"

"I don't think so."

Gardener stood and breathed a sigh of relief, glancing at Reilly.

"Treat it as normal?" asked the Irishman.

"I'm going to be in so much shit if this goes wrong."

"We both are."

Gardener finally turned his attention to the two driving licences. Both were a UK issue, both had the same photograph – the dead man on the ground. One had the name Conrad Morse. The other was Michael Foreman.

Gardener immediately recognised both names. He passed them over to Reilly, who read them and sighed.

"I wondered when this case would surface again."

"Question is," said Gardener, "who knows more than we do?"

Chapter Twenty-four

Anthony stared at the floor and saw a mountain of post and a stack of newspapers behind the front door – which was the reason he couldn't open it fully.

"What the fuck is going on here?"

He pushed harder, forcing the mound of paperwork to flatten out. The door opened wider. Anthony stepped in, dragging his suitcase behind him. Kicking the rest of the heap with his right foot he managed to spread it around enough so he could close the front door.

He hadn't been away that long, so why all the post? And what were the newspapers all about? Anthony had not read one for years – at least not in printed form. Most everything he read was digital.

He shivered as he realised the building was cold. Anthony couldn't understand that one. Despite not being home he'd left the heating on pilot. He felt the radiator – stone cold. He glanced up at the thermostat. It wasn't even on. Being digital, it required a current, so in order to confirm he had power he reached out for the light switch, flicked it down.

No light. No heat. He glanced to his right, down the hall to the kitchen, wondering what was going on. The contents of his freezer must be a mess. He ran over, pushed the door open. The kitchen was empty – totally empty: no fridge freezer, no microwave, and no furniture.

He glanced into the living room, staring into another empty space – aside from a table and four chairs – as if somehow, it had been left on purpose. The trouble he'd had at the airport was bad enough, but a totally empty house with no heating and no electricity was totally unacceptable.

Home was a three-bedroom detached bungalow in Manor Park, Burley in Wharfedale. Larger than average it had an extension for a swimming pool and a personal gymnasium, perched in its own grounds at the end of a private road, half a mile from his nearest neighbours.

In an agitated state, Anthony ran through every room. Each one was the same. The whole place had been cleared out. He didn't even have a fucking bed! It didn't have the feel of a burglary – more a house clearance.

He returned to the front door and the pile of correspondence. Staring at the floor, he murmured, "I have no idea what the fuck's happening with my life but I'm going to find out."

He reached for his phone. That would be of no use, it was still displaying emergency calls only.

Anthony needed to contact the others and the only way he could do that was from a public phone, which meant a walk to the Generous Pioneer, the pub at one end of the village.

First of all, he wanted to check through all the crap on his hall carpet. Whatever was happening to his life he was pretty sure someone was controlling it, and he needed to stop and think before doing anything rash, or drawing attention to himself.

Anthony picked up the post and the newspapers and walked to the table and four chairs in the living room.

He checked the newspapers first. He figured there must have been a copy of every single local and national daily, all of which had the lead story of the death of David Hunter. He checked the dates. None were recent – all of them from the night in question, and the following few days.

Who had kept all these? And why had they ended up here? Somebody was obviously trying to tell him something. But who, and what?

Sorting through the pile of letters he noticed that very few were junk mail. Npower and British Gas had written to him – two weeks ago. Both were final bills. They had been given readings and these were a settlement. He then noticed something else rather odd. They were addressed to the occupier, not him.

Further final bills came from the water company and the phone company. He did have a landline as well as a mobile. Both providers had written with final settlements. Other news came from insurance and investment companies – all sorry to hear the bad news, and that final settlements were being prepared.

Anthony flopped down in one of the chairs. He had absolutely no idea what it all meant. As far as he could see his whole life had somehow been switched off.

Why? Did all these people think – for some reason – that he was dead? Is that why everything was so final?

But he wasn't dead. So why did they think he was, and who had told them? Panicking, Anthony searched through more paperwork. His exclusive wine club had written to say they were sorry that his membership had been cancelled. He'd always been a valued customer and if he wanted to return at any time he was more than welcome.

So they didn't think he was dead.

He spotted a letter from Santander – his bank. Anthony reached out and ripped it open, his heart almost stopping when he saw the account had been completely cleared.

He jumped, causing the chair to fall back onto the floor. "What the fuck is going on?"

He found another bank letter: same story, no money.

If it was some bastard's idea of a joke, Anthony was not laughing. He'd rather his colleagues were not responsible but he couldn't think of anyone else – certainly no one clever enough.

But why would they do it? Had any of them actually gone away? Or had they conned him, led him to believe they had? And all the time, they *had* stayed back and – as far as he could see – completely wiped him out. Whilst he could understand them taking the money, he couldn't see why they would clear out his house. Or steal his car from the airport.

Anthony sat back down, tried to think rationally. Why was he so quick to blame his colleagues? They had never shown signs of robbing him in the past. All of them had worked well together. They'd had disagreements, ups and downs, but then all companies go through that.

Anthony ran his hands through his hair. Were they playing a joke on him? A pretty sick fucker if it was.

Another thought forced its way into Anthony's brain at jet miles per hour. He ran out of the living room, through the extension and past the swimming pool. He actually stopped to notice that all the water had been drained, before continuing, slipping into the small changing room at the side.

Like the others, the room was empty. He reached down to the false tile, pressing and shifting it to the right. The whole thing lifted out of the floor like a box. Anthony removed the top and reached in, breathing a sigh of relief.

Whoever had cleaned him out knew nothing of his emergency supply. Anthony retrieved the money – £5,000 in cash – all he had if the letters were anything to go by.

Dropping the safe back into the floor he left the house in search of answers.

Chapter Twenty-five

Gardener stood at the front of the incident room with a bottle of water in his right hand. Behind him were a number of whiteboards. Pinned to one were photos of James Henshaw, Zoe Harrison, and Anthony Palmer. To the other, a number of photos of Michael Foreman, taken at the scene of the crime on Bond Street, plus a whole host of information.

In front of him on a desk were the files the desk sergeant had found relating to the hit and run of David Hunter, with another steadily growing pile to the left, courtesy of DI Winter's cyber team.

In the next room he could hear HOLMES setting up their equipment.

The last of his officers, young Patrick Edwards, filed in, closing the door behind him. He was pleased that Thornton and Anderson had returned to work. And thankful that DCI Briggs was still down in London at a Metropolitan Police convention, which, no doubt, was all about the latest cuts to the police budget. Shona Pearson had returned as the SPOC for the latest meeting.

"Thanks for coming, guys," said Gardener, placing his empty bottle on the table. "Looks like we have our hands full with a new lead on the DPA hit and run."

Gardener went on to explain in detail the incident he had stumbled upon earlier in the day in Bond Street – from Millie Johnson entering the sports shop to his team arriving.

"Is he dead?" said Dave Rawson.

"I hope so," said Reilly. "I wouldn't like to be inside his skin if he isn't."

"So what happened to him?" asked Sarah Gates. "Did this Millie Johnson actually know?"

"No, but once I'd secured the scene I slipped back into the sports shop and to her credit she was still standing where I'd left her." Gardener held up a sheet of paper. "I have all her contact details here so I'd like someone to follow up and take a proper statement from her. We all know that once people have had time to think, all sorts of things come back to them."

"So this Michael Foreman, who's staggering all over the precinct," asked Longstaff, "had he been attacked? I take it he wasn't on drugs or anything."

"Not attacked in the sense of beaten up," replied Gardener. "According to what Fitz found he appears to have been injected with something. There was a mark to indicate as much on his neck."

"Oh no, we're not back to this again, are we?" asked Sharp. "Syringes in the neck job."

"Hopefully not," replied Gardener, remembering the problems they'd had with the Father Christmas murders.

"Do we know what he was given?" asked Bob Anderson, a solid dependable officer who could always be relied upon in a crisis. "Judging by the photos on that board he doesn't look too clever. Must have been something pretty bloody lethal."

"We're still awaiting the results from Fitz."

"He didn't have any ideas, then?" asked Thornton, another one returning from compassionate leave. Thornton and Anderson worked well together but Gardener was constantly reminded of a POW when he saw Thornton because of his thin – almost emaciated – frame.

"He did," said Gardener, "he thought it might be some sort of nerve agent."

"Here we go," said Rawson. "The Novichok nerds are back in town."

"It isn't a Hazchem scene, then?" asked Paul Benson.

Gardener glanced at Reilly, who remained silent. "I didn't think so."

"But it might be," Patrick Edwards pointed out.

"I hope not," replied Gardener. "I agree that he might have been given a dose of something rather nasty. In a short space of time his skin had blistered, and his throat swelled up, constricting his breathing. He was in constant agony before he died."

"If it is a nerve agent," said Rawson, "they'll shut Leeds down. We all know what happened in Salisbury."

"As far as I'm aware no one else has reported having similar symptoms, and I'm pretty sure they would have done by now."

"Let's hope you're right," replied Thornton.

"It might be worth checking with the hospitals," said Gardener.

"Where had this Michael Foreman staggered from?" asked Bob Anderson, leafing through one of the reports. "Did Millie Johnson say?"

"She didn't know, Bob," replied Gardener. "Hopefully, this is where you guys come in. Can we work it out from the statements you took this morning?"

With a rustle of paper, the team consulted their notes. Gardener listened intently to what they had to say. They had managed to construct Foreman's movements, which appear to have originated in Butts Court sometime after ten o'clock. He was definitely seen swaying around in Short Street, before finally making his way onto Bond Street.

"In that case," said Gardener, "we need someone on the CCTV from Butts Court. I know for a fact there is some. How did he get there? Did he stagger out from a building? Was he brought in and dumped from a vehicle?

If so, what was the vehicle and where did the driver go from there?

"We'll also need to follow up on the names and addresses of everyone who was questioned – including Millie Johnson – from Butts Court, through Short Street and onto the precinct at Bond Street. My guess is Michael Foreman will have been given his treatment somewhere else and dropped off. I wouldn't have thought it possible to do what was done to him outdoors and not be noticed."

Gardener turned to Reilly. "Sean, we have a PolSA team in place on Bond Street. Can you get in touch and tell them to widen the search in view of what we now know?"

"I have a witness named Dennis Frost," said Patrick Edwards, the youngest member of the team, who had an earring in one ear, "who works in the loading bay opposite. He saw a dark green Evoque leaving Butts Court pretty rapidly around ten." Edwards had played a blinder in a recent case and had gone up in the SIO's estimation.

"Good work, Patrick. Did he see the registration, or where it went?"

"No reg, sir, but the vehicle took off down Short Street. Mr Frost thinks the driver was male, but it all happened so fast, and he wasn't looking for anything suspicious at that point."

"Did he see Michael Foreman?"

"No," replied Patrick.

"Seeing as you can't drive straight down Butts Court because it's a dead end," said Reilly, "he's taken Short Street, and then had to go right onto Upper Basinghall Street."

"Where there are more CCTV cameras," added Gardener. "He could only have turned left onto The Headrow, so that's another set of cameras to check. Patrick, follow that up please. I want all the CCTV footage. Find the registration of the Evoque and see what we can learn from that. If we're lucky we might be able to compose a picture of *who* we're looking for. If we're really lucky, we might even get a photo of him."

"What about the other names on the other boards, sir?" asked Paul Benson. "Any information on them?"

Gardener let Shona Pearson take over. She quickly summarised in detail from the night of the hit and run to the present day, including the information in the attaché case and the bitcoin scam, and what they had discovered about a team known as DPA: real names, false names, and business premises that did not exist, registered to the company called V-Tech, that didn't exist either. She finally finished with the mystery surrounding the whereabouts of them all – apart from Michael Foreman who was now laid out on a mortuary slab.

"So this guy killed David Hunter?" asked Colin Sharp. "And somehow or other, he's laid low all this time?"

"We still don't know for sure who was driving," said Pearson, "but, yes, you're right in what you're saying, he *was* responsible for the banker's death in one way or another, and he hasn't been seen until today."

"I remember when all this happened," said Rawson to Gardener, "you spoke to James Henshaw's wife and you discovered *he* was missing. Is that still the case, or has he turned up as well, and does she know anything about it?"

"We need to speak to her again," said Pearson, also to Gardener. "When we spoke to her very recently she confirmed that James Henshaw was still missing but she has no idea where. He hasn't made any contact at all. To be honest, she's at her wits end. She's now harbouring suspicions that he's been leading a double life for years."

Gardener also summarised what they knew about the business premises in Leeds and the damaged Overfinch; that the accident hadn't happened where James had said, neither was the vehicle being repaired in Skipton like he'd also claimed. "We've been checking with Range Rover UK about the vehicle's tracker. They can't help because they've had no signal from it since the night of the hit and run."

"The first person we *have* seen from the investigation is Michael Foreman, and he's now dead," offered Pearson.

"Well he isn't just dead, is he?" said Rawson. "He's been made to die."

"Which suggests that someone might know who and where they are," said Bob Anderson.

"Maybe he's fed up of the fact that we haven't been able to come up with any answers," said Sharp, "taken the law into his own hands."

"Maybe," said Gardener. "But who's to say that one of the others isn't behind today's little incident? Is James Henshaw controlling it all? He's been clever enough to conceal everything from his wife."

"Or is he caught up in it?" asked Reilly. "Does someone else have all of them? Has this person had them all from the beginning, which is why we haven't been able to find them?"

"That's always possible," said Paul Benson. "We never found any evidence that they'd left the country. Have we found anything since?"

"Nothing," replied Pearson.

"But they could have gone," offered Sharp, "obviously using false names."

"We didn't get anywhere with facial recognition software," said Gates.

"So maybe they didn't leave," said Pearson. "Let's go with this theory that someone knows more than we do and has been keeping them prisoner."

"That's a bigger mountain to climb," said Reilly. "We'll need to go back through all the original witness statements to see if we can spot anything that might tell us who this person is."

Gardener could sense his team really had the bit between their teeth, and were definitely showing signs of hunger to proceed.

"So we have a hit and run, a cyber crime and the sudden appearance and death of one of the DPA team, Michael Foreman. All of these events are connected."

"So what's the plan, boss?" asked Bob Anderson.

"We need to cover the local airports again. I realise we did that before but in the event of one or all of them reappearing we need to go back and check again. It's possible that one of you guys might just ask a new question, which may produce a fresh lead. We won't know until we try. Drag up every scrap of airport CCTV you can find dating back to the night of the hit and run, and come forward to the last couple of days. I realise it's an awful job but it needs to be done.

"We'll need to coordinate with DI Winter at cyber crime, but I'd like someone investigating any or all online presence from then till now to see if it offers any vital clue about where the hell they have all been. There has to be something somewhere. Now that one of them has surfaced, their online presence could have started up again.

"We also need to visit David Hunter's bank again. Speak to the manager about his version of events; see if he remembers anything fresh. Or has anything else happened recently. I'd suggest someone gets onto that immediately. Banks are notorious for closing early and I want answers today, so whatever the bank manager thinks he's doing, he isn't."

Gardener turned and pointed to the whiteboards before continuing. "As for this lot, visit their homes again, find out everything you can. Speak to the neighbours. I appreciate they have all answered countless questions and they're probably sick of it by now but they'll just have to put up with more.

"Information we had said they operated from premises that have actually been closed for years; visit them again. Something might have been overlooked. But until his disappearance, James Henshaw had his wife believe he left for work every day. So where did he go? Where did any of them go?

"I've just had another thought," said Gardener. "Going back to cars. We drew a blank last time on the cars they drove, couldn't actually find anything. Can someone check all the lease companies and see if they have any vehicles registered to a company called V-Tech or Hammer Studios, like the Overfinch? Or maybe they registered them under DPA, another lead worth checking. These people must have been somewhere, and no matter how good they are at covering their tracks, there has to be a chink in their armour. We just have to find it."

Chapter Twenty-six

The first thing Anthony had done after leaving the house was catch a train into the centre of Leeds. From there he had found a sports shops and bought a holdall large enough to carry clothes, toiletries, and other items he purchased a few minutes later.

Anthony also needed a phone and the anonymity of pay-as-you-go was perfect for him because they were far more difficult to trace. He didn't load it up with too much credit in case he needed to ditch it and start again.

Following a coffee and a cake in an Internet Café he took advantage of their facilities to dig a little deeper into his financial situation. He was still flat broke, owned nothing, and, to his further amazement, didn't actually exist. Someone somewhere had wiped him out. His stomach felt incredibly heavy as he'd even discovered he'd been registered as recently deceased.

So who was responsible?

Anthony didn't have to think too hard for whom. It had to be the other three. *Was it one of them, or were they all in it together? And why? What had happened in the time they had all spent out of the country to bring about such a catastrophic result?* Anthony ran a check on his colleagues. No deaths had been registered amongst them.

He saw little point in returning home, so another internet search revealed a number of low budget hotels and guest houses within easy range of the airport.

He'd chosen well, a nondescript, slightly run-down establishment at the end of a tree-lined street. The landlord was more than happy for a cash only arrangement with no questions asked.

He'd only booked three nights in the bed and breakfast, and when Anthony saw the room he figured that was two nights too many. Cheap carpeting, faded wallpaper, windows that wouldn't open easily, and a bed made from granite with thin sheets – though they *were* clean. The only two pieces of furniture were an MFI wardrobe with uneven doors and a bedside cabinet ringed with tea stains on top. The room had no Wi-Fi and was not en suite. But what could he expect for £20 a night? God only knew what breakfast would be like.

Eager to rid the place of the musty smell, he managed to force a window open.

Anthony dropped his holdall on the floor and pulled out a packet of digestive biscuits he'd bought at a small store about a mile away when asking for directions. As he put the biscuits down they actually rolled away from him, toward the window. It was then that he noticed the bed was propped up on bricks.

"Jesus Christ, what the hell is this place?" Anthony was distraught to think of the life he had lived for the last few years. More money than he could ever spend, a beautiful home, staying in the best hotels anywhere in the world.

Everything had ceased with the flick of a switch. *But with whose fucking finger?* He'd only spoken to Michael once, five weeks previously. There had been no mention of things going wrong then. No one had called Anthony since.

He stood up, fuming. He needed to find out what was happening. The reason was almost certainly connected to the hit and run involving David Hunter. All the newspapers on his front doormat attested to that.

Something had come to light. Someone knew about it. It was either one of the others, or all three, and they were trying to sort the matter, or fit him up. But for what: why register his death and clean him out completely if they were fitting him up for something?

The only other option was that an outsider had stumbled across something. Instead of going to the police, maybe he had done his homework, figured out who they were and how much they were worth, and decided on a nice bit of blackmail. Maybe he or she had started with Anthony, intending to wipe out the rest of them in order.

One thing he was pretty sure about, the police were not yet involved, or they had no knowledge of their activities, otherwise they'd all be locked up by now.

Frustrated, Anthony left the hotel and headed someplace private so that he could make phone calls. Half an hour later he found himself in the big open space of Beckett Park.

Seated on a bench he made the first of those calls to Michael Foreman, which went to voicemail. The same thing happened when he tried to call James Henshaw and Zoe Harrison.

Anthony felt like death. *Were they ignoring him? Or had something really happened to them? Was the net closing in after all?*

Instead of being the first, maybe he was the last.

There was only one person left to call, Rosie Henshaw. She could be a little unpredictable but he would have to call her – see what she knew.

After a hesitation he called her mobile, which also went to voicemail. Seeing as James was the only member of the group who was married with children, life for him was somewhat traditional and he had a landline.

Anthony called that. After eight rings, a somewhat fractured Rosie finally answered.

"Hello?"

"Rosie?"

"Palmer? Where the hell have you been, you four-eyed, spineless, murdering parasite?"

"Pardon?"

"Deaf as well, are we?"

"I've no idea what you're talking about, Rosie?"

"You know bloody well what I'm talking about."

"Have you been drinking?"

"*You'll* need one by the time I've finished with you – if only to numb the pain."

"Put James on, Rosie."

"I wish I could."

"Why? Where is he?"

"You tell me. Last I heard he was in Brussels."

Anthony thought on his feet. "Oh, for the meeting."

"Oh, so *you* actually know something about it, then?"

"We all did."

"Michael Foreman must have suffered amnesia, then, because that beached whale didn't have a clue what I was talking about."

"When was that?" asked Anthony.

He thought the line had gone dead but then he realised Rosie was talking to someone else. The conversation was muffled. She must have had her hand over the receiver.

"About five weeks ago," she replied, when she finally came back to him. "Anyway, let's cut the bullshit, Palmer, because I know damned well that James was not in Brussels. He never even went there in the first place."

"So where is he now?"

"What do you think I am, a clairvoyant? The last I saw of him was when he walked out of here to take a trip to Brussels with, *supposedly*, you lot. That was weeks ago. The police told me he'd never even left the country."

"The police?" questioned Anthony, nearly fainting. "You involved the police?"

"I didn't have to. They've continually been knocking at my door and asking me questions to which I have no answers."

"About what?"

"What do you *think*, you cretin?"

"I'm not thinking anything," replied Anthony, "I'm asking."

"Does the name David Hunter mean anything to you?"

Anthony didn't reply. His mind was too busy thinking of the implications.

"Cat got your tongue, Palmer? Well, let me tell you how it stands right now, shall I? They know all about the hit and run in Burley in Wharfedale, in which you lot, including my husband, almost certainly played a part. They've been all over my house, and taken everything they thought was connected to that accident. They've studied all the airports. But, I'll give credit where it's due, you guys are brilliant at covering your tracks, because they can't find a damned thing, including you."

When Anthony made no reply to that outburst, Rosie asked him if he was still there.

"Yes."

"So go on, then, where are you?"

"I don't think it's a good idea to tell you."

"Nothing new there, then. Any idea what it's like for me and the kids, Palmer?" Rosie didn't give him the chance to reply. "No, you wouldn't have, would you? You've never had kids. They cry themselves to sleep every night wondering where their father is, and if he's ever coming back. What the hell am I supposed to tell them? That everything is okay and Daddy will be back soon?

Trouble is, if what they say is true, I don't want him back. You lot killed a man and his wife in cold blood and left them to rot. You all cleared off while the heat died down. I don't know what that makes you but I don't want any part of it, and I don't want my kids near it, either."

"Look, Rosie," protested Anthony, "let me try to explain."

She cut him off. "Don't bother. It'll simply be a pack of lies. Save those for the police. You know something, Anthony Palmer – if that even is your real name – you've never had anyone to think about but yourself. None of you have. Well that's okay, it's going to come in handy while you're still trying to hide from the police. And they will find you, you shitehawk, because they've also put a trace on my phone."

The connection died.

Chapter Twenty-seven

By the time the team had assembled in the incident room late in the evening, Gardener had updated the whiteboards with the information that had filtered in throughout the day. Sitting on tables at the side of the room were hot drinks, and snacks provided by a local bakery that Reilly was on good terms with.

Gardener addressed his team. "Thanks for coming. I realise it's been a trying day and we may not have covered much ground, but hopefully we'll add something further to the boards. I held a press conference about an hour ago."

That brought a chorus of noise. Everyone knew he hated the press, and why.

Gardener continued, "Has anyone gleaned anything from the witness statements?"

Bob Anderson and Frank Thornton had worked together; Anderson spoke up: "Nothing that we don't already know."

"One of the women who works in Waterstones noticed Michael Foreman on Butts Court around ten o'clock," said Thornton. "She'd popped out the back for a quick smoke and she saw him staggering away, toward the town centre. He had his hands around his face at that point."

"She didn't see anything else – anyone else?"

"No. Even though *we* know he'd been dumped," added Anderson, "she didn't see a vehicle."

"I'm working on that, sir," said Paul Benson. "After I'd finished speaking to Millie Johnson I drove back to the area and listed all the buildings and companies, so that we can prepare a list and work through it, and speak to more people, assuming CCTV doesn't reveal anything."

"I'm sure it will, Paul, good work. Did Millie Johnson have anything to add?"

"No. She'd been out to meet a friend for morning coffee. A lady named Stella Dent. After that, they'd both browsed the shelves in Waterstones before setting off in different directions. Millie Johnson never noticed anything when she passed Short Street, but saw him stagger around the corner when she was window-shopping. So what she said ties in with what everyone else is saying, but she couldn't add anything new."

"Have we interviewed Stella Dent?"

"Yes," replied Benson. "She confirmed what Millie Johnson had said about meeting up but saw nothing."

Usual frustrating stuff, thought Gardener. Something major happens and, even when there are a number of people milling around, no one sees anything.

"Patrick, please tell me you have something positive?"

Edwards resembled a rabbit caught in the headlights. He had a cup of tea in one hand and a half-eaten sausage roll in the other; the remainder was currently in his mouth.

"Does your mother not feed you, son?" asked Reilly.

"You're a fine one to talk," replied Rawson. "You're like a human trash can."

"There's too much waste in this country," said Reilly. "I'm doing my bit to help."

"What?" replied Thornton. "By storing it all in your stomach?"

Edwards had finished chewing and came to Reilly's rescue. "Got a registration, sir: LA20 PUR."

"Who owns it?"

"You're not going to like this. It's on a long-term loan to an Alfie Price."

Gardener rolled his eyes; here we go again. "Was it rented locally?"

"Yes, in Leeds."

"And you've visited the lease company, checked it out, seen all the paperwork?"

"Yes, but it was all done via computer and the photo ID was no one I recognised. It certainly wasn't any of them up on the board there."

"Did you get an address?"

"Yes. Apparently it's registered to a guest staying at The Old Swan Hotel in Harrogate but when I called them they'd never heard of the man. There were no records to backup the fact that he either was – or is – staying there. Apparently he told Hertz that he lived in London but he was up here on business for six months, so that's how long he needed the vehicle."

Gardener sighed, almost laughing. These guys were unreal.

"What about the London address?"

"A block of flats," replied Patrick. "I've checked the electoral roll against the paperwork. The address is real but the person isn't."

"Surely there's a paperwork trail," said Sharp. "What about the guy who does live there, has he received anything yet?"

"Still on it," said Patrick.

"Stick with it, Patrick, but don't waste a lot of time on it. I'm pretty sure it's not going anywhere." Gardener had to admit it was a clever connection. "Where did the vehicle go from Butts Court, do we know?"

"Yes. As Mr Reilly suggested–"

"Mr Reilly, now, is it?" laughed Colin Sharp.

"Hold your horses, son," said Reilly. "This wee young man will go far, he has respect."

"Respect my arse, he just doesn't know you as well as we do," added Rawson.

"Okay, lads," said Gardener, "go easy on him, he *has* provided the snacks." He waved his arm in Patrick's direction for him to continue.

Reilly smiled, raised his fingers to his eyes and then pointed at Rawson.

"It continued up Short Street, right onto Upper Basinghall Street and then left onto The Headrow."

"Which we suspected. Have we registered it with ANPR?"

"Yes, sir. Already done. I'm hoping to check the pings and all the CCTV cameras in the morning."

"That's something positive, we might strike lucky. But it still doesn't tell us who is behind it all. So far we have one dead body in the shape of Michael Foreman. With the others all still missing it could literally be any one of them."

"But we do have mention of somewhere new," said Sharp. "Harrogate."

"Good point," said Gardener, noting it down on the whiteboards. "We need to monitor this and see if Harrogate comes up anywhere else in conversation."

"As for who's behind it, they've all got motive," said Reilly. "They're all involved in the death of David and Ann

Marie Hunter. It must have been a pretty stressful time for them all. Wouldn't take much for one of them to crack."

"You'd have thought they'd stayed tight after something like that," added Benson.

"They obviously have," said Reilly, "but maybe time and stress have shown up the cracks. All that money, people get greedy. Maybe one of them has decided he wants it all for himself."

"Or wants a bigger share than any of the others," said Rawson.

"Or one of them has been siphoning a bit off without the others knowing," offered Benson.

"And now they've found out," said Gardener.

"Or it could be someone else," added Gates.

"We've all been talking about the possibility of it being one of the two men," said Gardener. "There are women involved."

"Ah, yes," said Anderson, "we can't rule out Zoe Harrison."

"I wasn't thinking specifically about her," replied Gardener, "James Henshaw was married. His wife may well have had enough of his double life."

"What possible reason?" asked Longstaff. "She's still got the house, and presumably a fair amount of money. Maybe that's all she needs."

"Perhaps she's not actually bothered about her husband," said Gates, "especially after what he's done."

Gardener nodded. "It could be any number of reasons but at the moment we just don't know enough. We still have a lot of blanks to fill in. Returning to the DPA team, have they all been out of the country and now they're back, or have they been here all along? Is it possible that someone else put all the pieces together a lot earlier than we have and held them hostage somewhere, and now he or she is releasing them one by one?"

Gardener's questions were halted by a knock on the door. Desk sergeant Dave Williams dropped in holding a piece of A4 paper. "This just came in, sir. A man called Jonathan Drake called in to register a complaint. He was attacked on Butts Court, shortly before ten thirty this morning by a man who was driving a green 4x4. He doesn't know what make, nor did he catch the registration, but it's a bit too much of a coincidence."

Rawson stood up. "I'm on it."

Chapter Twenty-eight

Anthony was laid on the bed in the guest house, totally bollocksed. He'd never had such a trying day in his life.

After Rosie had cut the connection, the first thing Anthony did was remove the SIM card from the phone and put it in his pocket. He then threw the phone in a bin. Only later, when he was on the bus going into the centre of Leeds did he realise how stupid it was to have done that.

Once in Leeds he bought another pay-as-you-go phone with about twenty pounds of credit. Returning to Beckett Park he discovered his other phone was not where he'd left it. No surprise there, then. Some skank would have it somewhere – not that it would do him much good, but it might help Anthony, especially if the police had a method by which to trace it.

He'd returned to the guest house about half an hour previously, exhausted but with no appetite. His brain however, had been on overdrive. A complete jumble of thoughts about who was doing what: *where the hell where they all, and what would happen now the police were involved? How much did they know?* Sleep was completely out of the question.

That would almost certainly lead to nightmares about him being chased by clowns – it always did.

Anthony sat up and rubbed his eyes. He jumped out of bed and crossed the room, switched on the travel kettle and made tea for himself. His stomach growled. He checked the biscuits. The few that were left would have to do.

With the tea made, Anthony sat down on the end of the bed, staring out of the darkened window. According to Rosie, everyone was missing and the police knew everything. So what to do and where to go from here would take some serious thinking.

Chapter Twenty-nine

"When did Jonathan Drake make the call?" asked Gardener.

"Just now," replied Williams. "I took it myself."

"Is he badly hurt?"

"Don't think so, sounds like it's just his pride."

"And you said we'd send someone round?"

"As soon as we could."

"Where does he live?"

"The flats near the university, about ten minutes away."

"Okay," said Gardener, eager to gain vital evidence but preferring instead to finish the incident room meeting.

"Dave, I appreciate your enthusiasm but if Jonathan Drake has just made the call he'll be happy to wait for us, so at least let's finish up here."

Rawson nodded and sat back down.

Gardener chose the subject of the airports next because he knew that Dave Rawson and Colin Sharp had worked in tandem.

"So far, sir, we've concentrated on Leeds Bradford," said Colin Sharp. "But we're no further on because we know that none of the names we have left the country. The situation is still the same."

"It was a long shot," said Gardener.

"We have requested that they try and find as much footage of the CCTV since the night of the hit and run but it's a massive job," said Rawson.

"We pretty much did the same with Humberside, and Robin Hood airports," said Bob Anderson. "We're going back tomorrow to go through what they've found but as Dave says, it's a massive job."

"I realise that," said Gardener. "I'll request some operational support officers to help out. Maybe if we can get enough of them they'll go through the boring stuff."

"Maybe we should try photo recognition again," said Longstaff. "It's possible they left the country using false names and passports, and maybe even disguises. But what if they've been a bit too clever for their own good?"

"What are you thinking?" Gardener asked.

"Well, now they've allowed the heat to die down, what if they've all flown back under their own names, using their own passports?"

Gardener smiled. "Well done, Julie."

"Makes sense," said Gates. "After all, we found both driving licences on Michael Foreman's body."

"Okay," said Gardener. "When you return to the airports take the photos with you again."

"Might be better if we take USB sticks with digital copies," said Gates.

"Yes," said Longstaff. "It's just possible that if they have returned using normal IDs, one or all of them just might have a criminal record for something that we've missed. Even if it was under completely different names, we might get lucky."

"Surprising how that can happen," said Frank Thornton. "But for a stroke of luck and a slip-up we might never have caught the Yorkshire Ripper."

"I know it's a tough job," said Gardener, "I really do, and I know what great work you guys are doing. All the legwork and no results can be discouraging, but all I can say is keep at it. Something will break somewhere."

In order to cover another subject, Gardener asked about the meeting with the bank manager.

"I was on that one, sir," said Sarah Gates, "but he's away until tomorrow morning. I said I'd be back first thing. His secretary put it in the diary."

"Okay. It's not ideal but it will have to do." He made a note on the whiteboard under the "actions" list.

"As we've already mentioned, we also need to consider the theory that someone out there might have them," said Gardener, "that we might very well have a vigilante to deal with."

That wasn't something the team relished. Not only would it make their job harder, trying to find the people they really wanted, but it suggested a completely unknown entity could be at work.

"Might answer for why their homes had been cleaned out," said Rawson.

"Which still gives us the problem of knowing who has done what," said Frank Thornton. "It still might *be* them lot, or one of them. Were they originally clever enough to see the writing on the wall, and cleared out themselves?"

"It's a possibility," said Anderson.

"If it is a vigilante," said Reilly, "he or she has been pretty bloody thorough, especially if they've been able to find out as much as they have, and stripped the houses, therefore removing any or all evidence."

"Good point, Sean," said Gardener. "One might even go so far as to say it has a hint of military precision about it."

The room descended into a strained silence. The task facing them was almost insurmountable. There was so much to do and it felt like a sheer race against time, with no idea how long they had, especially if a vigilante was at work.

Chapter Thirty

Alan Braithwaite had reached the end of the village where it met the main A65. Spike had done what he wanted, so the pair of them turned back. The weather was reasonably mild for the time of year, but a nice hot cuppa and a cooked breakfast before taking care of business would go down a treat.

As he entered the village he noticed the Frosts had had the wall repaired. And Wendy Higgins was approaching with Pouch.

"Morning, Alan, how are you this morning?"

"I'm well, thank you, Wendy. You?"

"Taking each day as it comes, but we're okay." As she said it she glanced down at Pouch.

"I was just looking at the wall, I see they've repaired it," said Braithwaite.

"Yes, I noticed that yesterday. Well, it's been three months and they've had the funerals for them both."

"I notice the Hunters' house has a 'sold' sign on it."

"Oh, it's gone, has it?" asked Wendy. "I spoke to David's brother, Roger, recently. He said there were a couple of interested parties."

"I expect he's glad to be rid of the place," said Braithwaite, "it can't hold any good memories for him."

The dogs sat beside their owners as if they had all the respect in the world for them, no matter how long the conversation went on.

"Terrible business," said Wendy, "have they caught anyone yet, do you know?"

"Not to my knowledge," said Braithwaite, bitterly. "People like that should be strung up. Two of the nicest people you could ever wish to meet, cut short in the prime of their life. Three months it's been and not a bloody word. Wouldn't have happened in my day. A short spell–"

Wendy Higgins interrupted him. "Yes, I know, a short spell in the army wouldn't hurt them." She placed a hand on his shoulder. "It didn't do you any harm. You said so last time, Alan. And I seem to remember telling you that your army days were behind you. You should leave it to the police."

"Don't seem to be getting anywhere, do they?"

"I doubt that will last forever. I can see you still have the bit between your teeth, Alan. How long *were* you in the army?"

"Twenty-five years."

"You must have seen some action."

"You could say that. Made it to the rank of sergeant. I wouldn't mind showing them lot some action."

Pouch suddenly stood up and yawned, as if his patience had worn thin.

Wendy Higgins must have noticed. "Well, like I said, there's no point you getting all revved up about it. I'm sure the police will get to the bottom of it eventually."

Braithwaite nodded but he doubted it.

As they bade each other a good morning, Wendy Higgins turned and addressed him again. "Was that a new car I saw you driving yesterday?"

He smiled, gently. "Yes, as you keep saying, I ought to take things easy. When you get to my time of life a bit of comfort goes a long way."

Wendy laughed and agreed. "Love the colour. Reminds me of a car my husband and I had when we were first married. British racing green I think the colour was."

Chapter Thirty-one

At the DCI's request, Gardener and Reilly were in an early morning meeting – a breakfast meeting it was called, though no one had anything in front of them. Reilly's stomach rumbled. Gardener felt pretty sure he would have eaten, and it was merely a protest.

Despite Briggs being the senior ranking officer, his office was no more luxurious than Gardener's. He had two desks, four chairs – apart from his own – and two filing cabinets. The room was carpeted, magnolia painted walls, with a number of prints attached. Apart from his computer and printer, Briggs had photos of his wife on the desk, and a coffee percolator. A small radio on the window ledge was tuned to BBC Radio Leeds.

Briggs had the policy book in front of him, in which Gardener had filed his report of the Michael Foreman incident.

Glancing at Gardener, he said, "Have we been a little economical with the truth here, Stewart?"

"We're not sure what you mean, Mr Briggs," replied Reilly.

"Which means you have."

Gardener took Briggs through everything they had found to date, emphasising that Michael Foreman was connected to the night of the hit and run and the death of David and Ann Marie Hunter.

Briggs glanced at the report again. Reading through it he quoted from a couple of paragraphs before lifting his head to meet Gardener's eyes.

"What kind of shape was Michael Foreman in?"

"He'd seen better days," said Reilly.

"From what we saw," said Gardener, "he was suffering. He had blistering red skin and there was a lot of swelling to his body."

"Had he been beaten up?"

"Didn't look that way to me. His tongue was swollen, so Fitz reckoned he would have had serious respiratory problems, nose and sinus pain."

"Did he say anything to you?"

"No, all he managed was a scream. Fitz seemed to think that they would almost certainly find fluid in his lungs. There was no sign of diarrhoea or vomiting, though he would have had abdominal pain."

"What were his movements like when _you_ saw him?"

"Erratic," replied Gardener. "His walking wasn't coordinated. When he was on the ground his body was trembling."

Briggs placed the report on his desk. "You know what's coming now, don't you? I have to ask this as a matter of form, did you at any point think to call it a Hazchem scene? Because it seems obvious to me that this man has been given something, and the first thing that springs to mind is a nerve agent. You realise how serious that could be?"

"I do, sir, but in my considered opinion it wasn't a Hazchem scene. In Fitz's opinion he'd been injected with something and despite the symptoms it wasn't considered to be contagious."

"Has Fitz confirmed that?"

"Not yet."

"So it still could be," said Briggs, sighing. He turned to Reilly. "What's your opinion?"

"I'm with the boss on this one."

"Christ," sighed Briggs, "you two are like glue. I'm not asking if you're siding with him. I'm not stupid enough to think you'd do any different. What I'm asking is, what's your opinion on what he was given; you've probably had more experience than anyone in this field."

"Judging by everything I saw, the staggering, the breathing problems, the obvious pain, it could have been any number of things but I don't think anyone has anything to worry about. Besides which, we've heard nothing else."

Gardener realised Reilly was also being economical with his summary because he hadn't seen any of those things. His partner had arrived on the scene after Michael Foreman had died.

Gardener intervened. "If I'd thought that it was a Hazchem scene I'd have called it."

"Okay," said Briggs, signing off the policy report, "there's no point labouring over it. I accept your decision. You seem to have it all in hand and you've got your team chasing up leads, but for God's sake, keep me posted." The senior ranking officer glanced up again and met Gardener's eyes. "If anything develops from this it won't just be your badge, we'll all be signing on."

"In all fairness," said Gardener, "if anything was going to develop it would have done by now. We'd have had half the population of Leeds filling every hospital corridor, and it would be all over the TV."

"Fair point," said Briggs. "I did see something on the news last night but they were very vague."

"That's down to me," said Gardener. "I made sure the press couldn't see too much of the scene on Bond Street. You know what they're like."

Reilly took over. "If we'd let them lot see what was going on they'd have started an epidemic on their own. The marquee was up in record time, and the boss man here said very little at the press conference."

Briggs' expression was priceless, as his bottom jaw nearly hit the desk. "You held a press conference?"

"There was no one else," retorted Gardener.

"You could have let him do it," said Briggs, pointing to Reilly.

"Are you kidding? There's no telling what he'd have said."

"You're too hard on me," said Reilly, "I speak the same language as you lot."

"I don't doubt it," replied Gardener, "we're just not quite sure on the order of the words."

Briggs laughed and closed the policy book.

"Okay, keep me informed of everything that happens. I know I'm changing subjects now, any news on your missing person case?"

Gardener cringed. He hated not being able to solve a problem, or apprehend a guilty criminal, but he knew that it was simply impossible to catch everyone. It may even be one of those cold cases that he would keep in an office drawer and take with him to his grave.

"Nothing, I'm afraid. As you know, he disappeared one night four months ago, never to be seen again."

"He'll turn up," said Reilly, "bad pennies always do."

"I wouldn't worry too much about it, Stewart," said Briggs. "We can't catch everyone. Someone is always going to slip the net; but he has a track record, doesn't he? Maybe five years down the line he'll show up somewhere with one of the travelling fairs and we might have our chance to nab him."

"Maybe," said Gardener, "but how many more women are going to suffer at his hands?"

"How many victims suffer every day in someone's hands?" countered Briggs. "We'll never apprehend them all, Stewart. But despite all that, never lose sight of the fact that you two do a bloody good job. You're out there all weathers and your dedication to the job and your team is as good as anyone I've ever seen, so don't beat yourselves up."

It wasn't very often Briggs gave out compliments so to hear that was music to Gardener's ears.

Reilly jumped in quick, changing subjects again. "How was London? Anything important we need to know?"

"No," sighed Briggs, placing his elbows on the desk and arching his hands, "usual stuff about police budget cuts, blaming it on anything but the truth–"

The phone cut short whatever Briggs was going to say. After three rings he answered.

"Briggs." The DCI's expression darkened. "Yes, he's with me now."

Briggs passed the phone to Gardener. "Who is it?" he asked.

"Williams, front desk."

Gardener took the phone. "David?"

"Just taken a phone call, sir, something I think you should know about."

Gardener's adrenaline started to race. "Go on."

"We have another body on Butts Court."

Gardener's heart sunk. His expression must have changed considerably because Briggs was mouthing the words "what's wrong".

"Where exactly is it?"

"Virtually the same place," replied Williams.

"How can that be?" asked Gardener. "We had a police presence there all night."

"I don't know all the finer details, sir."

"Who found it?"

"Lady called Elaine Kirk, she works for Slaters Menswear on Albion Street. She came out for a cigarette and found him."

"Same state?" questioned Gardener. "Staggering around?"

"No, definitely not. By the look of him he hasn't been capable of that for weeks. If what she's saying is true, you'll need to see this one for yourself. And my gut feeling tells me it's connected to yesterday's victim, which is why I'm calling you."

"Is he still alive?"

"Just."

"Have you despatched a PC to guard the scene?"

"Yes, and I've called an ambulance."

"Good, we're on our way."

Gardener replaced the receiver, wondering what the hell he was walking into, and whether or not there really was a connection to the death of Michael Foreman.

"What's happened?" asked Briggs.

"Another body on Butts Court; still alive, but only just."

"But you're already on two murder cases. I can't let you have another."

"I don't buy that, sir. My gut feeling tells me this is all part and parcel of the case we're already investigating from yesterday."

"What if you're wrong?"

"Then I'll hand it over."

Gardener could see that Briggs wasn't happy but he might have to roll with it.

"What state is he in? Did Williams say?" asked Reilly.

"Pretty bad, by all accounts, but this one isn't walking or staggering anywhere," replied Gardener.

"Where is he?"

"Behind the shops?"

"How the hell did he get there with a police surveillance?" asked Reilly.

"Let's go and find out, shall we, Sean?"

Both detectives rose and left the office.

Briggs shouted before they disappeared, "If it's anything like yesterday I want the Hazchem officers in. I don't want any chances taken, or any mistakes made with this one."

Gardener nodded before leaving but didn't reply.

Chapter Thirty-two

Shooting down Albion Street, onto Short Street, the two officers arrived at Butts Court to find it sealed off by a police car with flashing blue lights. As the vehicle blocked one side of the road, a PC stood in the gap at the other. A crowd of onlookers had already gathered, mostly from the unit across the street that had four loading bays, two of which had tractor units and trailers parked up.

Reilly pulled the pool car into the gap the PC vacated and both men jumped out, flashing warrant cards. Gardener heard raised voices, and the whine of the forklifts, banging about as they loaded and unloaded the pallets on the trucks.

"Where is it?" asked Gardener.

The PC pointed. "Down there, on the right, sir."

"How bad?" Reilly asked as both officers started to run.

"Bad enough for me to stay where I am."

Stepping to his right, around the corner of a building, at the rear of the shops, Gardener noticed a ramp leading to an underground car park. In front of him, the rear of all the shops had been sealed off with concrete posts, accompanied by wire fencing. He remembered years previously that it had been a popular area with the down and outs in Leeds, all of whom congregated here overnight.

Gardener noticed another police car further down Butts Court, which were very possibly the two officers who had been on overnight surveillance. He needed to talk to them but it could wait.

On the ground in front of him, huddled into what could only be described as a pile of rags – *like* a down and out – was the body. Standing behind the wire fence, a shop assistant cowered against the wall of the shop, arms folded, and as white as a sheet. She had a cigarette in her left hand but at the moment no attempt was being made to smoke it.

A PC approached Gardener as he knelt down to examine the body, realising that the crime scene was completely unimportant, but saving a life was. It had probably been contaminated anyway.

Reilly knelt beside him. "What in God's name has gone on here?"

Gardener noticed a hand and felt for a pulse. Faint though it may be, he *could* detect one. He wondered where the ambulance was.

"This guy will be lucky to live much longer. Will you call the station and get the team here as well?"

Reilly had his phone in his hand, barking his order into the machine, with an urgency that suggested he wanted everyone there by the quickest method possible.

Gardener flinched as he lifted the blanket covering the man, which literally stank to high heaven. He had no idea if the odour emanated from the blanket or the person. Nestled inside, very close to the body was a bottle of water.

Whoever he was he was dreadfully thin but at the same time bloated, reminding Gardener of pictures of starving children in Africa.

Although the man was dressed it was scant and Gardener could see beyond the clothing that most of his limbs were down to skin and bone but his belly was large and round. His eyes had sunk into his cheeks, which had drawn so tight to his skull that Gardener could almost see the white of the bone showing through. Most if not all of his teeth had huge gaps, and would very likely fall out if touched. What little hair he had sprouted through the dome of his head.

"He's been starved," said Reilly.

"Looks that way."

"How long, do you reckon?"

"God only knows but it looks like quite some time." Gardener glanced upwards. "Where the hell is the ambulance, Sean?"

"They shouldn't be too long, but you know what traffic's like this early in the morning."

The starved victim's breathing was very harsh and raspy, almost like the sound of a purring cat. Gardener had no idea what starvation did to your lungs but if the exterior of the body was anything to go by, they must be completely knackered.

He leaned in close, despite the smell. "Can you tell me your name, please?"

The man made no effort to reply. In fact, his eyes were closed and had been since the two officers had pulled up.

Gardener thought back to less than twenty-four hours ago, around the corner on Bond Street, with Michael Foreman.

He glanced at Reilly. "Best guess, Sean, how long would you say he's been like this?"

Reilly shook his head. "At least a month, boss." He glanced around and further down the street to the surveillance car. "How the hell did he get here, with those two on duty last night?"

"I have no idea but when we're finished with the shop assistant we'll go and ask them."

"We should really try and find some ID," said Gardener, "but what's going to happen if we move him?" He was convinced it was connected to yesterday's victim but realised it wasn't Zoe Harrison. It could be James Henshaw or Anthony Palmer, but the man was too far damaged to recognise from the incident room photos.

Gardener tried to talk to the victim again but there was no reply. He touched the man's hand. It was cold and pale, and he didn't even attempt to recoil from it.

"I don't think it will make much difference, Sean."

"We're not going to save him, are we?"

Gardener was about to answer when he heard an ambulance siren in the distance. He had no idea where it was but hoped to God it was the one they wanted. He stood up. "Sean, see if you can find something out from him; see if he'll talk. I'm going to speak to the shop assistant."

"Good luck with that one, she looks like she's in a trance."

Gardener walked over to the fencing, by which time another woman had joined the first one. Gardener stepped through the small gate.

"Elaine Kirk?"

The lady nodded but it was the other assistant who spoke. "She is."

"And you are?"

"Jean Lawford."

"Is she able to talk, do you think?" asked Gardener. He'd seen people in shock before.

"I'm okay," said Elaine Kirk. She was young, thin, late twenties, blonde hair, brown eyes, large nose, and wore round, wire-rimmed glasses. She had a North East accent. Jean Lawford was the opposite: twice Kirk's age, black hair tied up, plump, thirty years her senior, and spoke deep Yorkshire; not Leeds, maybe Sheffield.

"What time did you find him?" Gardener asked.

Kirk glanced at her watch and threw the unfinished cigarette on the ground. "About eight thirty."

"What made you come out at that time?"

"We hadn't been here long, got here about eight-fifteen. I'd had no breakfast so I decided to come through the back and put the kettle on before Jean got here, make us a cup of tea."

"What time did you arrive, Mrs Lawson?" Gardener guessed her marital status because of the wedding ring.

"Five minutes after. I'd brought a couple of bacon sandwiches in with me from Greggs. Can't say I've got the stomach for one now."

"Did you hear anything before you came outside?"

"No," replied Elaine Kirk. "Is he dead, like?"

"Surprisingly, no. So you only came out for a cigarette, no other reason?"

"No. Crafty fag while the kettle boiled. I've been trying to give them up but I don't think I'll bother after seeing him."

Elaine Kirk suddenly started shaking. In an effort to try and control it she immediately reached into her jacket and pulled out the cigarettes. "Oh, Jesus, I can't believe the state of him. What's happened?"

"Come on, Elaine," said Jean Lawford. "Let's get you inside."

"If you can bear with me, please, Mrs Lawford, I do have one or two more questions."

"Can't you see how traumatised she is?"

"It's okay, Jean," said Elaine Kirk. "I prefer to be outside. It's colder here. With the heat in the shop I'll faint, or throw up, and old misery guts won't want that."

Gardener continued while the going was good, aware that the emergency vehicle siren was much louder now. "Did you see anyone around, walking or driving?"

"No, nothing like that. Place was quiet as the grave…" Elaine Kirk stopped herself, realising what she'd said.

"And this was where he was; he hasn't moved at all?"

"What do you think? He hasn't got the strength to fart, never mind move."

"Has he said anything?"

"Not to me."

"Was there anything with him: bags, bottles, papers of any kind?"

"No, that was how he was, poor bastard. Anyway, I didn't check. You don't think I was going to approach him, do you?"

The ambulance drew up and the medics jumped out of the vehicle. One was tall and old with thinning grey hair. The younger one was stocky and balding, and immediately forgot his manners, or where he was. "Fucking hell."

"I'm going to have to leave you two ladies now, but I'd appreciate it if you stay around, we will need to take a statement."

"Doubt I'll be going anywhere," said Elaine Kirk.

As Gardener exited the fenced area, he heard Reilly explaining what he knew, which was very little.

The medics took over and both officers stood back. They asked routine questions – to which they received no answers.

The older man said he would retrieve the stretcher and a saline drip from the ambulance, whilst the younger one stood and spoke to Gardener.

"Where did you find him?"

"Here," replied Gardener.

"We think he was dumped during the night," said Reilly.

"We can see that he's been starved," said Gardener, "would you have any idea how long for, or what shape he's in; is he likely to make it?"

The medic whistled through his teeth. "Hard to say. Without water, he'd die after only a few days, three at the most, depending upon the temperature and other conditions. Starving someone but giving them just water, may well keep them alive for weeks; be bloody painful."

"Looks like that's what's happened," said Reilly.

The medic nodded. "It depends how fat they are to start with, and how well they metabolise their body fat. Using your own body fat to keep you alive makes you feel nauseous, because you can't replenish minerals like sodium. A patient's blood sodium levels eventually fall to the point where it induces delirium, and possibly a coma, then probably death. Without amino acids, the liver can no longer produce plasma proteins, and water then leaks out into the tissues and causes oedema fluid build-up – if the patient stays alive long enough."

"You seem to know your stuff," said Gardener. "How come you're driving ambulances?"

"Keep failing the exams," replied the medic, sheepishly. "Lose my bottle."

Gardener felt sorry for him.

The medic turned when his colleague called him over. As time was of the essence they figured it best to move the victim immediately, despite the ramifications. They had no idea if he would live, or if he did, how long it would be; but they knew for a fact that his best chance was not here, on solid concrete in the middle of Leeds on a cold February morning, despite it being mild for the time of year. Both men then discussed a technique they thought best for transferring him to the stretcher.

Either side of the body, they gently lifted him an inch from the ground and held him steady.

Still the victim made no sound.

"Okay?" said one of them.

His colleague nodded.

If Gardener thought the shocks had ended for the time being, what he saw underneath the body once it was clear and onto the stretcher, nearly stopped his heart and made his stomach lurch.

Chapter Thirty-three

"Hold it," shouted Gardener.

Both medics glanced in his direction with an expression that said "are you out of your mind, stopping us now".

Reilly knelt down and crawled carefully on his knees, retrieving a pair of disposable gloves from his jacket.

"Sir," said the medic, "if we have any chance of saving this man we need to get him to the hospital."

"Sorry," said Gardener. "When you get there I want his clothes."

"His clothes?"

"Yes, his clothes and his body are a crime scene. I need them removing carefully and bagging up."

"Right," said the older medic, "can we go now?"

"Yes," said Gardener, "I'll have two of my men at the hospital as soon as possible."

Gardener glanced at Reilly who had now collected the three items from underneath the victim. Gardener doubted he would like what he was going to see, but he knew he'd been right to persuade Briggs to let him have the job.

In his right hand, Reilly held two passports, and an A4 sheet of scrolled paper inside a plastic wallet.

Gardener glanced at both passports, aware that the first of his team had arrived in the distance, drawing their car up to the crime scene tape, further blocking entry to the street. A crowd had gathered, as usual.

He showed them to Reilly. "Jack Heaton and James Henshaw. No surprise there, boss."

"Certainly proves he isn't in Brussels."

"No, but the passports suggest he might have had every intention of going somewhere," replied Reilly.

"Unlike the others," replied Gardener, "I doubt he got there." He held up the A4 wallet, reading the quote on the paper:

> *When He broke the third seal, I heard the third living creature saying, "Come." I looked, and behold, a black horse; and he who sat on it had a pair of scales in his hand. And I heard something like a voice in the centre of the four living creatures saying, "A quart of wheat for a denarius, and three quarts of barley for a denarius; but do not damage the oil and the wine." Revelation 6:5-6*

Reilly finished reading and raised his head. "That's just brilliant. We've got a fecking religious nut on our hands."

"Where's the quote from?

"The Book of Revelation."

"What do you think it means?"

"I'm not sure. This stuff can be quite deep; might have more than one meaning. I'd have to think about it."

Gardener folded his arms and stared at the sky. "Someone's well ahead of us here, Sean."

"Who?"

"I had four in mind yesterday but Rosie Henshaw was one of them."

More of the team started to arrive, lining up at the end of Butts Court, waiting to be called.

Gardener continued, "We've now found two members of this so called DPA outfit who were involved in the hit and run which killed David Hunter: Michael Foreman and James Henshaw."

"Leaving Zoe Harrison, and Anthony Palmer," said Reilly, "so who's your third possibility?"

Gardener turned to face Reilly. "It's a long shot but I can't rule out Rosie Henshaw."

"First rule of thumb – always look at family."

"Her husband disappears after he's been involved in a hit and run in which two people die. His business partners also disappear; suddenly, one returns, and dies."

"She claims to know nothing about the hit and run. The damaged car is not where she believes it to be."

"Nor are the business premises," added Gardener.

Reilly glanced at the ambulance as it pulled away. "Now we find the husband in a critical condition."

"Where are the other two?" asked Gardener. "What does she know? Is she involved?"

"She might have known about everything from the start," offered Reilly. "Maybe she still has the other two holed up somewhere. But why would she turn on them; what sparked it off?"

"I've no idea, Sean, but we've seen enough murders to know that it doesn't take much."

"She'd have her work cut out with two kids to clothe and feed."

"She needs to be added to the list of visits. Let's see if she knows about Michael Foreman's death, and how she reacts."

As Gardener's team had all now arrived, he joined them out on Short Street. He very quickly briefed each of them on what he'd found before Reilly joined him.

Gardener glanced back toward Slaters Menswear. Both shop assistants had now returned indoors but the back door was still open.

"Time for actions," said Gardener, turning back to the team. "I'd like two of you in Slaters to take statements from the two shop assistants, and in fact anyone else who was around, or arriving for work at that time. It's a long shot because I believe the victim was placed here overnight. If on the other hand he wasn't and it *was* early this morning, someone may have seen something.

"Sean, can you go down there?" Gardener pointed to the surveillance car and the two officers who were standing beside it. "Find out what they know and ask them how the hell this could have happened when they were supposed to be on duty watching the place."

Reilly turned without question. Gardener knew it was exactly the type of job he relished.

"I need someone at the hospital. With the victim clear of the scene where he was found, his clothing is now a crime scene, as is his body. But they won't let you near him until he's stable. Stay there for as long as is necessary, and I need a progress report on his condition by the hour, or the minute if necessary.

"We need some operational support officers and all the forensic angles working, usual stuff: house-to-house, shop-to-shop, CCTV trawl from the cameras on the corner of the street, and I'm sorry to do this to you guys because I know you're already chasing up existing leads but I need everything we can get in time for the next incident room meeting."

"When will that be, sir?" asked Patrick Edwards.

Gardener glanced at his watch. "No later than three o'clock. But before you all go there is one big priority action and it really is a long shot."

"You want to know where he's been held," said Colin Sharp, "makes sense, I would."

Gardener nodded. "I said it was a big one, but you guys go about the actions I've given you. Sean and I will concentrate on that last one, which ranks in importance with speaking to Rosie Henshaw."

"She'll defo have to be told," said Edwards.

"She will, Patrick, but I don't want her to know we've found her husband just yet. I need to know if she knows about Michael Foreman, and what her reaction is either way. This will be a tough one, but we need answers, and fast!"

As his men dispersed, Reilly approached.

"This doesn't look good," said Gardener.

"Apparently they were relieved of their duty at midnight last night."

"By whom?"

"You're gonna love this. Detective Superintendent Palmer."

Chapter Thirty-four

Following a really awful night's sleep, Anthony had dragged himself out of bed an hour before, deciding breakfast might help him perk up.

That was a laugh. The dining room was another outdated box with peeling wallpaper, cobwebs, and a carpet held together through a variety of stains. Breakfast, which was not the usual full English, consisted of tea and coffee facilities, and two tables with individual packets of cereals, milk, pastries and an odd selection of continental meats and cheeses.

Anthony was hungry so he devoured a bowl of cereal, a plateful of meat and cheese, a bread roll, followed by two croissants and two doughnuts, all washed down with two cups of strong coffee. The quality of it all surprised him somewhat.

Back in his room, following a shower he was sitting on the end of the bed in a T-shirt, jeans and trainers, trying to figure out a plan of action.

Zoe Harrison had to be the key suspect in his downfall. Michael wasn't bright enough to complete such a task. He was a follower, not a leader. Besides, he didn't have the guts.

He doubted James was behind it either. He was a family man and perhaps the most stable of them all. Following David Hunter's death, James was the most concerned, and the least likely to draw attention to himself. It was also very possible that he had in fact made it out of the country. Probably started running before they found him.

Which left Zoe. She was brutal in nature, like the female spider that eats the male after copulation. She was also ruthless enough. They had all seen a new side to her on the night of the deaths. After all, she had not only killed David Hunter, but Ann Marie as well – calculated, and in cold blood.

Yes, Zoe was definitely in the running. Chances are she had been responsible for extinguishing him in cyber space.

So, what now?

Anthony realised that no one knew where he was, nor where they were able to contact him. They could email him but he didn't have to answer. Unless, of course, whoever had officially made him deceased had also disconnected his emails. He had a phone, but no one knew the number. He'd been careful to withhold it when he'd called Rosie.

However, she claimed the police had a trace on her phone. And although he was aware that pay-as-you-go was considerably more difficult to trace than contract, it probably wasn't impossible these days, so he'd still have to be careful.

The next and most likely thing to do would be to don a disguise. If the police were involved, they might have photos of him, which meant they would circulate them before long, and he would be noticed.

The next and most important thing to do would be to gain a little more freedom. For that he either needed a taxi, or a car, or possibly public transport. A taxi would be too expensive, and public transport too inconvenient. Which left only a hire car. But could you do that without the relevant documents? Anthony thought not.

Glancing around the room and at the state of the place, he figured he knew a man who might be able to help him. The owner was probably desperate enough for cash that he might consider lending Anthony his, or someone else's, car for the day, at the right fee.

Anthony was going to find out who was behind what was happening if it killed him. The only way to do that was to pay a few house calls.

Chapter Thirty-five

Stretched out on the bed, Zoe Harrison felt drained: low energy levels, joint pains, headache. She hadn't felt well for a couple of days but, in her opinion, her condition was slowly worsening. She couldn't be sure of the reason but she had an idea. Sleepless nights due to all the banging, hammering and whining of machines hadn't helped. God only knew what was going on.

At the other side of the room her computer monitor pinged.

She paid little attention, examining her skin instead, which was dry, coarse to touch. For years she had suffered with an overactive thyroid gland, more commonly known as thyrotoxicosis; her gland produced too much of the hormone thyroxine, which can speed up your metabolism. That meant medication for life.

She knew her heart rate was a little faster than it should have been, with occasional extra beats, indicating she may have atrial fibrillation which, left unchecked or uncontrolled could lead to heart failure, and possibly death. Not that she was under any illusion she would leave here in anything other than a box, but she was determined that she wouldn't go alone.

To ensure she'd remained healthy, Zoe had always tried to maintain a balanced diet, with calcium rich foods and supplements. Once again, it was a fine line. Some of those interfered with the Carbimazole absorption. Often, a gap of a few hours was enough to ensure no significant impact on blood thyroxine levels.

Since she'd been imprisoned here – wherever here was, and she had an idea – Zoe seriously doubted that the driver had been concerned about her diet, resulting in a feeling of serious lethargy. She barely had the strength to move from the bed, but she would have to.

She also needed to ask him for a vitamin supplement, and for it to work fast it had to be an injection.

The compromise would work both ways. The driver needed Zoe. He needed her brains, and her skills with a computer, which was why she was allowed access to one. After all, who else was capable of wiping out Anthony Palmer? A fortnight before he'd returned home, she had spent at least ten days eradicating any existence he might have built up. By the time he finally did make it through his front door, he would have a shock coming his way.

Strange how she hadn't been asked to do that for Michael Foreman or James Henshaw.

As far as Zoe was concerned, James was still alive. She hadn't heard otherwise. She doubted the same could be said of Michael. The Lord only knew what she'd been made to inject him with, but it wouldn't have been vitamins. As for Anthony's existence, she had no idea.

One thing she was pretty sure of, none of them would remain alive, which meant that Zoe had to concentrate on number one – herself. She may have spent all her life being a selfish bitch, and she may have done wrong on the night of the hit and run, but that character trait would help her survive.

Zoe figured she was being kept somewhere local, somewhere she knew. In her book, that could only be one place – the industrial unit they had all used for DPA business. It was big enough and secret enough for the driver to do what he wanted. And with the amount of noise he'd been causing it sounded like he'd been rebuilding the place.

Probing the computer she was beginning to recognise some of the characteristics of the programs they – as a team – had originally installed onto the server. The driver must have paid someone to make changes because there were areas she had been blocked from entering. She didn't think he was clever enough to sort that out himself.

But Zoe was. And she would find a route through.

She struggled but forced her body from the mattress and strolled over to the chair in front of the desk. The pinging sound had been an email from Rosie Henshaw.

Another one.

She'd had one yesterday. James' wife had been anxious to know what was happening. James had been missing for weeks. Rosie said Michael had been chasing him but even that had ceased. Yesterday, Rosie had received a call from Anthony, who had been as evasive as ever; either he didn't know much or he wasn't letting on. At least he was still alive, thought Zoe.

She spotted something concerning in Rosie's email. According to her, someone had been wandering around Leeds yesterday and had died shortly afterwards. She explained what she knew, but that was very little because there appeared to have been a media blackout.

Michael perhaps?

Zoe had obviously injected him with a lethal compound, that could lead to a painful death. God only knew what it was, but the driver, in her opinion, was ex-military, so it could have been anything.

She replayed the scene in her mind, remembering how odd it was that the driver kept his distance from the needle.

Why?

Was he frightened of what was inside the syringe; or was he actually frightened of the needle itself? A lot of people were. Was that the chink in Iron Man's armour?

Zoe glanced at the screen, deciding she would really test the water. She sent an email to Rosie telling her everything.

She sat back and waited for the fireworks.

Within minutes, the driver opened the door, dressed in a military uniform, wearing a snug fitting mask with holes for the eyes, nose and mouth. He carried with him a piece of A4 paper, which he placed on the desk in front of her.

"Don't be stupid, young lady."

"What do you mean?" Zoe played dumb.

"Do you honestly think I would let you play around with all this equipment, knowing how dangerous you are, without some form of security?"

Zoe lowered her gaze, silently elated.

"Please," she lifted her head, her eyes imploring, "don't hurt me. I didn't mean anything by it. I won't do it again."

"You're damn right you won't," replied the driver, "now you can resend that email and you will tell Rosie Henshaw exactly what I want you to tell her."

"I'm not feeling well," pleaded Zoe, "please, I need you to bring me an injection of Carbimazole, and a vitamin supplement."

"I will, when you've done what I asked." The driver leaned in closer. "And if you try anything like that again, I'll kill you. Think on, you're coming to the end of your usefulness, so don't push me."

As the driver stepped outside to grab a chair, he left the door open. With a quick glance at the roof of the building, Zoe knew exactly where she was being held prisoner. She would recognise that pipework on the ceiling anywhere.

All she needed now was a back door into her own computer system. Then she'd see who was pushing whom.

Chapter Thirty-six

Rosie read the email from James three times, trying to spot hidden messages or meanings. Problem was, it was short and sweet and to the point, sticking to the facts; not really the kind of thing he would normally write.

He claimed he was still in Brussels. *Lying bastard.* The meetings were complicated, therefore taking longer to strike a deal. *Who was he kidding?* He sent his love, and asked to be remembered to the children – didn't use their names, simply referring to them as the children – and said he would be home soon.

Rosie wasn't sure what to think. Despite the deception she still loved him and longed for him to be home. Part of her was elated that her long lost husband had finally made an appearance at last, albeit in cyber space. It proved he hadn't left her, or worse, was dead. Another part of her felt nothing but disgust and revulsion for what he had been accused of. *Did he really think he could kill someone and walk away from it all? Did he really do it?*

Was the email even from James? She doubted it, for a number of reasons. She'd heard nothing at all for weeks, and now a bolt out of the blue. And the phrasing, James wouldn't write and ask to be remembered to the children. No way. He would have referred to them by name.

But if he hadn't sent it, who had: and from where? Then again, why wouldn't he have sent one? She'd emailed not much more than half an hour back. Still, it was strange. Her head was a mess.

She raised her mobile phone and read it again.

The doorbell saved her from any further thoughts. When she answered she found two men on her doorstep. One was tall and thin with grey hair and a suit that had seen better days. The other was balding, wore wire-rimmed spectacles, and had very white teeth. His suit was smarter, more in keeping with a married man. He held a plastic folder in his right hand. Both had warrant cards on display.

"Mrs Henshaw?" inquired the tall one.

"Who wants to know?" demanded Rosie.

The smaller one answered. "DCs Bob Anderson and Frank Thornton. We're with the West Yorkshire Major Incident Team."

"Oh not this again," said Rosie, stepping aside. "You'd better come in."

She left one of them to close the door and continued through to the kitchen.

"I've just brewed up, would you like one?"

"No, we're okay, thanks, Mrs Henshaw," said the taller one. She couldn't remember who was who, despite having found out only seconds previously.

After she'd poured a drink she indicated for them to take a seat at the table. "I've told you lot everything I know. I can't possibly tell you anything else. I don't know where my husband is, and I know absolutely nothing about the hit and run. So what else can you possibly ask me that I've not already covered?"

"We're not actually here about your husband, Mrs Henshaw," said the smaller, smarter of the two. "We'd like to talk to you about Michael Foreman."

"Michael Foreman? What's that waste of space done now, assuming you've actually found him?"

"How well do you know him?"

"Obviously not as well as I thought," said Rosie, wondering why the hell they were here to talk about him.

"Well enough to call him a bald headed, squat nosed dumpling."

"Did I? When was that?" Before she gave them time to answer, she pressed ahead. "Well, whenever it was it was high praise for him."

"There's no love lost, then?" commented the one with the grey hair.

"Never has been."

"A few weeks back," replied the shorter one, opening his plastic folder. "We have transcripts here of a phone call he made to you."

"Oh, I do remember that," said Rosie. "I'm sure we had a thunderstorm that night and he called when I was trying to settle the children. I was bloody well fuming. I'd heard nothing from James since he'd gone to Brussels and then that idiot calls asking to speak to him and claims he knew nothing about a meeting in Brussels. Don't suppose you've found *either* of them, have you?"

Rosie took a sip of tea. "Anyway, never mind Foreman, what about my husband? Have you found him, yet?"

"We're working on it, Mrs Henshaw."

"Well you want to work a bit bloody harder and when you do find him I have plenty of questions of my own to ask him."

The pair glanced at each other with expressions that were hard to read.

"Did Michael Foreman have any family, or children?"

"Not that I know of. Who the bloody hell would have him?"

"When did you last see him?"

"Oh, Christ, to be honest I think I've only ever seen him twice in my life and I can't remember when either occasion was."

"Twice?"

"Yes, twice, or maybe three times. It wasn't often."

The smaller detective read through some paperwork he'd retrieved from a folder. "I gather that your husband and Michael were business partners. How long for?"

"About eight years, I think."

"Were you married to James when he started up the business with Michael Foreman?"

"And the other two idiots, yes."

"And do you know much about the business?"

"Not really, it's all a bit above me, computers and viruses and the like. All I know is they worked bloody hard; they were at it all hours."

"So you never saw much of them in the early days?"

"No, as I've said, they were all busy."

"And you don't find it odd that you never saw Michael Foreman other than two or three times?"

"We hardly moved in the same social circles."

"What about the other two partners?"

"Never saw much of them either, especially Zoe Harrison. She was even worse than Michael, totally unsociable. She spoke in bullet points, if she spoke at all."

"So there were no office parties where you could all get to know each other a little better?"

"It wasn't really that type of company," replied Rosie. "If it had been we still wouldn't have talked much. The best way to speak to Zoe was either email or text, even if you were in the same room."

"What about Anthony Palmer?"

"In all honesty, we did see a little more of Anthony. Although he was single he was more family orientated."

"Do you know if Zoe Harrison or Anthony Palmer had family?"

"Zoe's parents are still alive but I believe they moved abroad years ago. They left her quite a tidy nest egg, which she used to inject into the business. That was pretty much what got it off the ground."

"Any idea where they went?"

"No."

"What about Anthony Palmer?"

"His parents died some years back. I believe he had an aunt and uncle that he was close to, but I don't remember him talking about them much."

"So you wouldn't know where they lived?"

"No, but I had the impression it was local. Look, I don't mean to be rude, but what's this all about? You lot have been around here countless times, asked literally hundreds of questions, taken all my electrical equipment, which I've replaced at my own expense. I'm sure we've covered everything I know."

"Are you religious, Mrs Henshaw?"

"Religious? What the hell kind of a question is that? Am I religious? If I was, *He* certainly isn't doing a very good job of answering my prayers, is He?" she replied, pointing upwards.

"Were any of them religious; your husband or his business partners?"

Rosie shook her head. "Like I said, I didn't know them well enough."

"What about Anthony Palmer? You had any contact with him?"

"You have my landline records there, my phone is tapped, so you tell me."

"Can you please answer the question?"

"He called me last night but before you start I have no idea where from and he wasn't on that long so I doubt you'll have been able to trace it."

"That was when you called him a four-eyed, spineless, murdering parasite," said the smaller one, smiling.

"Why did you call him that?" asked the taller one.

"Figure of speech, officer." Christ, they were on the ball, thought Rosie.

"No love lost with him, either?"

"We weren't what you would call bosom buddies. Out of all of them I always thought Anthony Palmer was the better one, the more sociable one, and probably even the most helpful. Looks like I got that one wrong, didn't I?"

"Returning to the phone conversation with Michael Foreman, you also mentioned you'd been married to a bloke who couldn't tell the truth if he was given Pentothal. Do you have much experience with drugs or chemicals?"

Rosie stood up, the knot in her stomach tightening. "What the hell are you getting at? Are you accusing me of something?"

"If you could just answer the question, please."

"I'm a housewife for God's sake, not a chemist. My life is my children. We've already established that I'm not responsible for the hit and run so why the hell are you asking all these stupid questions. Am I under arrest?"

"Not at all."

"Then what's going on?"

"We're trying to get to the truth."

"About what? Because this doesn't sound to me like it has anything to do with the hit and run."

"On the contrary, Mrs Henshaw, it is connected."

"Do I need a solicitor?"

"Do *you* think you need one?"

"I haven't done anything. So why am I so concerned all of a sudden?"

"Where were you last night?"

"I was here, all night. Ask my children."

"Apart from your children, can anyone else confirm that?"

"There was no one else here, so no. And given that you have my landline records you'll see I never took or made another call last night."

"What about the night before?"

"Here again," replied Rosie. "What is going on?"

"We're just doing our job, Mrs Henshaw," said the smaller, friendlier copper, in a soothing tone. "And there are times when we don't like it but we still have to do it. Three months ago, a man and his wife were killed in a hit and run, which involved your husband and his business partners, all of whom went missing pretty much immediately afterwards. No one's seen anything of them since, apart from Michael Foreman."

"So you have found him?"

"Yes, Mrs Henshaw, we've found him," said the taller one.

"So why don't you ask *him* the questions you're asking me?"

"I'm afraid we can't."

"Oh my God…" Rosie's hands flew to her mouth. Her expression changed from one of abstract fear to growing concern.

With her legs trembling, she dropped back onto the kitchen chair. "Oh my God, that's why you're asking all these questions, isn't it? That man in Leeds yesterday was Michael Foreman, and he's dead. And you think it was me?"

Chapter Thirty-seven

They found Fitz in his office. The smell of fresh coffee hit them as they walked in. His desk, as usual, was clean and tidy and the only thing out of place was a small lunchbox to the left of his PC, containing a couple of sandwiches, two tomatoes, a chocolate bar, an apple and an orange. Gardener noticed the steam rising from the coffee cup. A classical music piece that he did not recognise filtered around the room.

Fitz glanced up at them. "Freshly brewed, help yourselves." He then glanced at Reilly. "Biscuits in the top drawer of the filing cabinet."

"It's not like you to give up the location so easily."

"That's because I want my office in one piece when you leave."

Reilly glanced at Gardener. "I don't know who he thinks I am."

"He has a pretty good idea."

Gardener chose a seat opposite Fitz, as did Reilly once he had the coffees and the biscuits.

"I take it you have something for us."

"I certainly do." Fitz finished up the sandwich he was eating, took a sip of coffee and wiped his hands on a napkin. He retrieved a folder from a desk drawer, placing it on the desk in front of him, pulling out a sheet of paper.

"I have Michael Foreman's dental records here so we know for a fact that it's him, although I don't suppose there was any doubt when we had *two* passports. What was the other one all about?"

Gardener took him briefly through what they knew about Michael Foreman, the night of the hit and run and the connection they had so far found to the others. He finished off with what they had come across earlier in the day – another body.

"In the same place?"

"As good as," replied Gardener.

"Someone's ahead of you."

"Be nice to know who," replied Reilly.

Gardener mentioned the quote they had found beside James Henshaw's body.

Fitz reached into his folder again. "That's interesting, because I found this stapled to Michael Foreman's back."

He passed over the A4 sheet of scrolled paper. It was identical to the one found beside James Henshaw, but the quote was different. Gardener read it before passing it over to his partner.

Then I saw when the Lamb broke one of the seven seals, and I heard one of the four living creatures saying as with a voice of thunder, "Come." I looked, and behold, a white horse, and the one who sat on it had a bow; and a crown was given to him, and he went out conquering and to conquer. Revelation 6:1-2

Reilly sighed and placed it back on the desk in front of him.

"I recognised it," said Fitz, "it's from The Book of Revelation. One of the Four Horsemen of the Apocalypse, namely Pestilence."

"The quote we found on James Henshaw this morning was also from The Book of Revelation," said Reilly. "That quote referred to Famine."

"Which is almost certainly what our killer did to him," said Gardener. "He starved him."

"Somebody obviously knows what's going on here," said Fitz. "I take it this James Henshaw isn't dead yet?"

"Not that we've heard," said Gardener, "but from what we saw of him I doubt he'll survive much longer, even with the best medical care."

"The important question for you two is where he was being kept," said Fitz. "He's obviously been holed up somewhere for quite some time, to be able to do that."

"We know that," said Gardener. "Whoever had James Henshaw very likely had Michael Foreman."

"When do you think he took them?"

"No idea," said Gardener. "But we're still left with the question of who."

"The other two are still at large," said Reilly, "so one of those two could be responsible."

"Unless it's someone who knows what happened and is taking their revenge on all of them," offered Fitz.

"It's a good bet," said Gardener, "but that only leaves us with one suspect, and she doesn't really fit the bill."

Fitz nodded but didn't answer.

"James Henshaw's wife, Rosie," said Reilly, "but I can't see how she could control everything so tightly when she has two kids to look after."

"Apart from that we are keeping a close eye on her, and she doesn't appear to have stepped out of line, so far," said Gardener. "We've read everything that the Bradford cyber team collated on her and I have my doubts."

"So, back to Michael Foreman, what killed him?" asked Reilly.

Fitz sucked in air through his teeth and pulled out another folder from the desk.

"I'm still awaiting the results of the screening tests."

"But you have a good idea."

"Yes, and I'm afraid you're not going to like it."

"Do we ever?" asked Reilly.

"In my opinion, what Michael Foreman had been given was a highly toxic substance, and it was administered by someone who really knew his way around the stuff. In rapidly dividing cells, blood, hair follicles, cells in the gut, sperm, bone marrow and cancer, it becomes obvious when the original cells die and are not replaced. In treating cancer you rely on cancer cells having a quick turnover and you stop the treatment before it causes cell death in other organs."

"Is that what he was given, an anti-cancer treatment?"

"Not strictly. I'm of the opinion he was given a dose of nitrogen mustard, which is related to mustard gas, some of which can be used as anti-cancer drugs. I think it was short term, probably administered as an injection not long before you found him. If it had been long term, we would likely have seen sickness, vomiting, hair loss, infection and anaemia due to low blood cell counts – just like the Russian diplomat who was given polonium some years back."

Gardener struggled to believe what he was hearing. "What is nitrogen mustard, and how do you get hold of it?"

"Nitrogen mustards were originally produced in the 1920s and 1930s, potentially as chemical warfare weapons," said Fitz. "They are vesicants, or to be more precise, blister agents, similar to the sulfur mustards. They come in different forms that can smell fishy, musty, soapy, or fruity. They can be in the form of an oily-textured liquid, a vapour, or a solid. But I don't believe it *was* a solid. I still think he was injected with the liquid form of the agent."

The mention of the word agent made Gardener shudder involuntarily. That led to nerve agents, which could lead to government involvement, especially when you considered where most nerve agents came from.

"But there is another complication that you might need to investigate," said Fitz.

"Go on," said Reilly, having risen from his seat to pour another coffee.

"They are also known by their military designations of HN-1, HN-2, and HN-3. To my knowledge," continued Fitz, "nitrogen mustards were never used in warfare. HN-1 was originally designed to remove warts. It was later identified as a potential chemical warfare agent. HN-2 was designed as a military agent, but that was used in cancer treatment. Other treatment agents now have replaced it. HN-3 however, was designed solely as a military agent."

"Has anyone used it?"

"Certainly not us."

"Is it contagious?" asked Gardener.

"If nitrogen mustards are released into the air as a vapour, you could be exposed through skin contact, eye contact, or breathing. If it's released into water, then you'd be exposed if you drank the contaminated water, or getting it on your skin."

"But you think this was injected in liquid form, so how likely is the exposure?"

"Very slight," replied Fitz. "You could be exposed by coming into direct contact with liquid nitrogen mustards but I don't believe either of you were."

"Is there an antidote if you are?" asked Reilly.

"No," said Fitz. "No antidote exists for nitrogen mustard exposure, the best thing to do is avoid it."

"Now he tells us."

"So which one of the three do you think he was given?" asked Gardener, not relishing the answer, or its implications.

"Without the results of the toxic screen I won't know for definite, but in my opinion he was given HN-3."

"And you'd get that where?" asked Reilly.

Fitz sat back, deep in thought. "There are any number of places on the black market, if you know the right people or the right place to look. If you two are going to start anywhere there's only one place I know in the UK."

"Go on," said Gardener.

"Porton Down."

Chapter Thirty-eight

Downstairs in a bathroom unit at the rear of the building, the driver opened a cupboard. Reaching inside he selected a sealed vial of iodine, and a vitamin supplement for Zoe Harrison.

His hand shook when he slipped it into the box of syringes. Before he even extracted the bloody thing he could feel his forehead sweating and his legs weakening.

He placed them in a small Boots bag before leaning back against the wall, calming his breathing.

When he felt ready he stood up straight, smiling about the fact that his prisoner thought she'd be given Carbimazole, a pro drug used to control an over-active thyroid; it stopped the thyroid gland from making too much thyroid hormone. Clearing out her riverside apartment, he had studied Zoe's medicine cupboard. A couple of hours' worth of research, both on the internet, and studying all her paperwork in a small wall safe she kept hidden behind an oil painting – how original – and he knew exactly what she was suffering from.

That had led him into researching things that were bad for her. People with hyperthyroidism should avoid preparations high in iodine because it can make the condition paradoxically worse. Additionally, in certain people it could provoke hypothyroidism.

Once he had emptied her cupboards he very carefully drained the sealed bottles of Carbimazole, replacing it with iodine, which was now beginning to take its toll. But it wouldn't be for much longer.

She really needed to avoid products such as kelp. They would almost certainly interfere with the thyroid function. He knew kelp was derived from seaweed, naturally high in iodine. According to Google, it was sometimes marketed as a "thyroid booster". He'd purchased it in dry preparations and tablets, grinding up both. As with iodine, kelp would have no health benefits for her at all.

Something else to avoid was soya, which also interfered with thyroxine absorption. That was more of a problem for him. She did not drink tea or coffee, or hot drinks of any description, only energy drinks. Soya milk would have been perfect.

Feeling calmer, he left the bathroom and headed up the stairs two at a time. He opened the door. She was still sitting at her desk, her hands flying across the keyboard.

Suddenly, as he closed the door, she went into a spasm, wrapping her hands around her stomach.

"About time," she said, through gritted teeth. "God only knows what's wrong with me."

He put the small bag on the table, retreating to the door, and standing with his back to it. Not that she would try to escape but he was taking nothing for granted.

She pulled everything out of the bag, inspecting it. She held the sealed packet containing the syringe in the air, at arms' length to her, and a little closer to him than he would have liked. His breathing quickened. He was beginning to wonder if she had cottoned on and was taunting him. All his research had told him that Zoe Harrison was by far the sharpest tool in the box. He was going to have to watch her more carefully.

Another forceful movement, probably another spasm, resulted in Zoe dropping the syringe.

The driver felt it was deliberate, as she'd made sure she threw the syringe toward him.

Once the spasm had allegedly passed she glanced at him, her arms still comforting her body.

"Can you pass that, please?"

He kicked it over. He doubted very much she could unseal it and do anything to him but his training told him not to take chances. As did his trypanophobia – if you were frightened of needles you stayed away from them.

She quickly picked it up, extracting the syringe.

"I'll give you some privacy," said the driver, slipping out of the room.

Chapter Thirty-nine

Entering the incident room, Gardener had a number of things on his mind but prioritising his actions was uppermost. Things had changed, and no doubt they would continue to, largely depending on what his team had to say.

He studied the whiteboards, which had been updated in his absence as the news came in. James Henshaw now had one to himself.

He took a sip of water and turned to face his team.

"Okay, let's see what we've learned in the small amount of time we've had. As you all know we discovered a second body in Butts Court earlier today, which we believe to be James Henshaw. From what we saw, Sean and I are of the opinion he's been held captive somewhere and systematically starved, kept alive with only water. That would have been excruciating. Underneath his body were a number of items, two of which were passports; one in the name of James Henshaw, and the other in his DPA character, Jack Heaton."

"You make him sound like a character in a game, sir," offered Patrick Edwards.

"Right now, he'll wish he was," said Reilly.

"Is he still alive?" asked Dave Rawson.

"I haven't heard anything to the contrary, Dave," continued Gardener. "Also underneath his body we had a quote on a scroll. Add that to what Sean and I discovered from Fitz earlier today, and this investigation has become a whole different ball game.

"Sean and I are now convinced that someone is taking revenge on the DPA team. Whoever it is, he or she means business, considering the extreme lengths to which they're going to administer justice. What we don't know is who's responsible? We appear to have a number of suspects in the frame but I'd like to go with what, if any, information you guys have found before I make any decisions."

Gardener turned to officers Thornton and Anderson. "One suspect now is Rosie Henshaw. Shortly after the hit and run, her husband, James, disappeared, as did the other members of the DPA team; one of his business partner's then shows up and dies in suspicious circumstances. This morning, her husband is discovered near to death and, to my knowledge, is still critical.

"That leaves two people from the DPA team, either still at large, or also being held captive somewhere. Finding them alive is imperative. What does Rosie Henshaw know? Is she involved? You guys paid her a visit today, what did you find out?"

Anderson took up the challenge. "Well, we know from Winter's notes that she's been living a lie, but whether or not she knows more than she's letting on is another matter." He confirmed what they already knew about false business premises and the Overfinch not where it was supposed to be.

"When we spoke to her today, sir," said Frank Thornton, "she claimed she hardly met any of the other members of the DPA team but she dislikes them intensely."

"Why?" Gardener asked.

"She wasn't very specific," replied Anderson, "but it was the expressions and the gestures when she talked about them that backed up her feelings. She said that Zoe Harrison was totally unsociable, reckoned that to communicate with her you had to send a text or an email even if you were in the same room. Although she did say that it was Harrison's money that started the company."

"She claims to have met Michael Foreman only twice," said Thornton.

"Twice?" questioned Gardener. "In how many years?" he asked, quickly searching his notes on DPA.

"About eight," replied Thornton. "Apparently they were not the type of company to socialise or hold Christmas parties. They rarely, if ever, got together and the only person she spoke positively about was Anthony Palmer."

"How so?"

"She reckoned he was more of a family man than the others. He had an aunt and uncle who lived close by but she didn't know where."

"But we do," said Reilly.

"Did *you* feel she was hiding anything?" Gardener asked. "Is she capable of what we've seen?"

"I don't get that impression," replied Anderson. "She's fiery, I'll give her that, but I think it's more of a passion for her keeping her family safe."

"I think she feels totally let down," said Thornton. "Her husband isn't the man she thought he was, and despite the fact that she didn't like the others, I don't think she thought they were capable of murder. That alone has turned her world upside down. Winter asked if he could put a tap on her landline so that if any of them called her at any point, the conversation would be recorded. Shona Pearson gave us those transcripts."

"Can you make sure we all have copies so one of us can study them?" Gardener asked.

Thornton nodded. "If you do, you can see that she's getting wound up by the situation that they have landed her and her children in. That's when she starts lashing out at them, calling them all sorts."

"Do any of the conversations reveal anything?" asked Gardener.

"Nothing we don't already know. Foreman was clueless and Palmer was evasive. She's the one on the attack, trying to drag information out of them."

"The most important being her husband's whereabouts," added Anderson.

"What happened when Michael Foreman called her?" asked Gardener. "Did Constable and his team follow up on that?"

"Yes, it took them a while to trace the call and when they did they had two men round to his apartment. It was empty."

"Of everything?" asked Reilly.

"No, just him. They returned on a regular basis before asking the caretaker to let them in. That was when they found it empty – cleared of everything. Caretaker was fuming because he knew nothing about it."

"And he didn't see anything suspicious? A caretaker usually has his eye on the ball. To clear an apartment out could take a couple of days. He didn't see anyone doing that – no removal vehicle?"

"Apparently not."

"And that was the last she heard from Michael Foreman?"

"Yes."

"Has she heard anything from Zoe Harrison?" asked Paul Benson.

"No, nothing," said Thornton. "But she had a call from Anthony Palmer yesterday."

"Palmer?" said Gardener. "Yesterday?"

"Yes. She went on the attack again," said Anderson. "He claimed he knew about the meeting in Brussels, the one that Michael Foreman apparently didn't know about."

"She had a go at Palmer," said Thornton, "called him all the names under the sun, tried to extract information from him and ended up by telling him the line was tapped and the call was traceable."

"Did we trace it?" asked Gardener.

"Yes. Through the cell masts we managed to put it somewhere in the location of Beckett's Park."

"That's in Headingley," said Dave Rawson.

"Did you check the place out?" Gardener asked.

Thornton nodded.

"I suppose it's too much to expect we found the phone," said Gardener.

"No, but it's a big area," Thornton replied. "Do you want us to get some extra help on it?"

"I doubt we'll find anything but it's worth a try," said Gardener. "Has the phone been used since?"

"No."

"He's obviously ditched it," said Sarah Gates.

"Okay," said Gardener, "someone keep on that one."

Thornton and Anderson were two of his most experienced, which is why he asked, "Do either of you suspect Rosie Henshaw is in on this?"

The room grew silent. "I know we shouldn't rule out anything or anyone," replied Anderson, "but I really don't think she's that good an actress."

Thornton agreed.

"Apart from that, we have her landline and mobile tapped. If we've found no suspicious calls it seems unlikely," said Gardener. "As I've said, let's have a copy of those transcripts and I'd like someone to go over them with a fine toothcomb. Pressing on, do we have anything on the green Evoque?"

"I have, sir," said Patrick Edwards. He tapped a few keys on the computer, which was linked to a projector, with a screen on the wall at the opposite end of the room. Everyone turned to see what Patrick had unearthed.

Butts Court in Leeds appeared in extreme clarity. The green Evoque pulled up. They noted the time. A man dressed in a white protection suit stepped out of the car and round to the back.

"What the hell is that?" asked Dave Rawson.

"It doesn't look good," replied Anderson. "That's the kind of thing Hazchem would use."

At the mention of that word, Gardener's stomach swelled. If it *was* a Hazchem suit, it would suggest he needed protecting from something nasty, which would not go down well with Briggs. It could also suggest that it was someone with a background in the police or the military. The other option was that he simply didn't want to be seen.

The man in the suit opened the vehicle tailgate and dragged Michael Foreman out of it, onto the concrete, past the ramp leading to the underground car park and then into the corner near the chain-link fence behind the shops.

Then the hoodie appeared.

"There's Jonathan Drake," said Rawson.

Each member of the team moved in closer as Jonathan Drake suddenly started to film the event. The man in the suit grabbed the phone, put it in his pocket and swiftly took care of Drake, disposing of him at the bottom of the ramp.

"Is that how Jonathan Drake described what happened?" Gardener asked.

"Pretty much," replied Rawson. "He beefed it up a little, made out he'd put up more of a fight."

"Stupid question, I know, but did he get a good look at the man in the suit?"

"No. Not enough to identify him."

"Did he recognise the voice?" asked Reilly.

"No."

"What happened when he came round?" Gardener asked.

"Nothing. Everyone had disappeared. Michael Foreman had gone, and the man in the suit and the Evoque, along with his phone."

"Did he give you his phone number?" asked Julie Longstaff.

"Yes. I put a trace on it," said Rawson. "Nothing has happened with the phone since the attack. It's been switched off, and no doubt the SIM card removed because there is no signal."

"That guy in the white suit obviously knows how to handle himself," said Reilly. "Everything he did was swift and clean, professional. Almost, dare I say it, military?"

Gardener thought about it and then pressed Patrick Edwards about the Evoque's movements.

"After leaving The Headrow it disappeared for a few minutes before doubling back. The next ping was on the A61 Roundhay Road. We lost him after that; still trying to get the information."

"Where does the A61 lead to?" Gardener asked.

"North of Leeds: Thirsk, Ripon, Harrogate. Could be any of those places, sir," replied Edwards.

"Okay, keep plugging away. I suspect the man with the Evoque is the one impersonating the police officer in the early hours of this morning. It could be Anthony Palmer. It wouldn't be the first time we've been fooled by someone dressing up and impersonating a police officer."

"Why would Anthony Palmer pose as a policeman and use his own name?" asked Reilly.

"To make us think it was too obvious to connect," said Gates.

"Hiding in plain sight, you mean?" said Longstaff.

"He's had some nerve, though, hasn't he?" said Rawson. "Posing as an officer, and relieving our two of their duty to carry this out."

"Wouldn't take a lot," said Reilly. "Boring shift, sleepy officers. This guy comes along, offers them some shut-eye at home in their own beds. Come back first thing, they're gonna jump at it."

"Meanwhile he ships his next victim in without a hitch," said Sharp.

"It's a possibility," said Gardener, "or is it someone else altogether, who knows as much – if not more – about the incident, than we all do?"

"That seems obvious," said Benson, "which brings us back to Rosie Henshaw and another possibility."

"Go on," said Gardener.

"Is she working *with* someone – Palmer being the most obvious?"

"But why?" asked Gardener. "What's the endgame?"

"Can't be the money," said Reilly. "They appear to be rolling in it anyway, and if her husband dies, she'll inherit it all."

"Maybe," said Sharp, "but if all this money has been made illegally, how will she stand? Can she keep it?"

"That's a good question, Colin," said Gardener, "but not for us to decide."

"Knowing this lot," said Reilly, "they won't have everything in one basket. There's bound to be shit loads of money in a Swiss bank account somewhere."

"Or is Rosie working with Zoe Harrison?" asked Patrick Edwards.

"Maybe she just fed us a pack of lies about what she really felt for Harrison," said Benson.

"All good points," said Gardener. "But the person in the Evoque was male, which suggests three people involved. That's too many for my liking, gets too messy."

The door to the incident room opened and DCI Briggs walked in, his face impassive, his mood sombre.

Gardener read the signs. "What's happened?"

"News just in, James Henshaw has died."

Chapter Forty

Gardener placed his bottle of water on the desk. "Two down, two to go."

Briggs took a seat at the back of the room, allowing Gardener to continue. "When?"

"About half an hour since."

It would be pointless checking on Rosie Henshaw's whereabouts. James Henshaw was beyond help when they found him. He seriously doubted she'd have had either him or the others holed up somewhere with everything else going on in her life, and her every movement being watched. Although everyone was a possible suspect, he still didn't think she was top of the list.

"Looks like Sean and I will have to pay a visit and break the bad news, and very probably coerce her into identifying the body. In that case, can we try to look a little closer at James Henshaw? According to Winter's team, his last movements never put him at the airport."

"Where did they put him?" asked Rawson. "Does anyone actually know?"

"No," said Anderson. "According to his wife he left the house intending to go to Brussels for a meeting that he never made. From Winter's notes, we discovered that he never even boarded a flight. Why was that? Where did he go?"

"Or, where was he made to go?" said Thornton.

"How did he get to the airport?" Gardener asked. "Did he have a taxi booked? If so there must be a record. Did one of the others pick him up?" The senior officer glanced at Bob Anderson. "Bob can you call Rosie Henshaw and find out if she knows?"

Bob Anderson nodded and left the room, returning a few minutes later. "Palmer picked him up."

"Back to square one," said Gardener, "so we don't know where either of them went and in which direction they were heading."

"If she's telling the truth, Stewart," said Briggs. "Isn't she a suspect?"

"Technically, yes, but a lot of what we've so far uncovered shows it would be very difficult for her to pull it off."

"But not impossible," countered Briggs. "If she really hates her husband, and the rest of them for what they've done to her and the kids, she could be capable of anything. Also think about the way women kill, usually from the inside, very rarely anything as direct as a knife or a gun. What happened to both Michael Foreman and James Henshaw started on the inside. I know it's not very nice but she will have to be questioned more closely."

Gardener nodded, unable to dispute anything Briggs was saying.

"Sean and I will handle that one. There was mention of the airports just then, has anyone had any luck?"

"We might be able to help there, sir," said Julie Longstaff. "Sarah and I spent most of our time there today with some operational support officers and a couple of super recognisers."

Gardener had his fingers crossed. "What did you find?"

"Digital ID and photo recognition software pulled something up," said Gates, "and fortunately for us, the airport archives all the CCTV so the super recognisers came into their own."

"They managed to spot three of them," said Longstaff. "Michael Foreman, Zoe Harrison, and Anthony Palmer on their return into the country. From that we have information of when they left, where they went, and when they returned."

"Seriously?" asked Gardener, unable to believe that sometimes good news came into an incident room as well.

"We're still documenting it," said Gates, "but we're pretty confident we can make something of it."

"This backs up something that was mentioned yesterday," said Gardener. "Maybe they went out under false names and disguises but they've had the nerve to return as themselves. Everything the DPA did seems to have been online, which means there must be a record. I realise they were brilliant at covering their tracks, but there has to be a trail somewhere, so speak to cyber crime again. Maybe returning as themselves is the mistake we needed."

"We're pretty sure that's what happened. They all went out on separate days, all within a week of the hit and run," said Longstaff, "and they all came back on separate days. None of them were together. They were all in different parts of the world. Michael Foreman was in Miami; Anthony Palmer in the Bahamas; and Zoe Harrison in New Zealand."

"Do we know what names they used?"

"I think they must have been card players at some point," said Gates. "We have a Jack Spade, and an Alf Diamond, but get this, Zoe Harrison chose Hunter as a surname."

"Jesus Christ," said Reilly, "they're nothing if not inventive."

"When did they come back in?" Gardener asked.

"Michael Foreman was first," said Gates, "six weeks ago. Zoe Harrison came in three days later, and Anthony Palmer as recent as Monday of this week."

"This week?" questioned Gardener.

"Yes," said Longstaff, "and apparently there was an incident with a clown, involving security. We're still checking but it involved Anthony Palmer."

Reilly clicked his fingers, and Gardener nodded. "Roger Hunter told us that Anthony Palmer was petrified of clowns, so what was the incident?"

"We're not sure," said Gates. "Apparently a new carrier was having an open day and clowns were present when Anthony Palmer passed through the lounges. The CCTV didn't show a lot but it looks like he spotted the clown and fainted."

"There was a doctor on hand," said Longstaff, "he was checked over, given some tea and then he left, but we're still working on where he went from there. We need to check more of the CCTV."

"None of this tells us who is responsible for what's happening now," said Briggs. "Two of these people are still at large: Zoe Harrison and Anthony Palmer. On top of that, there is still one more person in the picture. Rosie Henshaw. Have we any idea yet where these people operated from, and whether or not it is still being used by one of them? That might help."

"All houses have been cleaned out completely," said Dave Rawson.

"I'm not sure if this will help," said Gates, "but we also now know what cars they drove and we have the registration numbers from the airport. Like the Evoque, they are all on lease with the defunct company V-Tech, all using the DPA names. Problem is, the cars are all missing, including Anthony Palmer's."

"What about the account?" asked Gardener. "Is it still open?"

"No," said Longstaff. "But it was only closed two weeks ago."

"That's interesting," said Gardener. "How long were they leased for and how was it all paid?"

"Leased for six months and paid in full," said Gates.

"And now the account has gone," said Gardener, "just like them and the cars. Can we find out who closed the account?"

"The cars could be wherever the victims are," said Reilly.

"They could be," agreed Gardener, "but that would have to be somewhere big and possibly remote, all of which make it very difficult for Rosie Henshaw to control."

"Only if she's working alone," added Reilly.

Gardener glanced at Sarah Gates. "Were each of these cars parked at the airport and taken from there?"

"We believe so," she replied, "we're still checking the CCTV to see if the owners removed them, or someone else, and which way they went."

"Excellent news," said Gardener, updating the whiteboard. He turned back to his team. "I keep thinking about them all being holed up. We know for a fact that the unit they supposedly had is derelict, a dead end, but if they had somewhere else they operated from, what's to say that whoever is running the operation hasn't got them all in their own place?"

"But that would need to be a big industrial unit," said Briggs. "Especially if they have all the cars in there, and the vehicle used in the hit and run, and this green Evoque that we keep seeing. So the question then is, why would a company who specialise in computer viruses need a big unit?"

"Why would they need a unit at all?" asked Gardener. "They could all have worked from home."

"Maybe there was a lot more to it than computer viruses," said Rawson.

"Could have been a smokescreen," offered Gates. "Maybe they just rented a big unit somewhere whether they needed the space or not."

"For what?" Gardener asked.

"No idea," offered Longstaff, "but let's face it, money was no object. And if one of them had this in mind all along, the big unit would be perfect."

Gardener figured they may have hit on something. "Okay, point taken. I need someone to start checking units and warehousing within a fifty-mile radius."

"I'll take that, sir," said Patrick Edwards.

Gardener was beginning to appreciate Edwards. He was young but willing, rarely shied away from anything he was given, and often volunteered for jobs other people wouldn't want.

"Excellent, Patrick. Get Benson to help you. But before you guys go anywhere, I'm afraid we still have more information for you."

Chapter Forty-one

A collective sigh rattled around the room but Gardener understood it. Sometimes the mountain continued to grow and you could see no way of scaling it. He picked up the two scrolls containing the biblical quotes, now sealed in evidence bags.

"We've now discovered that two of the victims each had a paper scroll accompanying them."

"I never saw one on Michael Foreman," said Rawson.

"None of us did. It was stapled to his back."

"Stapled?"

"Yes," said Reilly, "four, one in each corner of the scroll, and they were heavy duty. I reckon whoever did it wanted the scroll to stay where it was because they were embedded into bone."

A few of the team winced and sucked in breath.

"What do they say?" asked Sharp.

"They're biblical references."

"Great," said Thornton, "we're not dealing with a Bible basher as well, are we?"

"I'm going to let Sean explain them."

"Hang on a second," said Rawson, retrieving his phone from his jacket.

"What are you doing?" asked Reilly.

"I'm going to record it and translate later."

Reilly stuck two fingers up as the rest of the team cheered. When the noise died and the tension dropped, Reilly stood at the front.

"They are from The Four Horsemen of the Apocalypse, as described in the last book of the New Testament. It's the revelation of Jesus Christ to John the Apostle. The chapter basically tells of a book, or a scroll in God's right hand. It's sealed with seven seals. The Lamb of God opens the first four of those seven seals, which summons four beings that ride out on white, red, black, and pale horses.

"Now, interpretations differ in most accounts, but the four riders are seen as symbolising Pestilence, Famine, War and Death. The vision is that the four horsemen are to set a divine upon the world as harbingers of the Last Judgment. One reading binds the four horsemen to the history of the Roman Empire, an era that followed The Book of Revelation being written. In other words, they are meant as a symbolic prophecy of the subsequent history of the empire."

"So who was wearing what?" asked Sharp.

"When we found James Henshaw this morning, his scroll represented Famine; extreme scarcity, especially of food."

"Guess they got that one right," offered Rawson.

Reilly nodded. "That refers to the third horseman, who rides a black horse. He's popularly known as *Famine*, because he carries a pair of scales. He's trying to show us the way that bread would have been weighed during a famine. Other people see him as the 'Lord as a Law-Giver' and what he's holding are scales of justice."

"So what do the DPA have to do with all this?" asked Frank Thornton.

"Probably nothing," said Reilly. "This says more about the person who has them. He's picked out a method of killing and made it fit with what he wants. Whether or not he's trying to send a message is another matter."

"Maybe he isn't," said Sharp. "He might just be trying to throw us a curveball, send us in another direction that's not relevant."

"Sir?" said Anderson. "You shared that quote with us this morning, so we brought it into the conversation with Rosie Henshaw, asked if she or any of the DPA were religious."

"And no doubt she said no."

"Pretty much," replied Thornton. "It wasn't emphatic, as if she was trying to protest too much. She said that not one of them had a religious bone in their body."

"No surprise there," said Gardener, nodding to his sergeant to continue.

"Michael Foreman took the guise of the first horseman, Pestilence."

"So what killed him?" asked Briggs.

Reilly glanced at Gardener, who hesitated, knowing his answer would cause a shitstorm. "HN-3."

"Pardon," said Briggs.

"Nitrogen mustard, sir."

Gardener went on to reveal exactly what Fitz told them. What it was, how it affected Foreman; that it was not a Hazchem scene, and why, and the possibility of where it *could* have come from. He then asked Reilly for the Pestilence interpretation.

Reilly nodded but Briggs stopped him in his tracks and he took over himself. "The origin isn't clear. Some translations of the Bible interpret plague, disease, or pestilence in connection with the riders in the passage following the introduction of the fourth rider; 'Authority was given to them over a fourth of the Earth, to kill with sword, and famine, and plague, and by the wild animals of the Earth.' But it's a matter of debate as to whether the passage refers to the fourth rider, or to all four of them together."

"Where did you learn about that, sir?" asked Gardener.

"The wife," said Briggs, "she's into all that shit."

Another round of laughter told Gardener what his team thought of the biblical angle. Aware of the time and eager to move things along, he said, "I don't want to pour cold water all over the biblical theory but it's something else we will have to consider and take note of. There could be something in that book of revelation that might point us in the right direction. The other thing we have to do is feed it into HOLMES and see what it throws out."

"Given what you've just told us, we need to talk to Porton Down," said Briggs.

"Good luck with that one," said Gardener.

"We've juggled around the people we know who could be in the frame for this," said Bob Anderson, "but considering what we've just heard, how likely is it that any of these people would have access to anything from Porton Down?"

"Which puts someone else in the frame altogether," said Thornton. "Someone we don't even know about."

"Basically, is that someone now playing God, comparing the death of the Hunters to the four horsemen?" asked Bob Anderson.

"It's very possible?" said Gardener. "We need to answer all these questions. Someone needs to speak to Porton Down, using whoever's help we need to get that information."

"That might be tough," said Briggs. "But I have a contact in the Force Intelligence Bureau."

Gardener knew the FIB assessed all intelligence that came in, before sanitising it to make sure it didn't compromise anyone.

Sensing that was everything, Gardener addressed the team. "Okay, guys, sterling effort from everyone. We still have a lot to do and once again, time is against us." He glanced at his watch. "Let's meet back here at nine tonight."

As the team dispersed, Gardener waited while Briggs left the room and called his partner over.

"Something else came to mind during that incident room session but rather than bring it up, I wanted your take on it."

"Go on," said Reilly.

"We've neither seen nor heard anything of Roger Hunter recently?"

"Not since the funeral. He did say he was putting the house on the market for a stupid price to get a quick sale before returning home."

"And where's home?"

"He never actually said."

"What he said was very little," replied Gardener. "He also implied that he worked in government but he didn't say what."

"Which could be anything."

"He made it sound like we'd have to upset quite a number of apple carts to get the information."

"Are you thinking he's responsible?"

"I have no idea," said Gardener. "If anyone has a motive, he does. Maybe it's worth checking to see if the house has sold; if not, is he still around? If he is, update him on what we've found, and find out if he knows anything more. But more importantly, we might need to upset one of those apple carts because we could really do with finding out more about him. If only to clear him and perhaps make sure he isn't on the list either."

Chapter Forty-two

Ablutions complete and bathroom duties finished, Anthony was back in his room, sitting on the edge of the bed.

He still didn't feel clean. How could he? The guest house was a dump, with little in the way of hygiene standards. The sheets in his room hadn't been changed. *Who was he kidding?* The bed hadn't even been made. He was sharing a bathroom down the corridor with Lord knows how many other people, where he actually had to clean the bath *before* he jumped in.

About to think things through, a news anchor from the TV on the wall led with the story of a man who had died in horrific circumstances in the centre of Leeds yesterday. Anthony wouldn't have bothered too much but he heard the words hit and run.

Jumping off the bed he increased the volume.

"The victim, known as Michael Foreman, was seen wandering around Bond Street in a very distressed state…"

A picture of Michael appeared on screen and Anthony nearly collapsed. His legs weakened, and he felt pins and needles in his arms and the ends of his fingers.

The news crew were talking to eyewitnesses, whose accounts were moving. Michael had been wandering around, searching for help, screaming out in pain – almost blind.

What the fuck had happened to him? thought Anthony, staring at the screen.

The Calendar news team confirmed the police had been on hand very quickly and the whole scene was cordoned off whilst they dealt with the incident. It appeared that Michael Foreman had died pretty soon after, leaving the scene in an ambulance. The police were appealing for more witnesses to come forward. They had not revealed what Michael had died of.

Anthony couldn't believe it. He felt hollow, and cold, and close to breaking down. *What the hell had happened to their lives?* They had had everything: successful business, nice homes, flash cars. More money than they could ever have spent. One mistake. One mistake was all it had taken to ruin everything.

Anthony grabbed his bottle of lager, taking a deep, long swig, thinking over his day.

As he'd suspected, the owner of the guest house knew someone who knew someone who had a car that was surplus to requirements. Fifty pounds cash with no questions asked and he'd had the keys and the car before ten o'clock.

He'd actually started with Michael's apartment in Skipton. He wasn't surprised when the caretaker informed him it had been emptied, and that the police were calling on a regular basis. It was the same story at Zoe's riverside apartment. When he dropped by Rosie's house in Ilkley, the police had actually been there. He'd seen them enter the house from the opposite side of the road.

What in God's name was going on? How much did the police know? More to the point, who was responsible for the carnage? Who had killed Michael?

There were two prime suspects as far as he could see. Zoe Harrison or James Henshaw.

Rosie claimed James had never made it to Brussels. Maybe he hadn't. What if James had had a change of heart, decided he didn't like what had happened, wanted to fix things?

The same could be said of Zoe. She was completely fucking ruthless when it came to business. The cold-hearted way in which she disposed of Ann Marie was unparalleled.

Anthony swigged more lager. They could both be in it together, though it was a long shot. Zoe and James were complete opposites.

It was still possible that they could have ripped him off and fucked off.

But why would James do that? He had a wife and family – more to lose.

Another thought hit Anthony. *Was it Rosie? Was she responsible for the mess and the destruction?*

Anthony's thoughts were then dealt another serious blow, when three faces appeared on the TV screen, wanted in connection with the hit and run of David Hunter, and the death of his wife, Ann Marie, in Burley in Wharfedale three months previous.

They had pictures. And he recognised them all: Zoe, James, and himself.

He lowered his head and covered his face with his hands. It could be all over now.

How long did he really have left before the net closed in on him?

Desperate for answers, Anthony suddenly had a light-bulb moment, one that was worth hanging on to.

The DPA safe cyber forum address where they could be contacted if all else failed.

It had to be worth the risk.

Chapter Forty-three

Rosie opened the front door to the sound of the bell and immediately saw red.

"Brought the cuffs, have you?" She stretched out her arms and held out her hands. "Ready to cart me away?"

Both officers pulled out warrant cards. One was very smartly dressed in a jacket, shirt and tie, trousers, and for some bizarre reason a hat with a hole in it. The other wore a bomber jacket and jeans.

"Mrs Henshaw." Gardener held up his card.

"This is police harassment." Rosie walked off, leaving the door open, as she had earlier in the day for the other two.

Gardener and Reilly followed. Rosie ended up in the kitchen, taking a seat at the table.

She immediately jumped up, wandered over and removed lemonade from the fridge, took a glass from the cupboard above her head and poured one out.

"Would you like one?"

"Please," said both officers in unison.

When all three were seated, Rosie went on the attack again. "I'm really sick of this. *I'm* not the criminal here, but you lot are treating me like one. I haven't done anything and you're just hounding me. I'm just pleased my children are having a stay over. Why aren't you out there catching real criminals – like my husband?"

"It's your husband we've come to talk to you about, Mrs Henshaw," said Gardener. "When was the last time you saw him?"

"Weeks ago, when he left here for a meeting in Brussels."

"A meeting that he never made."

"So I've heard."

"And you haven't heard from him in that time?"

Rosie sighed, drinking lemonade.

"No. He sent one or two emails at first. Then they dried up and I heard sod all."

"And you didn't think that odd?" asked Reilly.

"Of course it was bloody odd, but what could I do about it? I made calls and sent emails but they all went unanswered. Next thing I knew I had Michael Foreman ringing me up, asking for James. Then Anthony Palmer."

"You've had no contact with Zoe Harrison?"

"No. Not that I'm bothered. And then I find out that Michael Foreman is dead and two officers come here and accuse me of it. Well, don't worry because I've already been on to my solicitor. I'll be speaking to him first thing in the morning. I probably should have spoken to him weeks ago."

The two detectives glanced at each other with expressions that Rosie couldn't read but doubted it was anything good.

"What is it now; found another one dead?"

"Mrs Henshaw, we're not accusing you of anything," said Gardener. "Perhaps I can explain something to you that might help you see it from our point of view; your husband and his business partners were involved in the hit and run back in February, in which a man was killed. His wife also ended up dead. It seems that all the people in the car went missing shortly after the accident. We've established that – apart from your husband – they left the country but have since returned. Until now, they haven't been seen, but they are dying in mysterious circumstances."

Rosie clamped her hands to her mouth. *What did he mean, they are dying in mysterious circumstances?*

"Oh my God. The man who died was Anthony Palmer's uncle? And he killed his own aunt?"

"It's looking that way."

Rosie stared across the kitchen for want of anything better to do, trying to put her thoughts together; trying to rationalise them, especially when her instinct told her that whatever these two were there for would be of no benefit to her.

"As yet, we don't know," said Gardener, "but it puts us in a very awkward position where you're concerned."

"Why?"

"We're not sure whether to treat you as a possible suspect…"

"Or what?" asked Rosie, preferring not to hear an answer.

"Or the next victim, which is something we'd like to prevent."

"What the hell do you mean, next victim? Have Zoe and Anthony been found dead as well as Michael?"

Once again, the two detectives glanced at each other.

"As yet, we haven't found Zoe Harrison or Anthony Palmer," said Gardener.

"So what are you–" Rosie stopped mid-sentence, the implication of what they were saying becoming all too evident.

"It's James, isn't it? You've found James."

"Mrs Henshaw, is there anyone you'd like us to call to come and stay with you?" asked Gardener.

"Just tell me."

"We could call a Family Liaison Officer to come and stay with you," said Reilly.

Rosie felt her insides swell up to twice their normal size. Her legs turned to jelly and her hands suddenly felt numb. She felt sick, and they hadn't even told her anything yet.

The tears rolled down her cheeks. All the time she had spent cursing James for what he had done, explaining to the children that he was on business and would be back soon, and that secretly she was wishing him in hell.

They do say be careful what you wish for.

"Please... what's happened?"

"I'm really very sorry," said Gardener, "but we think we may be the bearers of bad news. We discovered another body this morning in Butts Court."

"Is it James?"

"Mrs Henshaw, does your husband have any distinguishing marks anywhere on his body?"

Rosie was answering on autopilot. "He has a birthmark, on his right thigh."

Gardener nodded at Reilly.

"It's him, isn't it?"

Rosie remembered the email from James earlier in the day. "Wait a minute, no, it can't be. I had an email earlier today."

"An email?" asked Reilly. "What time was that?"

"Eleven o'clock this morning." After she'd said that she felt stupid, it wouldn't be anything but morning, they hadn't reached eleven at night. "How can that be?"

"You're sure it was from your husband?"

Rosie wasn't. "I thought it was... at first."

"What do you mean?"

"Well, when I reread it and thought about it afterwards, it didn't sound like James."

Floods of tears streamed down Rosie's face. She stood up and walked over to the window, pressing her hands onto the draining board, unable to stop the flow, despite what she had thought about James in recent weeks.

Gardener followed her. "Are you sure there is no one we can call for you?"

Rosie was struggling to breathe, let alone string a sentence together. She reached across the worktop and grabbed her mobile. On the contact page she found Michelle's number. She handed the phone to Gardener.

"Please," she sobbed, pointing to her best friend's number.

Gardener passed it to Reilly, who immediately stepped out of the kitchen.

"I'm really sorry to land all of this on you, Mrs Henshaw, but there are two further things I need to ask."

Rosie simply nodded, unable to speak.

"Did the email come through to your phone?"

Rosie nodded.

"May we take it? Once we analyse it, it might tell us who sent the email and where from?"

Rosie nodded and buried her head into a kitchen tissue, sobbing and shaking. Reilly came back into the room, nodding. "She's on her way, Mrs Henshaw."

Rosie nodded, finally managing words. "And your second question?"

She could see the compassion in Gardener's eyes. He really did not want to ask the obvious question. "Oh, God, please don't ask me to identify him."

Rosie collapsed in a heap.

Chapter Forty-four

Anthony was sitting in a late-night café in Headingley. His day had been brutal. After finding a chemist he had dyed his hair, swapped his glasses for contacts, worn a fake moustache and bought a leather jacket and jeans.

Thirty minutes previously he had been over to Beckett's Park again but swiftly left after he had spotted what he suspected were police, more than likely searching for the phone he had disposed of yesterday.

He was sitting at the back of the room, completely out of earshot of everyone else, staring at the untouched latte in front of him. Not that he had a great deal to worry about. The other people in the café were students and he may as well not have existed for all the attention they were paying him.

His head was a mess. *Who the hell was picking them off? James? Zoe? Rosie? Someone else altogether – someone he either didn't know or hadn't considered?*

The café owner was cleaning and setting a table in front of him. He stared at Anthony but said nothing. At the front of the shop a group of excited students cheered and shouted, and squealed with laughter at something on one of the phones.

Anthony picked up his own phone. It was no good. He needed to speak to someone, and Rosie was probably the only person. He hadn't been able to connect with Zoe or James, nor had he received any reply to his email at the safe address.

The line was answered after two rings but Anthony didn't recognise the voice. He stared at the phone, making sure the number was right.

"Hello?" the voice repeated.

"Is Rosie there, please?"

"I'm sorry, she can't come to the phone right now."

Anthony had no idea who he was talking to but it must be someone who knew her. "Is she okay?"

The line grew silent, the reply taking forever. "Who are you, please?"

"My name is Anthony Palmer, I'm a friend of her husband, James."

"I'm really sorry, James died earlier today."

Chapter Forty-five

Gardener was dog-tired. So was his team. He knew it. They knew it. But there was a real buzz in the air as they entered the incident room, giving him the impression that some good news had broken.

Gardener was leaning against the wall, with his partner, Reilly. He grabbed a bottle of water and a Bounty bar from a table. Healthy eater he may have been but he'd always had a weakness for the popular coconut and chocolate bar. The Lord only knew what Reilly was eating but he was using both hands.

Dave Rawson grabbed a coffee and a sausage roll.

"I think you'd better hold your horses there, my wee friend."

Rawson glanced at Reilly. "What are you on about?" questioned Rawson, laughing. "Don't know why I'm asking that, I understood him better with a mouthful of food."

Reilly ignored the jibe. "I'm not sure I can let you have anything to eat there, son, not after your earlier misdemeanour."

"Oh, come on, where's your sense of humour?"

"Another thing I don't have, according to you."

"Come on, boss." Rawson glanced in Gardener's direction. "Have a word with him."

"He might have a point, Dave, you *were* a bit hard on him."

"I see, like that, is it? Well, if you don't feed me I won't have enough strength to impart the important information."

Gardener glanced at Reilly. "He does have a point."

"I'll let it go this time."

Once the team had filed in – including Briggs – and were seated, Gardener nodded and signalled he was about to start. Shona Pearson slipped in before Gardener started talking.

"Good to see you've all made it back. Judging by the air of excitement I gather we have something further to work with."

Dave Rawson stood up, finished a swig of tea and opened a thick file in front of him, spreading papers around.

"Me, Julie, Sarah and Shona have been with cyber since we finished this afternoon. I think David Hunter made a lot more headway than he would ever be credited for."

"Do tell," said Gardener.

"We've all known DPA were involved in the hit and run, but why and how was another matter," said Rawson.

"We also felt that there must have been a track record somewhere about their activities," said Gates.

"They've been conning people since day one," said Longstaff, "and all of it online, and all of it practically invisible because of their skills."

"It was the bitcoins that finally gave them away," said Shona Pearson.

"Yes," said Gardener, "DI Winter said something about that. He reckoned if you were good enough you could follow the trails."

"Winter's team have," said Rawson. "They've been at this longer than we have and they've been concentrating on a series of online scams, which is what DPA have been doing from the beginning."

"That's what made them the money and gave them the confidence to go large," said Gates.

"Okay," said Gardener, "let's have it."

"They all had a scam of their own," said Longstaff, picking up one of the files. "Let's start with Zoe Harrison, the romance mule."

"The what?" Reilly asked.

"Romance mules usually fall prey to romance scams, which are all online. They're deceitful romantic interactions with unsuspecting victims. These fraudsters work to gain the trust and affection of mules. They then use that relationship to commit fraud. The majority of the time, the victims haven't a clue they're involved in a fraud scheme, or a criminal act, until it is too late.

"Zoe Harrison created fake profiles using stolen photographs and false names on a number of dating websites, social media sites, blog forums, and support groups. She worked a number of victims all at the same time, beginning with contact. Almost immediately she went into private chat rooms and used emails or chat sessions to gain their confidence."

Gardener sighed, shaking his head.

"What's wrong?" Rawson asked.

"Who else do we know that did all of this?"

"Robbie bloody Carter," said Reilly.

"It's obviously a bigger market than we thought," said Gardener. He nodded to Longstaff. "Carry on."

"She usually took three months to form the relationships," said Longstaff. She acted as if she was in love with them, creating a bond, sharing life stories. She made sure there was a decent distance between them all. In one case she forged a relationship, despite claiming *she* lived in Eastern Europe. She promised to visit as soon as she could. Once she'd gained their trust, she asked them to receive and transfer money on her behalf."

"How did she manage that?" asked Colin Sharp.

"She used a variety of excuses," said Gates. "Experiencing banking-wire issues due to a foreign account, claiming she needed money to pay for a family member's funeral. Or she claimed she was in the middle of a divorce and needed some assistance pawning jewellery, and having the funds sent through Western Union. In one case, the jewellery the woman received was stolen from fraudulent online auctions, and she unknowingly became a mule in Zoe's scheme.

"In another she claimed to be military personnel stationed overseas who needed assistance accessing their funds due to being in a war zone. She tricked a fifty-year-old man called Christopher Barlow in the West Midlands into allowing his personal bank account to receive and send money as part of a scheme to finance terrorists."

"Terrorists?" shouted Reilly.

"I know," said Rawson, "takes some believing, doesn't it?"

Reilly shook his head in disbelief.

"According to a leading newspaper, the victim believed he was corresponding with an affluent businesswoman in her early forties whom he met on an online dating site. The woman claimed she needed to pay some of her employees in the UK, and would only trust payments coming from a UK bank account. Once Barlow agreed, she began to wire large sums of money into his account and he would prepare and send cheques on her behalf. He was eventually charged with a criminal offence because he did not report the illicit incident to the police. There are literally hundreds of instances that Winter's team believe she was involved in but we don't have all night."

"Okay," said Briggs, "take us quickly through what the others were involved in, otherwise we'll be here till Christmas."

Pearson took up the conversation. "Michael Foreman was involved in a WFH scheme. Work-from-home schemes are fake job offers that are used by fraudsters and mule herders, to entice witting or unwitting individuals into providing bank account details for the purpose of receiving an Automated Clearing House deposit or counterfeit cheque. They are then instructed to electronically transfer funds to a third party, often in another country.

"Mules are also told to make transfers to the third parties through a money-service business, such as Western Union. Occasionally, mules will deliver cash in person to representatives of the crime group. This type of transfer usually involves a mule who is a willing participant in the illegal scheme."

No one interrupted. It was late, they were tired, and Gardener felt it best if he simply let his team say what they had to, and then try to deal with the aftermath.

Pearson continued, "WFH offers are usually cleverly created to look like legitimate companies. Sometimes they use recognisable trademarks, or logos, or names to create apparent legitimacy. Fraudsters often use a variety of methods for potential victims such as spam emails, job search sites and online classifieds or social media.

"The job application process for some opportunities even requires applicants to be interviewed by a company representative, and maybe even sign an employment contract. Individuals who succumb to these types of fraudulent job offers are often financially distressed due to extended unemployment or other financial hardship.

"Even though the job offers will seem suspicious to many, those who feel they don't have anything to lose will give it a try. Unfortunately for them, most mules are only used once and will never see a commission. There is also a significant chance of being arrested and being a victim of identity theft later on, because the fraudsters have all the personally identifiable information they need, such as the mule's national insurance number.

"Here's an example: a woman was on Indeed looking for a job when she found a WFH administrative assistant opportunity. She applied for the job, and that's when things took a strange turn. She hadn't even accepted the position when a package containing a cheque for £3,450 arrived at her door. Along with the cheque, the envelope contained detailed instructions to deposit the cheque into her personal bank account, keep £400 for herself and send the rest via two separate MoneyGrams to different individuals in West Africa. She realised it was fraud and reported it."

"How come Michael wasn't caught at that time?" asked Reilly.

"Couldn't trace him," said Longstaff. "These guys were far too clever with computers, clever enough to completely dispose of a trail as they were laying it."

"Christ," said Reilly. "I think we're in the wrong job."

"I think you're right, Sean."

Rawson took the reins and filled them in on James Henshaw. "He was the real wizard behind the company. He dreamed up most of the scams, but he was also the brains behind the computer viruses."

"What did he start with?" asked Gardener.

"His was the Secret Shopper Scheme."

"Christ," said Reilly, "I've never even heard of this stuff. Is this what they have to contend with in cyber crime?"

"Every day," said Pearson.

Rawson continued. "The secret-shopper mule usually falls prey to a secret-shopper scam, which is similar to the WFH scheme. It's an employment-based scheme designed to lure victims with offers to earn extra money for shopping at certain stores, or having the opportunity to keep the goods that are purchased in exchange for 'evaluating' the customer service, among other things, while visiting the store.

"Like the WFH scheme, these scam advertisements and websites are designed to look legitimate and blend in with other genuine secret-shopper programs. Likewise, recruitment is performed in a similar fashion using spam email and employment site advertisements.

"The scams often include evaluating a money-service business such as Western Union or MoneyGram. Shoppers will receive a counterfeit cheque that may be worth several thousand pounds. They will be instructed to cash the cheque and use their local Western Union or MoneyGram to send proceeds to a designated third-party account. The shoppers are told to keep a certain amount for themselves and email the fraudster their rating of the service.

"The Better Business Bureau issued a warning of one such scam business called Pinecone Research. This is an example of how fraudsters use legitimate-looking businesses to trick victims, since Pinecone Research Panel is an actual company.

"James targeted a number of people with the secret shopper scam including many abroad. One such victim was a British Army veteran called Gerry Russell, who found securing full-time employment difficult after he'd completed his military career. Whilst using the internet, he saw an advertisement for a mystery-shopper evaluation job and applied.

"Russell's assignments were easy. He would receive cheques via bogus parcel companies and deposit them into his personal account. He was instructed to purchase prepaid cards with the funds from Green Dot, a provider for prepaid Visa or debit MasterCard cards. Once Russell had the Green Dot cards, he would call his manager and provide the card numbers and the amount. After the second 'assignment,' his bank withdrew £3,000 to cover the cost of the counterfeit deposits. Russell reported the incident to his local police station, but there was little that could be done.

"Henshaw made a serious amount of money using the scam. He was also clever enough to cover his tracks, and because his machine ran through a number of servers it was almost impossible to detect."

"This reads like a Grisham novel," said Gardener.

"Doesn't it?" said Pearson. "Wait till you hear about Palmer."

Gardener glanced at the clock on the wall. "What did he do?"

"He ran the lottery and inheritance scam. Palmer would inform his victims that they have won a lottery or a sweepstake, or are set to receive an inheritance from an unknown deceased relative. He would initiate the scam through a number of ways, such as email, telephone, letters, faxes and social media. Once victims responded to his communications, he then required proof of identity to facilitate the payment transfer.

"In reality, he was gathering information to potentially steal the victim's identity. The next thing he did was mention legal issues, taxes, insurance, probate fees or delivery costs. Such a scam was a form of the advanced fee scams, though the difference was that Palmer used the victims as unsuspecting money mules.

"One of the ways he did it was to offer to assist potential money mules with paying the fees mentioned above. He informed the victims that the payments were coming from legitimate clients. What they actually did was come from other victims' accounts. He then wired funds into the mule's account; on rare occasions, he used stolen or counterfeit cheques. Once the mule had received the funds, Palmer instructed them to keep a portion and send the rest to another account, effectively turning his victim into a money mule.

"A recent article in The Yorkshire Press reported of an elderly couple in Wellington Hill in Leeds. They were informed that they had won an international sweepstakes. Anthony requested fees in advance, and the couple agreed. Soon after, more and more sweepstakes mailers came in, and the couple kept engaging Palmer, believing they were winning.

"Once the old couple was deep in debt, Palmer offered to hire them as representatives for the bogus sweepstakes company he had created. Large sums of cash began to arrive at their home, where they would repackage them and mail them out. They would receive commissions for their work as their payment. Sadly, they were the couple that had lived next door to his parents, which proved Palmer's incapacity to feel or become emotionally involved, despite knowing you."

"Has anyone spoken to these people?"

"No," said Anderson, "but Frank and I will pay them a visit tomorrow."

Longstaff added a little more. "In another case, a forty-five-year-old man living in Middlesbrough, Barry Cooper, is facing money-laundering and theft charges after he allegedly fell prey to Palmer's Jamaican lottery scam. After he lost all his money, Palmer offered him a deal. The man could work as a mule for the cyber criminals, and they would help him recover his money. The victim was so desperate that he agreed, thus moving from victim to perpetrator."

"It never ends, does it? Someone needs to ring the Middlesbrough police in the morning, see what they can tell us about that," said Gardener. "How the hell did they work all this out?"

"The things is, Stewart," said Briggs, "none of this tells us who is responsible for what's happening now."

"I agree, sir, but if we can trace something in their past, it might give us a clue to where they could be now, particularly if we're trying to find a needle in a haystack like an industrial unit from where they operate."

Briggs nodded but he didn't seem convinced.

"So how did they go from this relatively small-time stuff to the big one with David Hunter's bank?" asked Gardener.

"They've been involved in everything," said Gates. "Stolen cards, fraudsters shop-to-drop. Spy software. At one point they were offering an online service of bank robbers for hire; thieves replacing money mules with prepaid cards. A couple of years back the FBI were investigating theft of $139,000 from Pittsford, New York."

"What, and they were involved?" Reilly asked.

"Seems so," said Pearson, "but the big one was when someone was sold a lemon in Internet Banking. We finally discovered this was the precursor to the bank scam involving David Hunter."

"What happened?" Gardener asked, taking a seat.

"Be quicker if I just read this out," said Pearson. "I haven't had time to study it all. An online bank robbery in which computer crooks stole £50,000 from a Glasgow car dealership illustrated the deftness with which cyber thieves were flouting the meagre security measures protecting commercial accounts at many banks. But it was small fry compared to what James really had in mind.

"At 7:45 a.m. Monday, 1st November last year, the controller for Auditech, a Glasgow-based Audi dealer, logged into his account at RBS, Glasgow, to check the company's accounts. Seven hours later, he logged back in and submitted a payroll batch for company employees totalling £40,000. The bank's authentication system sent him an email to confirm the batch details, and the controller approved it.

"The controller didn't know it at the time, but DPA had already compromised his Microsoft Windows PC with a copy of the Octopus Trojan, which allowed James to monitor the controller's computer and log in to the company's bank account using his machine. Less than an hour after the bookkeeper approved the payroll batch, bank records show, DPA logged in to Auditech's account from the same internet address normally used by the dealership, using the controller's correct username and password.

"The attackers cased the joint a bit – checking the transaction history, account summary and balance – and then logged out. They waited until 1:04 p.m. the next day to begin creating their own £50,000 payroll batch, by adding four new 'employees' to the company's books. The employees added were in fact money mules recruited through work-at-home job scams to help crooks launder stolen funds.

"Auditech's controller never received the confirmation email sent by the bank to verify the second payroll batch initiated by the fraudsters, because the crooks also had control over the controller's email account."

"Is that everything?" asked Gardener.

"I wish," said Gates, "you can see the size of this file."

Gardener glanced at Briggs. "I agree with the DCI, it is very interesting, and I appreciate everything you've done in bringing this to the incident room, but we're no nearer to finding out who is killing *them* now."

"There's every possibility we could be even further away than we thought," said Briggs. "Think about how many people they've crossed. All the information we have picked up would require the entire UK's police forces on it full time to make a breakthrough."

Gardener sighed and took a seat. The previous incident room meeting had given them some hope. He didn't feel the same way now.

"Does anyone have any good news?" he asked.

Patrick Edwards raised his hand.

Chapter Forty-six

Patrick swivelled his chair around to his computer station, which was once again connected to the overhead projector. He tapped a few keys and the screen came to life.

"I've got some more good CCTV footage from Butts Court, which concerns our friend, Superintendent Palmer. It's not brilliant because it's relying on street-lighting."

The scene was peaceful enough. A Vauxhall Astra pool car was parked up. Gardener moved in closer, if you peered at it for long enough you could see the two officers on watch. The passenger seat appeared to be reclined and the officer had his hat over his face. The other was reading a book.

Before Edwards said anything, Sergeant David Williams dropped into the room and took a seat. Chances were he'd finished his shift and was interested enough to see what was developing.

On the screen that Edwards was operating, the infamous Green Evoque pulled in behind the Astra, making the driver's side harder to spot because it was lined up with the kerb.

The door opened and the officer stepped out, dressed in full regalia of uniform and peaked cap. He closed the door of the Evoque and straightened his cap and walked towards the Astra, with his head still down. He appeared to be holding his throat.

"Stop it there, Patrick," said Gardener. "Can we enhance that?"

"Not enough to get a good look at him. I've tried."

Gardener still requested it. The software gave them a close up but as Patrick Edwards had said, it was grainy. "Anyone recognise him?"

The officers shook their heads.

"What about the build?" Gardener asked.

"He's not very tall," said Sharp, "if you look closely he's about the same height as the Evoque, which doesn't make him tall."

"He looks a bit chunky," said Reilly.

"So," said Gardener, "are we finally looking at Anthony Palmer?"

"I know who we're not looking at," said Bob Anderson.

Thornton said what Anderson was thinking. "Rosie Henshaw or Zoe Harrison."

"Still doesn't mean one or both are not involved in this," said Briggs. "They might need the man for the heavy work."

"The build suggests it's the same person we saw in the chemical suit," said Rawson.

"I'll second that," said Gardener. "Okay, Patrick, start it up again."

The man in the uniform walked toward the Astra, alerting the two officers to his presence as he tapped on the passenger window of the car. Once the window was opened he leaned in and spoke to the officers.

"He's very confident," said Paul Benson, "look at him, he's leaning into the car so he was obviously close enough to be recognised."

Gardener jumped on it. "Have we spoken to those two? Surely we have a description."

Colin Sharp consulted his notes, reading through what was said. "I'm afraid not. According to what they were saying his cap was very low down on his head and he was wearing a scarf. The lighting behind him made it hard to see his features clearly."

"A scarf?"

"Yes, apparently he complained about how cold it was and the scarf was covering most of his face because he had a cold and he didn't want to breathe all over those two."

"Brilliant," said Briggs. "He really has thought of everything."

As the scene unfolded, the two constables were laughing and smiling with Superintendent Palmer. Finally, the constable leaned back, the car was started, and they pulled off.

The officer waited before opening the tailgate and removing the bundle. He placed it exactly where they had found James Henshaw. As he walked away there was no movement from that bundle. He glanced at the camera and nodded before jumping into the vehicle, turning it round and pulling off, out of picture.

"He knew the CCTV wouldn't identify him," said Gardener.

"Where did the vehicle go from there?" Reilly asked.

"Pretty much the same route as last time," said Edwards, "but interestingly enough, the Evoque *has* pinged a camera today."

"What time?"

"Around twelve thirty."

"Where?"

"The A658, Harrogate Road."

"Going into Harrogate, or coming out?" asked Reilly.

"In."

"Interesting," said Gardener, "the vehicle is on long-term hire to an address in Harrogate that doesn't exist. The chances are that is exactly where our man is – Harrogate."

Gardener turned to Gates and Longstaff. "Did either of you find out where and how the vehicle was paid for?"

"I spoke to Hertz. It was paid upfront, the Evoque is long term, a one-year lease."

"One year?"

"Yes, it was paid BACS from a bank account that is now closed. In fact, it was closed shortly afterwards."

"I accept that," said Gardener. "I know how careful these people are, but is it possible to keep hounding Hertz and see if they can dig a little further, find something that might point us in another direction? Find out which bank it was and then pursue them and see what they can tell you."

"What about the house clearances?" Thornton asked. "He must have used something big for those. Do Hertz have a large white van on hire anywhere in that area?"

"Maybe using the same account?" added Anderson.

That point brought the team to a halt. Gardener realised it was something that had been overlooked so he seized the opportunity. "I want someone on that first thing in the morning. And while I'm thinking about it, Patrick, when you've finished here go to the press office and get them to put out an appeal for that green Evoque. If anyone thinks they have spotted it they are to give us a call."

Gardener quickly changed topics. "What about industrial units, have we gained any ground?"

The response was negative again. They had very obviously been busy with all the online stuff, but now the spa town of Harrogate had come into the equation more than once.

"My gut feeling tells me that we might need to concentrate on units on industrial estates in Harrogate."

Gardener turned and updated the whiteboards. When he'd finished he addressed the team.

"Keep digging into these vehicles. Now we need to concentrate on the industrial units in Harrogate. That place could be the key to everything here."

He glanced at Colin Sharp. "Anything on their personal vehicles?"

"Zoe Harrison's car stood out like a sore thumb. It was a Ferrari Diablo."

"Oh my God," said Bob Anderson, "crime certainly does pay."

Sharp nodded. "CCTV shows it leaving the airport on February 15th, around midday. I fed the information into the system but there haven't been any pings since that day. Anthony Palmer had a 7-series BMW. This is interesting, CCTV shows it being driven away on Sunday of this week, also around midday, which was, of course, the day before he landed back in the country."

"Meaning it was stolen," said Reilly. "Why didn't he report it?"

"Good question," said Rawson, "obviously had plenty to hide and didn't want us lot sniffing around."

"So how did he get home?" asked Gardener.

"Had to be a taxi," said Benson.

"Maybe," said Gardener. "Job for you, Paul. Find the taxi driver or the bus driver that took him home. We know for a fact that he is still at large, so he wasn't abducted and taken to wherever the others are, still making him a possible suspect, or victim. What about Michael Foreman's car?"

"He had an Audi TT. According to the caretaker of his apartment block it was parked there for a few days and then it pretty much disappeared after he moved out."

Gardener bristled. "He never told us that before, did he? Check the system for pings. One of these cars may have been seen somewhere."

"If we go with your gut feeling, boss," said Reilly, "that somewhere could be Harrogate."

Gardener nodded. "Colin, I believe you were also checking the pay-as-you-go phone that Anthony Palmer had in Beckett's Park."

"A bit of news on that. It was bought at the O2 shop in Leeds. Receipt made out to Alec Prince."

"There we go again," said Patrick Edwards. "Same initials. Anthony Palmer, Alfie Price, Alec Prince."

"Can we get any more on that?"

"Afraid not. Pay-as-you-go."

"No cameras in the shop?" asked Rawson. "I find that hard to believe."

"They do have cameras," replied Sharp, "but they don't cover all of the shop, and the only shot he was seen in, he had his back to the camera."

"I know it's a tough question, Colin," said Gardener, "but did he look anything like the man in Butts Court?"

"Sorry, sir, neither one was clear enough. The only thing I will say is similar build."

Gardener updated the boards again.

"Okay, did anyone have any luck with Porton Down?"

"Not yet," said Briggs. "I've put the call in and started the ball rolling but I've no idea how long it takes. A government establishment like that might take ages to come back to us."

"If at all," added Reilly.

"They'll have to come back to us," said Gardener, "even if they don't care to admit anything. A place like that could say everything tallies up even if it doesn't, and then they'll start their own investigation and we'll probably never know."

Gardener ran his hands through his hair and down his face. "I want to thank you all for what you've done here, you've pulled a double shift and filled in lots of blanks. For that you can be pleased with yourselves. But we still have one big question remaining, that we have yet to answer. Who is killing people?"

Chapter Forty-seven

Gardener was sitting in a car. It was late, dark, cold and desolate, and he had no idea where he was.

The engine wasn't running; the lights and the radio were on, but there was no sound emanating from the latter. As he glanced through the windscreen he figured he was in a large car park, or on a piece of wasteland, but there were no buildings nearby. He couldn't see any trees, or any lights, yet he could still see quite clearly.

Glancing at the passenger seat, he noticed he was alone. He wondered where Reilly was. If they were investigating a case, he should be close by.

Within the blink of an eye Gardener was outside of the car. To his left he saw a stretch of river with a narrowboat running along it. The man at the back, steering it, gave him a wave.

Nothing made sense. Since when did you have a river running through a car park?

Gardener's phone rang. He reached into his pocket. Staring at the display he didn't recognise the number but he answered anyway.

"Stewart, it's your mother. What time will you be home?"

Gardener didn't answer.

"Don't be late, I don't want you out on your own when it's dark, there's a lot of strange people around."

"How old do you think I am, Mum?"

The line disconnected, leaving Gardener staring at the device.

When he'd replaced the phone in his pocket the landscape had changed completely. He was now in the middle of an industrial estate, with buildings all around, a chain-link fence, and good lighting. A number of cars drove by on the road on the outside of the fence.

The building he was standing against had an aluminium exterior with a number of windows on the upper level for the offices. In the distance on his right he saw a roller shutter door, and next to that a smaller metal door that was open.

Standing in front of it was Sarah. He'd recognise the shoulder-length blonde hair anywhere. Not to mention the white leather jacket he had bought her for her birthday. She was also wearing jeans.

"Come on, we don't want to be late." She beckoned him over.

"On my way," he shouted. For what, he had no idea.

Sarah disappeared through the door and he followed her. The inside of the building was huge but not well lit. There were so many corridors he thought he was in a maze. He could hear music playing from speakers he couldn't locate. He had no idea what it was. All he knew was how strange it sounded; some lunatic was singing about somewhere in the night, and turning to the right, when something clicks inside of your head. Then there would be trouble ahead.

"Chris?" shouted Sarah. It was distant, so she must be.

Gardener took off down one of the corridors, not knowing where he was going or why.

"Chris?" Sarah shouted again. "Where are you? It's getting late and we're supposed to be meeting your father."

What the hell was she on about, thought Gardener.

He took more corridors, which didn't lead anywhere. Sarah shouted for Chris at least three more times and each one grew successively louder, and scarier. She sounded really worried.

Desperate, Gardener started to run, feeling unsettled. If he didn't find her soon, something bad might happen.

A sudden gunshot and a scream stopped him in his tracks.

"Sarah," he bellowed, moving as fast as he could.

First one corridor, then another. He could hear Sarah's sobs. She sounded panicky. He really needed to find her, especially if a nutter with a gun was in here.

Gardener turned right and found himself in the car park again, but his car wasn't there anymore. Sarah was laid on the ground, holding her stomach.

He ran over, dropped to his knees and cradled her head in his arms. Blood seeped through the gaps in her fingers.

Suddenly the fear in her eyes became all too evident.

Sarah wasn't frightened for herself because she was staring ahead of him, over his shoulder.

Gardener turned and saw a man bearing down, his hand in the air. Something glinted as it came down. It could have been a screwdriver, or a knife, or anything. But he had no idea.

"Stewart, watch out."

Too late. The blade buried itself between his shoulder blades.

Gardener shouted, clutching his shoulder. His elbow slammed into the headboard and he bounced out of bed and onto the floor, knocking over the lamp from the bedside cabinet in the process.

"Shit," said Gardener.

He hadn't had a nightmare for some time.

Chapter Forty-eight

As Wendy Higgins was walking back into the village with Pouch, Alan Braithwaite was heading out toward the main A65 with Spike.

"I was wondering if I'd see you," said Wendy, "you're a little later this morning."

Braithwaite nodded. "Didn't have the best of nights." He glanced down at Spike, who was now sitting with Pouch.

"Oh dear, you're not sickening for something, are you?"

"Might be coming down with something."

"You do look a little tired," replied Wendy. "You want to be careful. How's the new car?" she asked, in an effort to change the subject. She knew how men didn't like to admit a sign of weakness.

"Not driving much for pleasure at the moment," replied Braithwaite.

"Oh dear, it's not faulty, is it? I know what modern cars are like. You pay thousands for them and the garage have them more than you."

"No, nothing like that. Just a bit busy at the moment."

"I thought of you yesterday," said Wendy, realising he didn't want to elaborate. "That awful business with the Hunters and the hit and run. The police are appealing for witnesses. There was an awful incident in Leeds in which a man died. There were some photos, and they're looking for a man who drives a car like yours."

"Oh, really," replied Braithwaite, as if he didn't know what to say.

"Yes, it's all over the newspapers and the TV, quite a nasty business."

Pouch suddenly stood up and strolled into the garden of The Malt public house, sniffing around the benches. Spike joined him.

Wendy Higgins continued. "I was talking to Mary Fellows about it, one of my neighbours. She reckons she's had some inside information."

"From where?" asked Braithwaite.

"She never said, but her husband is quite high up in one of the newspapers, I think. Anyway from what he heard, it was something nasty. They think it's to do with the military."

"Why?"

"I'm not sure, but there was mention of dangerous chemicals involved. She didn't tell me what. I hope it's not catching. Anyway, I'm not going into Leeds until it's all sorted. You've no idea what goes on. Could be terrorists… could be anything."

"I think you might be letting your imagination run away with you, Wendy."

"Well I think he's right. It has all the hallmarks of the military."

"What does?"

"Whatever happened," she replied. "Keeping it all secret, like the army always do. You should know."

Pouch and Spike returned. Wendy Higgins placed the lead around the dog's neck. "Anyway, I'll have to get on."

She bade Braithwaite and Spike goodbye but turned before they had moved ten yards. "You mark my words, when it all comes out you'll see I'm right."

Braithwaite nodded.

"What was it you did in the army?"

Braithwaite hesitated but finally answered. "Medical corp. Anyway, Wendy, must dash."

All the way home, Wendy Higgins thought about that conversation.

Once inside the house, with fresh tea made, she studied the newspapers and whatever Google had to offer about the incident involving Michael Foreman, becoming increasingly concerned.

It really did sound as if someone with military experience had been up to no good. Furthermore, she thought, there *was* mention of chemical warfare. And she simply could not remove the idea of the large green 4x4 from her mind. The newspaper did ask for anyone with any information whatsoever to come forward.

Wendy Higgins was torn in two but she still reached for her phone.

Chapter Forty-nine

Gardener and Reilly met Rosie and her friend, Michelle, inside the hospital corridor that led to the mortuary.

"Thank you for coming, Mrs Henshaw," said Gardener. "Are you sure you're okay with this?"

Rosie was dressed in black: jumper and jeans and an outer coat, as if she was ready for the funeral. She held a handkerchief to her eyes, which were red rimmed.

Gardener figured she couldn't have had much sleep. Neither had he.

"I don't have much choice, do I?"

"I'm really sorry," he replied, "if there was any other way."

Rosie nodded, introducing Michelle. She was also dressed in dark colours, blue instead of black. Gardener was struck by how alike they were. They could have passed for sisters.

He led the way. Reilly walked ahead and opened the doors into the room. Michelle supported Rosie, as if she was going to crumble at any moment, and Gardener wouldn't blame her.

On the inside, the room was spotlessly clean, smelled fresh. A small table and chairs stood to the left, with a vase of flowers. The glass window in front of Rosie revealed a gurney on the other side, with a body underneath a sheet. Rosie stepped up to the glass, sobbing, shaking. She was fragile – nothing like he'd seen the previous evening, or the fiery woman his officers had described.

Death had a way of doing that.

"My sergeant and I feel it best if we show you his right thigh, the one with the birthmark."

"Why?" Rosie asked. "What have they done to him?"

"Let's just say, we don't think it's necessary for you to see all of the body, Mrs Henshaw," said Reilly.

"Why? Isn't he all there?"

"Rosie, love," said Michelle, "I think these gentlemen are trying to save you from too much distress."

The room descended into a short silence. No one knew what to say. Rosie eventually nodded and the assistant appeared at the other side of the glass and lifted the sheet.

Rosie did crumble, falling to her knees. "Oh my God, James, what have they done to you?"

Gardener nodded and the sheet was replaced. Both officers supported Rosie out of the room and across the hall to the cafeteria. The SIO ordered four teas and had them brought to the table. The atmosphere in the café was altogether more pleasant, but it couldn't have been any worse. The tables were clean, the staff friendly, and the light background music helped.

Allowing time to pass, Gardener asked Rosie if she was okay.

She nodded. "Who's doing this?"

"We're giving it everything we've got, Mrs Henshaw, but as yet we haven't found the suspect."

"What did they do to him? James?"

"I'm not sure it's something you need to know, Mrs Henshaw."

"I do." She took a sip of tea. "He was like a skeleton. Looked to me like he'd been starved. Was he?"

She was staring directly at Gardener. He wasn't going to lie. "We believe so."

"Drink your tea, Rosie," said Michelle, "no point upsetting yourself."

The tears rolled down her cheeks. "What am I going to tell the kids?"

"We'll have plenty of time to work on that one," replied Michelle.

Rosie glanced at Gardener. "For what it's worth, I know I'm not Anthony Palmer's biggest fan, but he wouldn't do that to James."

"What makes you say that?" Gardener asked.

"James was closer to Anthony than the other two."

"That's the name of the man who called last night," said Michelle.

"Anthony Palmer called last night?" asked Gardener, the policeman's instinct immediately surfacing.

"At the house?" asked Reilly.

"Yes," said Michelle.

"Did he say where he was?"

"No. The conversation – if you could call it that – lasted less than a minute. He asked if he could speak to Rosie and I told him James had died."

"What time was this?"

"About eight o'clock."

"When you told him what had happened to James, did he say anything?"

"Nothing, the line went dead."

"I'm sorry to ask you this at such a bad time," said Gardener, "but did you hear anything in the background that might give us a clue to his whereabouts?"

"No, not really. I heard voices but I don't think he was in a pub."

Gardener apologised and left the table, withdrawing to the corner of the room. He reached into his jacket, drew out his own phone and made a call to the station. He gave them Rosie's home number, and the exact time and length of the call. He said he wanted it triangulating and he wanted the results in five minutes or heads would roll.

He returned to the table, noticing her complexion had improved a little.

True to form, his phone rang a little after five minutes later. Gardener answered and was given the information he needed.

"Anthony Palmer made the call from somewhere in Headingley," he said to Reilly.

Chapter Fifty

Reilly pulled the pool car to a stop in front of a three-bedroom detached bungalow in Manor Park, Burley in Wharfedale, home to Anthony Palmer. The pair of them jumped out and approached the front door. Though he felt foolish, Gardener still rang the bell.

There was no answer, as expected.

"Didn't actually think he'd be home, did we?" asked Reilly.

Gardener shook his head. "He's not likely to be, Sean. This is the last place he'll be if he's responsible for the deaths of the others."

Reilly glanced around the property, through the windows, and then turned back to his partner. "Rosie Henshaw surprised me when she said that she felt Anthony Palmer wasn't responsible for James' death."

"Yes, I thought it a bit odd," replied Gardener. "Everything we know about him says otherwise. And even if he isn't, he certainly has to bear some responsibility for the death of David and Ann Marie Hunter."

"Judging by how Michael Foreman was disposed of, it has me doubting that Palmer was involved. That HN-3 shit won't be easy to get hold of."

"You're probably right," replied Gardener, "but starving someone is well within his remit."

Gardener glanced around, still unsure where it was all leading. "Do me a favour, Sean, will you have a look around the back?"

Reilly nodded and took off. He was back within minutes. "Nothing there. Christ, you want to see the size of this place. There's two really big rooms, not sure what one is but the other looks like a swimming pool."

Gardener rolled his eyes. "Like you said yesterday, Sean, we're in the wrong job." He checked his watch. "Right, there's nothing doing here, why don't we drive through the village and stop off at the Hunters' place, see what we can pick up there?"

The journey took all of five minutes. Pulling up in the drive, the Hunters' residence appeared to be equally as nice as Palmer's bungalow, though not as big. One main difference between the two properties was that Highway Cottage had a sold sign bolted to the outside wall.

Gardener glanced back down the drive but he couldn't see one on the main road leading to the property.

"Will you do the honours again, Sean?"

As Reilly walked around the back, Gardener glanced through the windows. The furniture was still in the same place as when he and Reilly had visited Roger Hunter some time back. He knew the funerals had taken place and he had not seen or spoken to Roger since, but the sold sign suggested he might still be around somewhere.

As Gardener turned, he noticed the neighbour in her garden opposite. She smiled and said morning and he racked his memory banks for a name, which slipped into his brain at the very last second.

"Morning, Mrs Poskitt," he said, strolling over and showing his warrant card, not because he wanted to question her, but more a reassurance that he was not a burglar. "We're looking for Roger Hunter, you haven't seen him around, have you?"

She was an elderly woman with grey hair tied up in a bun, which elongated her thin face. She was dressed in garden denims that bore green and brown stains, and a quilted bodywarmer, and Wellington boots. "I can't say I have, not for some time."

"When you say some time, how long are we talking?"

Poskitt placed her tools on the ground and thought about that question. Eventually, she replied. "Maybe five or six weeks now."

"As long as that?"

"Well, not to talk to. I have seen him popping in and out."

"How does he seem?" Gardener asked.

"Busy," replied Poskitt. "He doesn't stay too long. But then I can't say I blame him. This place must hold some awful memories for him."

"Okay," said Gardener, nodding and tipping his hat. "Thank you for your time."

As he turned, she spoke again. "Mind you, I do find it very odd."

Gardener glanced at her. "Sorry."

"I didn't see a for sale sign."

Gardener glanced back at the house. "When did the sold sign go up?"

"Can't have been much more than a week. I went out to the shops one morning and when I returned, it was up. But I never saw a for sale sign. They always put a for sale sign up before a sold sign, don't they? Which is why I think it's odd."

Gardener thanked her and strolled back to the property as Reilly came around to the front.

"No one home, boss. Everything looks like it did last time."

Gardener nodded, studying the sold sign. Although it was bolted to the wall it was dark brown at the bottom, suggesting it *had* been in a garden at some point. He stared down the drive to the road. It was always possible, he thought. But as the neighbour had pointed out, she had not seen a for sale sign, indicating she didn't know it was on the market, so why would anyone else?

He reached for his phone and dialled the number on the board, which, strangely enough, was a Harrogate estate agent.

"What's going through your mind?" Reilly asked.

The line was busy so Gardener hung up and told Reilly about the conversation with Poskitt. He rang the number again, which was answered on the second ring. He asked to speak to the manager.

An older sounding lady said she *was* the manager – Ms Reynolds. Gardener introduced himself and asked about Highway Cottage.

After a few minutes, and a tapping of keys, she asked. "In Burley, you say?"

"Yes," replied Gardener.

"I'm afraid we have no property of that name on our books. Or even one for sale in Burley at the moment. It's definitely our board, is it?"

"Yes," replied Gardener, "I'm looking at it now."

"I'm really sorry, officer, but I don't know what to say. It definitely is not one of ours."

"Do many people steal these boards?" Gardener asked.

"Not often, but it does happen. Funnily enough, we did have one stolen last week."

"Where from?" asked Gardener.

"Here in Harrogate," replied Reynolds, "about a street away from the office. We asked our man to go and take it down and put it up somewhere else. When he returned he said it wasn't there." She laughed, which sounded more like a horse whinnying to Gardener. "Anyway, it's not as if they cost much."

Gardener thanked Reynolds for her time and then relayed that conversation to Reilly.

"Might not be this one," said Reilly.

"True, but it's odd."

"Okay," said Reilly, "but it still doesn't prove anything." He turned and pointed to Sheila Poskitt. "She didn't see anyone putting the sign up so we still have nothing to go on."

Gardener agreed and called the station to find out if Briggs had any information from Porton Down. Williams took the call and said that he had not put anyone through as yet.

"But I do have a message for you," said Williams. "Where are you?"

"Burley," replied Gardener.

"Perfect," said Williams. He then relayed the call from Wendy Higgins and gave Gardener all the details and asked him to call round to see Alan Braithwaite.

Chapter Fifty-one

Anthony Palmer's head was a shed.

Unexpected news and a completely sleepless night can do that to you. He was sitting in an Internet Café in Headingley, on his fourth coffee since five o'clock that morning, having caught the owner unawares, who had claimed he didn't open till six but took pity on Anthony and served him coffee, then eventually breakfast. Anthony had then taken a bus into Leeds and strolled around till he found a different Internet Café to the one he'd visited the previous day.

There was something to be said for being completely oblivious to your circumstances and hoping things will turn out right. With his predicament however, the chances of that would be impossible.

Michael's death had shocked him. James' demise had devastated him. Following a conversation the previous evening with an unknown female, Anthony had left the café in search of a pub, downing plenty of alcohol when he'd found one that suited. It was nearly empty and had no atmosphere. He started with beer, moved to wine, and finished with a couple of shots.

Back at the guest house, sleep was never going to happen. His head was completely spinning.

It still was.

Who was responsible? Zoe was the obvious choice. She was a machine, incapable of feelings, with such an iron will that she rarely allowed anything to compromise her plans. She had killed David Hunter without a second's thought.

Then she'd finished off Ann Marie with a baseball bat when she'd stumbled upon the accident. What's to say something in her head hadn't cracked and she now wanted everyone else out of the way?

Anthony stared at the screen, itching to log on to the safe cyber address that the DPA had, to see if Zoe had sent anything – though he doubted it. Should Zoe be responsible, she wouldn't want to communicate with him at all. If she wasn't, she might already be dead.

Leaving only him, with no answer as to who it actually was.

The only other possibility would be Rosie, but could she kill her husband? Rosie was hot-headed, short tempered, but not really given to rash behaviour. He could imagine she might want to dispose of three of them – but why James? He was the father of her children. Try explaining that one to them.

It could always be someone else. The DPA team had certainly put enough noses out of joint. The trouble with that last thought was where to start. It could be anyone, from anywhere, from any time.

Anthony bit the bullet and found the site for the safe cyber address and logged in. That wasn't so easy. The login required a number of different passwords and configurations, some of which were random, requiring a search of the old memory bank.

A skinny waitress in a short skirt and black leggings passed by his booth. "Can I get another coffee, please?" asked Anthony.

"Sure thing," she replied, without so much as a glance.

Having passed the first test, he typed in the password for another. Eventually the screen led him to the next page, where he typed in the final information.

His heart skipped a beat when he saw he had a message.

The excitement level rose when he noticed it *was* from Zoe. That meant she wasn't dead – yet.

He opened it to find a lot of text, which was almost certainly unlike her, but the style pretty much confirmed it was. By the time he finished reading what she had to say, he nearly vomited.

Anthony jumped up. Exiting the booth, he collided with the waitress. The coffee went all over the floor and the cup and saucer smashed. Her expression said it all: wide eyes, mouth open, hands round her head.

"Sorry," said Anthony, noticing everyone else staring at them.

"No problem, I'll get you another."

"No, sorry, no time." He passed her a five-pound note and ran out so fast he nearly left a trail of smoke.

Chapter Fifty-two

Fail to prepare, and you prepare to fail. The driver wasn't going to.

He was sitting in one of the offices, staring into the mirror, waiting for what lay ahead.

It was twelve weeks since the Hunters had died. Not died – had been killed in cold blood by a bunch of thieving, murdering, parasitical bastards. It was bad enough that they ran him over but to drag his weakened body over to the electric box, hide him from view and fuck off was completely unforgivable.

The driver had had many sleepless nights since the incident, repeatedly thinking about what they had done. Every time he'd end up thinking, wondering, had David Hunter actually still been alive when they were moving him? Had he known what was happening when one of them dragged him as far away as they could, to cover their mistake? Had he died alone? What were his last thoughts?

The driver felt hollow. When he thought of how he'd passed the last twelve weeks, avenging their deaths, it had all been worth it. He had taken no pleasure in the acts of torture. That was the soldier in him, something he had been trained to do. He simply wanted them to feel a little of what they had dished out.

Each and every one of them had been easy to dispose of. James Henshaw had accepted his death well before the end. Starving someone was quite simple. Watching the realisation and the defeat in their eyes when they knew there was no way out had brought a little satisfaction.

Michael Foreman believed right until the end that he would be forgiven and that the driver really *wouldn't* kill him. His demise had been far quicker than James' – but equally as painful.

As for Zoe Harrison, she wasn't sure what to think. The driver didn't know if she had accepted it or not but he really admired her spirit. Right until the final second, ever the fighter. She simply would not give up. Even now she was trying to set him up, pit him against Anthony Palmer, which he found hilarious.

They thought they had a safe cyber address. A place where no one could spy on them, see what they were saying, and what they were doing. The driver laughed to himself. It wasn't as safe as they had assumed. It mattered not that Palmer had changed his phone, rendering his listening useless. He didn't need it. Those silly bastards were doing his work for him.

Fail to prepare, and you prepare to fail. That's what they had taught him in the military. That's what they were doing now. They thought that together they had the upper hand; that the driver didn't know what they were up to. They were failing to prepare.

He cracked his fingers. He was tired, but the end was near. He'd spent the entire last week rearranging the unit, making it unrecognisable. He would have the upper hand in the end. He knew Anthony Palmer was on his way. He suspected the man would be feeling pretty smug after the information Zoe Harrison had given him.

What a shock he would receive when they finally met.

Staring into the mirror, the driver realised he was about to play his trump card. He'd spent time on his research. He knew exactly what troubled Anthony Palmer, especially when he had seen it all first-hand at the airport.

The driver laughed. Palmer would shit his own body weight when they met.

Chapter Fifty-three

"What are you doing?" asked Brian.

"Watching him," replied Sam.

"Why? What's he up to?"

"I'm not sure."

"Then why are you watching him?"

Sam was sitting on the long wooden seat in front of a unit called Transmech, which was situated on the Industrial Park on Crimbald Cragg Close near Harrogate, opposite one called CDC. Only now, the name had been changed to Blockheads.

"I've been watching him a while now," said Sam. "All those cars sitting outside must have been inside. He's moved them. He's been in and out of the place all week in that white van of his, loading and unloading gear, all sorts of stuff; no idea what he's up to."

Sam offered Brian a sandwich from a large box, containing four roast beef in granary, two yoghurts, two chocolate bars and a couple of packets of snack tubs containing nuts – not to mention a variety of fruit. Brian had no idea where the hell he put it all because he was as thin as a lathe.

Neither of them had what you called a stressful job, or one that overworked them or provided any exercise. They were both draughtsmen, which involved hours sitting at a desk, staring at drawings all day. If Brian so much as sniffed one of the chocolate bars he'd put a stone on.

"Something about him is obviously bothering you."

They'd been friends for fifty years. Born around the same time, grew up on the same street, went to the same school and spent a lot of time together after school and outside of work, taking part in similar sporting interests: darts, snooker, badminton. Only difference was, Brian was married but Sam was a confirmed bachelor. He was also very intelligent, loved puzzles and studied people. He couldn't help it.

"It is, but I can't say what. Maybe he's taken over from them four that were in there before."

"Probably why he's changed the name," said Brian.

"But what kind of a company is Blockheads?"

"If it's anything to do with the uniform it must be some kind of military establishment."

"If it was anything to do with them surely there'd be a lot more people hanging around."

"Well, I don't mean government," said Brian, "maybe it's something to do with an Army & Navy store."

"It's a big place, and why still only one person?" said Sam, glancing at his friend. "And there's something else that bothers me – the same bloke was sat here a few weeks back. Middle of the afternoon, not long after we'd finished dinner."

"What was he doing then?"

"Watching that place. He brought some dinner with him, and a flask, and he was sitting there for about two hours."

"Then what did he do?" asked Brian.

"Don't know. I was sitting at my desk so I was able to watch him for quite some time. I went to make a cup of tea and when I came back he'd gone."

"Well, there you are, then. He's taken over the place."

"So if he was taking over, why sit outside observing for an hour or two?"

"Perhaps checking it out. But if you're that bothered why don't you report the matter?"

"Who do we tell, and what do we tell them?"

"Just a minute." Brian stood up.

"What's up?" asked Sam.

"That green four-wheel drive, just inside the fence."

"What about it?" Sam asked.

Brian adjusted his glasses but he still couldn't see it. "Can you see the number plate from here?"

"Don't be stupid, I can only just see the car."

Brian walked over to the chain-link fence, glanced at the plate and made a mental note, before returning to Sam.

"What was that all about?"

"Before I came out to join you there was a report on the news, from the police, asking to keep an eye out for a dark green Evoque that's been involved in something."

"What?"

"I can't remember now."

"Is that the one?"

Brian felt odd inside, weak. He sat down on the bench. "I think so." He stared at Sam. "And there's another four-wheel drive a bit further back; a white one. All the left-hand side stoved in."

Sam stared back at Brian. "What the hell's going on?"

"I don't know. But now you know who to ring and what to tell them."

Chapter Fifty-four

What a fucking mess, thought Anthony.

Greed. Self-absorption. Vanity. Call it what you like, it all led to the same thing. Failure.

Anthony reminisced about their humble beginnings, when each of them had nothing. Dead end jobs, where you worked all hours and earned very little but had so much fire, so much energy, so much determination to change the world, and everything in it. Make a name for yourself.

Well they certainly did that but for all the wrong reasons. They started with Zoe's money, but instead of going down a straight and narrow path they took the road into darkness, which meant they must all have been bad apples. No surprise they ended up the way they did. Michael and James dead; Zoe possibly – he didn't know, yet. Anthony was on his way to certain death, despite what he had brought with him.

He was sitting on the wooden seat in front of Transmech. He knew the company had been there some years but he didn't know anyone in it.

Anthony stared over at CDC. What used to be CDC. The Lord only knew why the name had been changed to Blockheads but Anthony could guess. That's what they were.

All of their vehicles were outside, which surprised him. The white Overfinch that he hadn't seen since the accident – still damaged. A green Evoque accompanied it, Zoe's Ferrari Diablo, Michael's Audi TT, and his own BMW.

There was also a big white Mercedes van. Anthony knew nothing about that. He'd never seen it before. Whatever the driver – as Zoe had called him, because that's what he apparently called himself – was up to, he had really done his homework.

That thought frightened him even more. What did he have in store for Anthony on the inside?

Would it matter?

Not that Anthony was feeling confident at all but he had digested Zoe's email. She'd told him all about the person who had them, how long he'd had them and what he'd done to James and Michael.

Sitting on the seat, Anthony wondered whether or not he should have called the police. That man had committed murder. Kettle, pot, black came to mind, halting that thought.

Calling the police would have been a bad idea. If he had, they would have been here by now, arresting him for the murder of his uncle and aunt. He would have spent the rest of his life in prison, which might have been easier than going up against the driver, given what he'd heard.

However, self-preservation kicked in, and Anthony decided he would take his chances. If he came out of it alive, he would still be free, possibly penniless, though he suspected he could work on that one. He'd never survive prison. He simply couldn't do it.

Anthony stared into the carrier bag he'd brought with him. On Zoe's instructions, in case everything went tits-up, he'd obtained a can of mace pepper spray. He had a rope and a gag. The other two items had been much harder to come by and had cost him most of the money he had left. He stared at the largest syringe he had ever seen in his life; not that needles bothered him but the one in the bag sent a shiver down his spine; it would certainly fucking bother the driver. Next to that was the empty vial; what it had contained, he had no idea. He didn't ask any questions when he'd bought it.

The syringe was fully loaded.

He was as ready as he ever would be. If he was correct in his assumption as to who the driver was, Anthony was up shit creek without a boat, never mind a fucking paddle.

He grabbed the bag and stood up, staring at the industrial unit, wondering what was ahead, and how the hell it was going to finish.

He could only hope.

Chapter Fifty-five

"Here you go, get that down you." Reilly passed Gardener his tea.

The SIO scrutinised the porcelain cup. "You made this yourself?"

"Well Briggs didn't, and you can tell by the cup it's not that crap out of the machine."

"Well done," replied Gardener. "Didn't realise you were house-trained."

"There's a lot you don't know about me."

"There's a lot I'd rather *not* know," said Gardener.

"You'll miss me when I'm gone."

"Maybe." Gardener laughed. "But not for your tea-making abilities."

The door to the incident room was open and Gardener noticed members of his team flashing by, carrying documents, holding conversations. Something was happening.

Most of his team slipped quietly into the room, pretty dejected if their expressions were anything to go by. He didn't much fancy chairing the incident room meeting because they had very little to go on. God knows they needed a break but when and where it would come from he had no idea.

Most of them poured a cuppa and took a seat, spreading folders around, opening chocolate bars. Before anyone said anything, Sergeant David Williams rushed in, waving a file.

"Sir? Need to speak to you."

"Sounds urgent."

"It might be."

All eyes faced the front and all ears were pinned back.

"Just taken a call from a man called Sam Coulthard. He's a draughtsman, working for a company called Transmech. They have an office on an industrial park in Harrogate."

At the mention of those magical words, everyone stopped eating.

"Go on," said Gardener.

"About six weeks ago, Sam and his colleague, Brian Thatcher, noticed a man in military uniform sitting on a bench outside of Transmech, watching the unit at the opposite side of the road, called CDC."

"What was he doing?" asked Reilly.

"Apparently nothing. He had some dinner with him and a newspaper. Sam Coulthard watched him for quite some time…"

"Alright for some," said Rawson, "when he's supposed to be working."

"Lucky for us he did," continued Williams. "Anyway, he got up to make some tea and when he came back the man was gone. Same bloke was at the unit yesterday, doing exactly the same thing. He is also at the unit today. For the last week he's been in and out of there with a white van, loading and unloading gear."

"What sort of gear?" asked Colin Sharp.

Williams appeared flustered. "I don't know, and will you shut up while I'm trying to get on with it?"

"Get you," said Bob Anderson.

"Yeah," said Thornton, "what's eating her?"

Williams ignored him. "Anyway, apart from the van there are another five or six vehicles in that compound. One is a white Overfinch. The other is a green Evoque. I asked him for the registrations of all the cars."

Williams spread his paperwork around on the desk. "It's definitely them: a Ferrari Diablo, an Audi TT, and a BMW. Registrations all match up and are on the list for the DPA team."

"Have we finally found them?" asked Reilly.

"Looks like it," replied Williams.

"At last," said Gardener. "Address and postcode, please, David."

"Do you want me to arrange some backup, sir?"

"No need, we're all going." Gardener faced his team. "Coffee break over. Grab your coats."

DCI Briggs walked through the door. "Gardener, Reilly, my office now!"

With that he disappeared.

"What's eating him?" Gardener asked Reilly.

"No idea, but it must be catching because Williams is in the same mood."

"What do you want us to do, boss?" asked Rawson.

"Hang fire while we sort this out," replied Gardener.

Chapter Fifty-six

"Sorry about that," said Briggs, "but I needed you in here immediately."

Reilly glanced around, sharply.

"What are *you* looking for?" Briggs asked him.

"The fire."

"Sit down, smart arse, I've got some stuff here that's going to make your hair fall out. Did you find out anything in Burley, by the way? Williams told me he'd given you a lead."

"We know it's not Alan Braithwaite," said Gardener.

"Same car but different registration," added Reilly.

"And he's been really busy for the past two weeks moving his sister into a care home," said Gardener. "She has advanced dementia."

"Sorry to hear that," said Briggs. "Anyway, given what I've just heard, *I* know it's not Alan Braithwaite, either."

"What have *you* heard?" asked Gardener, glancing at the document Briggs had in front of him, which must have been a hundred pages long.

"My friend from Porton Down finally called me back," said Briggs. "I explained what our problem was and he went off to check the stocks of this HN-3 stuff."

"And?" asked Gardener.

"He was pretty bloody cagey when he called back. He wouldn't exactly admit that anything was missing."

"What did I tell you?" said Gardener.

"What did he say?" asked Reilly.

"Just that there was a discrepancy and they needed to check it out further."

"And then arrange their own investigation and that's the last we'll hear of it," added Gardener.

"Not quite," replied Briggs. "He said he didn't know too much about the stuff. He knows how dangerous it is, and what it can do to you."

"So do we," said Reilly.

Briggs continued, "I asked him if I could talk to someone who did know more about it. After all, if it's been used once it might be used again and we need to know what to expect and how to deal with it. He said there was only one man we could speak to, who knew the stuff inside and out, because he had a hand in developing it. But apparently he's been on compassionate leave for three months, since the death of his brother."

"Pardon?" said Gardener, his skin prickling.

"I think you know where I'm going," said Briggs. "It's David Hunter's brother, Roger."

Gardener rolled his eyes. "That figures. He told us he had a position within government," said Gardener.

"Wasn't joking, was he?" added Reilly.

"So where do they think Roger Hunter is now?" asked Gardener.

"They don't know," said Briggs, "because they haven't heard anything from him. Every time they call him the phone goes to voicemail."

"It's all falling into place," said Gardener. "David's brother. Given the type of man he is, he's obviously going to want some kind of revenge and he's not prepared to leave it to us."

"So what type of an animal are we dealing with here?" asked Reilly.

"One who likes to mess around with chemical warfare, and shouldn't be crossed by the sound of it," said Briggs, holding up the thick file. "And that's only the start of it, I have his records here."

"Those are his records?" asked Gardener. "What the hell is he?"

"Pretty bloody dangerous," replied Briggs. He opened the file. "He doesn't take prisoners. What we're dealing with here is Robocop on steroids. Started out as a Marine Commando, 45 CDO RM at Lympstone. He underwent six months Commando training, completing the All Arms Commando Course. When he had passed his fitness and CDO tests he was only awarded the infamous Green Beret.

"He was then posted to the Falklands where he picked up a Distinguished Service Order, and a George Cross, the first British medal to be created for bravery, equal to the

Victoria Cross as the nation's highest award for gallantry, for the night attack on Two Sisters."

Gardener shook his head and ran his hands down his face. "Looks like they've picked the wrong man to mess with here."

"So have we," added Reilly.

Briggs rattled more paper around.

"During 1985 he was stationed to keep the peace in Killean, County Down."

"Bet that was no problem to him," said Reilly.

"In December of the same year, the Provisional IRA launched an assault on the RUC barracks in Ballygawley, County Tyrone. Two RUC officers were killed and the barracks was completely destroyed by the subsequent explosion. Roger Hunter received another campaign medal, to match the one he'd received for serving in the Falklands.

"Then in 1991, The Commando unit was deployed to Northern Iraq on *Operation Haven* at the end of the Gulf War. By that time he'd reached the rank of Corporal, but sustained a serious injury, resulting in a broken ankle. He was pensioned out of the Royal Marines, but not before he received The Distinguished Service Medal."

Briggs glanced at the pair of them. "The list is endless. The man is a war hero."

"With all due respect, sir," said Gardener, "he might be a war hero, and I appreciate his family have been killed but it doesn't give him the right to take the law into his own hands."

"That is impressive, though," said Reilly. "What was it he said to us when we spoke to him? He operated better on his own." Reilly turned to Briggs. "What did he do then?"

"Went to Porton Down and studied a whole load of nasty shit in the chemical warfare department. Since he's been with them he's been decorated twice, and I think he was one of the team responsible for developing this HN-3 crap. I know he's capable of doing what's been done. I mean, to be honest there's probably only him that could wipe this lot out with such precision."

Gardener stood up and told Briggs what Williams had told the team before they were dragged into his office.

"Oh Jesus," said Briggs, "so he has the unit in Harrogate and he's there now?"

"Yes," said Gardener, "and we're on our way."

Gardener turned but his partner had already disappeared. As he shot out the door after him he heard Briggs shouting something about backup and being careful and not to let the Irishman start World War Three.

Chapter Fifty-seven

Covertly scurrying through the compound, dodging in and out of vehicles, Anthony approached the main entrance. He noticed the roller shutter door and the small metal door to the side were both shut, so he had no option but to go through the front door. He didn't think darting around was doing much to conceal him anyway. He figured Roger would be watching his every move.

With little need for a reception area – because they rarely received visitors – the four of them had decided to go basic when designing the unit. No point spending money unless you had to. Three glass panels with a door made up their entrance. Once you were through that door you entered a small lobby, with magnolia painted walls, and a waist-high wooden counter with a false computer monitor and keyboard for effect. A chair stood behind, and four more were positioned around the room, with a door leading into the warehouse.

Anthony glanced behind him. He wasn't happy about what he was going to do. He was completely outclassed but he had little or no choice. He'd never been a violent man. Most of the kids at school had picked on him because of his brains. He couldn't fight back because no one had taught him how, and he lacked the killer instinct.

He checked the carrier bag once more before slowly opening the front door and peering inside. The place was deathly quiet – as it used to be. If he made the faintest of noises he would telegraph where he was. But he would do that anyway because they had a CCTV camera in the corner of the room, and another above the door into the unit.

As Anthony took another step forward he heard a strange sound, one that stopped him dead in his tracks, and brought a halt to his breathing. He wondered if that lunatic was crouched behind the counter, waiting.

The high-pitched moan came again, and someone breathed in. It didn't sound like Roger, but then it wouldn't. He'd give nothing away.

Anthony dropped to his knees and carefully opened the bag, removing the syringe, and the pepper spray. See how he liked that combination. He crawled over to one of the chairs and placed the bag with the rope and the gag on the floor underneath it. If he completed his mission he could come back for those, and completely disable King Kong.

Who the fuck was he kidding?

Someone suddenly called out his name and Anthony nearly shit his pants. He actually ducked and tried to become part of the floor before rolling over to see who it was.

There was no one there.

The sound came again.

"Zoe?" said Anthony.

As difficult as the one-word sentence was, she replied, "Yes."

Anthony sat up, stood up, and dashed around the side of the desk. What he saw freaked him out.

Zoe was laid on the floor beside the chair. Her hair was limp and her complexion pale. Zoe's eyes were bigger than they should have been, as was her neck. She was taking quick, shallow breaths. She appeared dehydrated and Anthony would swear she had lost weight.

"Zoe? What the hell has he done to you?"

"Doesn't matter," she croaked.

Despite everything that had happened and no matter how wrong they had been, or what Zoe had done on the night of the hit and run, it nearly broke Anthony's heart to see her now.

He reached down and cradled her head in his arms, as if she was a newborn child. She may as well have been because Anthony realised how incredibly frail she was. He suspected she didn't have long.

"Please, tell me, what's he done?"

She took her time in answering. "I think he might have got the better of us at last."

Zoe then smiled. "I'm so sorry," she said.

"What for?"

"Everything. If it wasn't for me, we wouldn't be in this mess."

"It doesn't matter now," said Anthony.

"It was me…" Zoe stopped speaking and suddenly started coughing.

Anthony tried harder to comfort her, pulling her a little closer, as if by tightening his grip he would somehow stop the coughing.

Eventually she did. "It was me… who wiped you out. He made me."

"I realise that. No one else would have been clever enough."

"I didn't want to."

"It doesn't matter." Anthony was on the verge of tears himself. Michael and James had gone. Zoe was close, and within the next few minutes, Anthony was sure to be facing certain death.

"Did you bring everything I asked?"

"Yes."

"Good. He's frightened stiff of syringes." Zoe paused, drawing breath, calming down. "You probably won't have to use it. I'm sure he'll cave in at the sight of it."

"I'll use the bastard anyway."

Zoe smiled again. "That's the spirit. Go get him, tiger."

Anthony would rather not. "What about you?"

She took her time in replying. "Don't worry about me."

"You need an ambulance, Zoe."

"No. No time. Finish him off… and then me and you can start again. We'll show the world that no one messes with DPA."

Tears rolled down Anthony's face. Whatever wrong they had done, didn't seem to matter. With DPA it was all for one and one for all – the four musketeers. Hurt one, you hurt them all.

Zoe's eyes widened and she drew in a breath.

"What's wrong? Are you in pain?" Anthony carefully laid her on the floor and pulled out his phone.

Zoe waved her hand. "Told you. No time. Go now. Sort him out. Then you can sort me out."

She smiled again and Anthony felt a wave of revulsion for Roger Hunter, despite the fact that he had been the victim from the beginning.

He held Zoe's face in his hands.

"You're right, girl. You and me against the world."

Chapter Fifty-eight

Reilly brought the pool car to a halt inside the gates, parking up behind the other vehicles.

Gardener jumped out and studied them. He glanced at the white Overfinch and strolled over, staring into the interior from the smashed passenger door window. There were fragments of glass across the seats, the dashboard, and the carpet, all of which were covered in white dust from the airbags. A baseball bat laid on the back seat.

"What's happening?" said Reilly.

"This is obviously the vehicle that killed David Hunter. No wonder it was never seen again."

Gardener glanced at the industrial unit when he heard footsteps behind him. Two men in their early sixties approached. One was tall and thin with grey hair and glasses; the other short, fat and bald, but no glasses.

"Are you the police?" asked the thin man.

"Yes," replied Gardener.

"It was me that called you," he said, offering his hand. Gardener saw no reason not to shake it. "Sam Coulthard. I called you about this place. This is my mate, Brian. We work over the road at Transmech."

"Thank you," said Gardener, "but it's probably a good idea if you two observe from the other side of the gate."

"Oh we're not stopping," said Brian, smiling, "crime scene and all that. We've just come to tell you we saw another bloke walking into the place a few minutes back."

"Did you recognise him?" asked Reilly.

"Yes. He used to work here but I don't know his name."

Gardener figured that it must have been Anthony Palmer. "Well thank you for letting us know. We'll take it from here."

Gardener turned and walked toward the unit, giving neither of them a chance to elaborate. As he reached the glass-fronted office he heard more cars pulling into the compound.

The rest of his team had arrived. One parked up near the pool car, and the other two blocked the gate. Everyone alighted and trotted over.

"What do you know?" said Rawson.

"Nothing… yet," said Reilly.

"We were about to have a look round when those two came to let us know what's been happening."

"Has something?" asked Colin Sharp.

"Yes," said Gardener, "apparently Anthony Palmer is here. Or so we believe."

"What, here? In this building?" asked Longstaff.

"We think it's him," said Reilly.

Rawson glanced around, peering at the upstairs windows.

As Gardener studied the side of the building he noticed the small metal door next to the large roller shutter door was ajar.

"Right," said Gardener. "I have no idea what's happening in there, if anything is. We need to split up and cover the building equally, blocking any and all exits. Colin and Dave, I'd like you two round the back, see if you can find a way in.

"Bob and Frank, can you two cover that side door and make sure no one leaves? Paul, Patrick, Sarah and Julie, can you come with us through the front entrance?"

"Have Ant and Dec said anything else about the place?" asked Frank Thornton. "Have they seen anyone else?"

"No. They said they'd seen someone walk in but that's all," said Gardener.

"So no one's seen Roger?" asked Bob Anderson.

"They wouldn't know Roger," said Reilly.

"What I'm getting at is this: is Roger armed?"

That silenced everyone. It was something Gardener hadn't really considered.

"I know he's military but I don't think he thinks he needs anything to see this lot off," said Reilly. "They're no match for him and he's proved it."

"Fair point," said Sharp, "but we have no idea what kind of finale he's planning, have we?"

"No," said Gardener, "and we're not going to find out standing here. I'm with Sean, I don't think he's armed so on my head be it."

"Might not be your fucking head that comes off," said Rawson, laughing, nervously.

"If it is we'll bury it with honours," said Reilly.

"You're all heart," said Gardener, "let's get moving."

Each of the men set about their tasks. Gardener and Reilly turned and walked toward the offices with Paul Benson, Patrick Edwards, Julie Longstaff and Sarah Gates.

"What if he's in there, sir?" said Patrick.

"He'll definitely be in there, son," said Reilly, "it's just a case of where."

"That's not what I meant. What if he's in the offices?"

By the time it had been said, Gardener was pulling open the door, peering inside. He saw an office, a computer, chairs, and CCTV cameras. The only other thing of note was a carrier bag abandoned under one of the chairs, which he figured was alien to the scene.

"All clear," said Gardener.

Everyone trooped inside. Gardener studied the room, noticed a pair of feet behind the counter. He motioned to Reilly to approach with caution.

Reilly pointed to the others to remain where they were, whilst he crept around the side of the counter.

He bent down, standing back up within seconds. "Too late," he said.

Gardener walked forward. "Who is it?"

"Zoe Harrison, but she's not looking her best."

Gardener reached Reilly and bent down. The Lord only knew what Roger Hunter had done to her but the end would not have been pleasant, especially considering how he'd treated James Henshaw and Michael Foreman.

"What do you think?" he asked Reilly.

"No idea, boss. Something nasty – looking at her."

Gardener stood up and faced the only door in the room that would take them into the unknown.

"Well, he's not in here, is he?"

"So he must be in there." Reilly nodded to the door.

Gardener glanced at the others. "Can you stay here, make sure no one comes through the door and tries to leave."

"Unless it's us," added Reilly with a smile.

Chapter Fifty-nine

Once through the door, Anthony received the first of two shocks. One was the fact that it was pitch black, and his eyes were completely unaccustomed to it. He immediately turned tail, reaching for the door handle. When he found it and tried to turn it, nothing happened. The door wouldn't open to allow him back into the reception area.

How the fuck had he done that? thought Anthony.

Sheer panic rose within him and he tried again but nothing gave. With a deep sigh and a resignation, he turned to face whatever unknown horrors Roger had in store for him.

Then the lights came on.

He blinked furiously, holding on tightly to the mace and the syringe. They held very little comfort for him anyway but if he lost *them* he'd probably lose his mind.

As his eyes adjusted he found himself in a corridor, constructed of wooden boards. Around two feet in width, it stretched about ten feet in front of him. He glanced upwards and immediately recognised the roof of the warehouse, with its criss-cross steel beams and large domed lights. Although he considered it, the walls were too smooth and too high to climb so he had no choice but to move forward.

He was grateful that the building beyond the reception was deathly quiet. Yes, it meant he had to be careful about making any noise and telegraphing his approach but Roger Hunter had built the contraption, so he would know exactly the route Anthony was taking. He twisted his head to make sure. With no choice, Anthony moved forward, seething with anger and resentment, mainly for what had happened to Zoe and the others. *Roger Hunter might well want revenge but did he have to go to such lengths?*

Reaching the end of the corridor, Anthony turned right into another corridor that headed left at the end. He tried to make sense of where he might be in the warehouse but he soon gave that up as a bad idea. The building was bloody massive. Even if he knew now, he probably wouldn't by the time he'd finished the maze. *If he finished it!*

Anthony glanced behind, knowing that it would be nigh on impossible to creep up on him at the moment, unless Roger had followed him through the reception door.

Anthony scurried back to check. All was clear. He returned to his position and headed left. The panelling was still the same so he would have little choice but to go the way of the corridors.

The third corridor however, ended in a T-junction. So now he did have a choice.

Anthony wasn't keen on that. What if he chose the wrong way? He supposed it didn't really matter. He was here at Roger's mercy so there wouldn't really be any right way.

He reached into his pocket, pulling out a coin. Heads he went right. Tails he went left. He placed the pepper spray and the syringe on the floor whilst he flipped. It landed heads up so he picked up his stuff and headed to the right.

At the end of that corridor he came up against a door. Anthony turned tail and slipped back the way he came so he could take the left turn, where he also came across a door at the end, so it mattered not which route he took. He suspected they would also be one-way doors again.

He was really pissed off with Roger's games. *Why the hell didn't he simply come and finish him off like the others? What the fuck was the point of games and puzzles?*

He was about to scream out in frustration but caught a grip of himself – bad idea.

Anthony grabbed the handle and twisted it. He decided that he would hold on to it so that he could return if he needed to.

That didn't work. As soon as Anthony went through the door the lights went out and something brushed his face.

Anthony yelped like an injured dog, dropped the mace and the syringe and let go of the handle. The door slammed shut.

"For fuck's sake," shouted Anthony, all thoughts of not giving away his position having gone, like the lights.

But they came on again quite quickly.

Anthony picked his weapons up, stood up and turned, wishing he hadn't. He was no longer in a corridor of wooden panels but a hall of mirrors.

Then the music started.

Chapter Sixty

Gardener slipped through the door and Reilly followed him. As it shut, Reilly turned and made a grab for the handle.

When it wouldn't open he turned to his partner. "Good idea, that."

"What is?"

"A one-way door. You can come through it but you can't go back."

"Doesn't help us," replied Gardener.

"Roger's not after us. He wants to keep Palmer in here."

Gardener turned and surveyed the corridor; it was long and narrow with smooth wood-panelled walls.

Reilly glanced upwards. "What the hell is that shit playing in the background?"

"No idea," said Gardener, following his partner's gaze, "but for some reason it sounds familiar."

Reilly nodded to continue. "Let's get moving, otherwise we'll be here all night."

Gardener nodded, walking to the end of the corridor before venturing the only way he could, to the right. The end of that corridor led him into turning left. When they reached the end of that one, they had a choice.

Gardener stopped. The music was still bothering him. He definitely had no idea of the song or the band but the familiarity was haunting.

"What now, boss?"

Gardener's phone sprung into life. He pulled it out of his pocket and noticed Dave Rawson's number.

"There's a door at the back, boss and it's open, do you want us to go inside?"

"I think not, Dave. You and Colin stay at the door and make sure no one leaves. We're not sure yet if this place is booby trapped in any way and I don't want either of you risking your lives."

"Sure?" asked Rawson.

"Yes," replied Gardener.

"Will do."

Gardener put the phone back in his pocket. "Right, Sean, time to split up. You take the left and I'll go to the right."

Reilly nodded but before he set off, Gardener spoke to him.

"And, Sean? No heroics. If there's anything you don't like the look of, get on the phone."

Reilly nodded.

Gardener figured he'd be better off talking to the wooden panels. He walked further down the corridor, took a right and came across a door. He wasn't too happy about the situation but he suspected he knew Roger Hunter well enough not to have rigged the place with explosives or anything dangerous. Hunter was on a mission and Gardener and Reilly were not a part of it.

Gardener opened the door and stepped into the cavern of the warehouse. As the door closed it suddenly hit him why the music was familiar.

It was strange and haunting and the lyrics contained something about the night, and turning right. And when something clicked in his head there would be trouble ahead.

Chapter Sixty-one

Liverpool, 1992, the Big Top all over again.

Or it might as well have been.

He was surrounded by mirrors. Tall ones, short ones, wide ones; round mirrors, oval mirrors, square mirrors. Wooden frames, metal frames, gilt edged surrounds. Frames with different colours: black, gold, white, chrome. The whole place was filled with mirrors and it was a fucking mess, like Anthony's mind.

The overhead lights were reflected in each and every one of them. Some of the mirrors were normal and others were fairground attractions. He had seen a dozen different reflections of himself: normal, short, fat and dumpy with little or no head. Stretched out like the Peperami Man. He'd seen himself wide, thin; little legs, long legs. You name it, every variation possible he had seen.

Where the fucking hell had Roger Hunter found all of these? Some were free-standing, others were *in* corridors – some of them actually *formed* corridors instead of the wooden panels. Anthony would be lucky if he ever found his way out of the building.

But he wasn't meant to. That wasn't what Roger had in mind. Zoe, James and Michael were all dead. Logic stated that he would be next and it wasn't because he was the only one left. Anthony had to die whatever the running order.

How to survive was the major problem here. Not only was the hall of mirrors unsettling him, the music was doing little for his state of mind. He had never heard that song on a good day, and doubted he ever would.

He relived the fateful day back in Liverpool when he'd been parted from his mother. On his own it had been unsettling, but he could have coped because he knew she was in there somewhere. He knew she would come to his rescue.

She wouldn't today, though. There was no fucker coming to save him today.

But the awful music had spelled doom and gloom from the first time he'd heard it, and had done ever since.

All he needed now was a clown.

Anthony suddenly slunk to his knees, whimpering. Why had that thought entered his head? A clown was the last thing he needed now. He never, ever wanted to see a clown again for as long as he lived.

"No, no, no…"

Anthony dropped the pepper spray and syringe, covering his face with his hands.

"No, no… please don't do this to me."

Anthony snorted, almost choking with the size of the sobs. *Why was it happening? Why did it keep happening?*

But deep down, he knew the answer to that one.

In short, Anthony was a bastard. He had never cared about anyone but himself. And if the truth be known, neither had any of the DPA team, which was why they made such a good quartet. They were hard and brutal and were able to make split second decisions without emotion when it counted.

Which had done them absolutely no favours in the long run. It certainly hadn't helped three of them. And it was unlikely to benefit him, either.

The music suddenly stopped, spreading the whole place with a deathly silence.

Oh, God, no. Anthony glanced upwards: left, right, his head spinning like a top. He reached down to the floor, grabbing the syringe and the mace.

He wasn't sure which he actually preferred – the silence or the music.

Suddenly, on the other side of the mirror, he heard a movement. It was slight and, if pressed, he would have said it was a footstep.

Anthony stopped breathing, trying desperately to rise to his full height without making a sound. One of his knees clicked, which sounded like a whip cracking. Anthony froze.

He glanced left and right, and up again, hoping to Christ whoever it was had not chosen to come around the other side of the mirror. Maybe they were doing exactly the same as him.

They? Who the hell were they? It could only be Roger Hunter. There was no one else in here. It was him and Roger. So that's who had to be on the other side.

The music started again.

Somewhere in the night
Turning to the right
Something clicks inside of your head
A taste of mystery
Creeping all in
Shadows of the unknown dread

Superstitious feeling
Superstitious feeling

Anthony crouched back down, too terrified to move. He wanted to stay there forever, no matter how bad the situation, no matter how many mirrors, and no matter how many times he had to put up with that dreadful song. If he could stay here without moving, nothing bad would happen.

Not a chance. Whoever was on the other side of the mirror, moved; and the mirror moved slightly.

It was enough for Anthony. He knew he couldn't stay there all night, or even the next five minutes. Because whoever was there, sounded like he was coming round.

Anthony made up his mind. It was now or never. No turning back. Time to grow a pair of bollocks.

He stood up straight, nearly dropping the mace.

"Oh, fuck…"

Regaining a little composure he eased off the top, raising the syringe in his right hand as high as it would go.

> *The flashing of a light*
> *Slashes through the night*
> *Changing colours in the face*
> *You meet a stranger's eyes*
> *Gripping like a vice*
> *Noises shouting out a face*
>
> *Superstitious feeling*
> *Running all around my head*
> *Superstitious feeling*
> *I don't know why but I think that I'd be better off*
> *dead*
> *Oh yeah*

The words were haunting him. There were plenty of flashes of light and changes of colours.

Anthony took a deep breath, preparing himself.

In a split second he ran around the mirror; the lights suddenly dimmed, momentarily obscuring his view.

He raised his left hand and sprayed the mace into his opponent's eyes.

A scream followed, hands gripping a face.

Anthony drove the syringe into Roger's shoulder and pressed the plunger all the way home. He hoped that whatever was in there was enough to kill a dinosaur.

> *There's trouble up ahead*

My mind is flashing red
And evil's just around the bend
You're in a cold embrace
Lost without a trace
It's getting very near the end

Superstitious feeling
Running all around my head
Superstitious feeling
I don't know why I think I'm goin' outta
My head

Anthony was back around the mirror within seconds. That's all it had taken. Seconds. Evil was no longer around the bend. He had seen to that.

As the music came to an end, Anthony listened intently. He could hear nothing from the other side.

Yes. Yes. Yes.

He was so relieved. He had done it. He had survived an encounter with Godzilla.

Elated, Anthony ran back around the mirror to gloat. Job done.

Only it wasn't.

The man bunched up in the foetal position at Anthony's feet was not Roger Hunter.

Chapter Sixty-two

Reilly found Gardener on the floor, hunched up, his hands near his head but not covering it. His senior officer's face was damp; his eyes were closed and slightly inflamed. He had a syringe in his shoulder with the plunger pressed home. His hat was turned upside about eighteen inches away from him, close to a can of pepper spray. He was unconscious.

"Stewart," he called. He didn't receive a reply and he didn't think he would.

"What happened to you, son?" he said quietly, checking for a pulse. It was good. Gardener was still breathing.

Not knowing what was in the syringe, Reilly was very reluctant to move his partner. *Who the hell had put Gardener's life in danger? Roger Hunter?* Reilly doubted it. Though he suspected Roger was responsible for the carnage, he really didn't think he would put an officer's life at risk and, in all honesty, Roger's beef was not with the police.

That left Anthony Palmer. Perhaps he'd decided he had little left to lose and was prepared to go out in a blaze of glory.

Whoever had done it, sitting here trying to figure the matter out wasn't helping either him or Gardener.

He pulled out his mobile and called the station. When the desk sergeant answered, Reilly went straight into the conversation.

"It's DS Reilly. I have a man down."

"Who?"

"The boss man, DI Gardener. We're in pursuit at the industrial units in Harrogate. The St. James Business Park, about three miles out of the town centre on Grimbald Cragg Road. No idea what's wrong but he's unconscious with the biggest syringe I've ever seen sticking out of his shoulder."

"Ambulance on its way."

Reilly broke the connection. The music started again.

"Oh, Jesus," he said to himself, glancing upwards. "If I find out who is responsible for this fucking racket I'm going to stick that syringe up his arse." He glanced at Gardener. "Never mind what he's done to you."

Reilly checked his position. He was alone. He grabbed his phone and called Dave Rawson.

"What's up?" asked Rawson.

"The boss man's down, I need you in here, now."

"Oh, Christ. Colin as well?"

"No, leave him at the door."

Reilly called Bob Anderson next and issued the same instructions: Anderson in, Thornton out.

Reilly checked Gardener's pulse again – still good. God only knew what was in the syringe but if luck was on his side it may only be a sleeping compound.

The question was, what did he do now? Stay with his friend and partner, or go in pursuit of the maniac responsible?

Chapter Sixty-three

Anthony was terrified, and in more trouble than he'd ever been in his life.

He was trapped in a maze of mirrors with literally no way out that he could see, being pursued by a madman, intent on ending everything; and he'd lost the only defence he had – the syringe and the pepper spray. He was being forced to listen to the world's unluckiest song. To top it all, he'd probably killed someone.

Anthony snorted and rubbed the tears from his eyes. He'd turned left and right so many times in an effort to leave he was now dizzy, with no idea where he was. He glanced upwards but the criss-cross beams and the domed lights gave him no indication.

He stood in front of a mirror, glancing at the reflection. What a mess. He was thinner than usual, with his blond hair spiked up in places. His glasses were smudged, and his complexion as rough as sandpaper. The latest fashions that he was normally up to date with had gone. He now wore jeans and trainers with a black T-shirt and a padded jacket.

He glanced upwards once again, wondering where it had all gone wrong.

The music stopped and a voice broke the silence.

"Where's your needle, Anthony?"

Anthony's testicles shrunk, his spine bent, and his stomach swelled. His legs felt hollow but heavy. His bottom lip quivered.

"Turn around, son. Face up to your mistakes."

Anthony did as he was told, slowly. What he saw took him close to fainting, and the brink of madness. He remembered thinking a short while ago – before he'd committed murder, again – that the last thing he wanted to see now was a clown.

"Oh… My… God!"

"Yes, Anthony, you might well need the help of your God to get out of this one."

Roger's laugh almost suited his demonic appearance. Dressed in a one-piece maroon suit, he had one hand on a false extended belly, and the other pointing directly toward the mirror, as if taunting. His face was bizarre: a long crooked nose, hollow eyes like that of a skull, and heavy make-up made him completely unrecognisable. God only knew what he had used to create the sweet, sickly smell.

Anthony backed away immediately, into the mirror, which was pretty solidly embedded into a wooden panel wall about twelve feet square. The rest of the area had more mirrors, and there were a number of entrances. With nowhere to go – it wouldn't matter because Roger would find him anyway – he stood with his back to the mirror and his arms by his sides, his hands pressed so hard against the surface they were white.

Roger moved closer, to within six feet of Anthony. "But before we get to the point of you praying for help, I have a question for you."

Anthony didn't reply.

"Just tell me why, Anthony?"

He found his voice, however faint. "Why, what?"

Roger raised his hand and pointed his finger. "Stop taking liberties. We have very little time, so I want to know why you and your psychotic friends killed my brother and his wife?"

"What are you going to do to me?"

Roger flew at Anthony, driving his fist into the mirror at the side of his nephew's head, smashing the glass. "Answer my question!" he shouted, so loudly and so severely that Anthony moved his head and tried ducking.

Roger caught him and slammed him back against the mirror, holding him by the throat. Once he seemed satisfied, he let go and retreated to the six feet mark.

"Answer my question," he repeated.

Anthony was aware of the silence. The song had not started again.

"We didn't mean to."

Roger nearly climbed the walls again. "Didn't mean to! You've all said you didn't mean to. You must have meant to do something to them. No one sets up a meeting at midnight, armed to the teeth to just talk."

Roger moved in closer. Anthony squirmed, his legs weakening, not to mention his bladder. His mind was a complete jumble of thoughts. *What could he do? What was Roger going to do? Were the police in here; would they come to his rescue?*

"It wasn't me," blurted out Anthony. "I didn't want any part of it."

"That's something else you've all said," continued Roger. "You've all blamed each other. According to your statements you were all driving the car. How is that possible? There's only one driver's seat, you couldn't all fit in it."

"It was Zoe," shouted Anthony, "all Zoe's idea. She was the mastermind."

"Rubbish," said Roger. "Stop blaming the dead when they're not here to defend themselves. No *one* person masterminded this little operation. And even if they did, you were all in the car. You were all responsible. What I want to know is, why?

"After everything they did for you. They looked after you when your parents died. They steered you in the right direction, helped you become the successful businessman that they thought you were. David even set up a meeting for you with his bank."

"Fat lot of good that did," said Anthony.

Roger's expression changed. "What are you trying to say; that because the bank turned you down, made a bad decision – in your opinion – my brother was held responsible and eventually killed?"

Anthony couldn't answer, though he knew it was part of the reason. DPA wanted to hit back at the establishment: the banks, the government, everyone who yielded some sort of power over the small businessman. He never intended to kill anyone. That was an incident beyond his control.

"That was it, wasn't it?" said Roger. "One knock back from the bank started you lot off on a life of crime."

"It wasn't one knock back, we were all knocked back, more than once."

"So what?" shouted Roger, moving to within two feet of Anthony, who slid down the mirror, ending up on his knees, his hands covering his head.

Roger leaned in and whispered into his ear. "How pathetic. Thirty-six years of marriage wiped out by the stroke of a pen. You held a negative decision against my brother when he had nothing to do with it, and you nurtured that grudge for so long that you eventually took *his* life, his wife's, and countless others, I shouldn't wonder."

Anthony was sobbing but somehow found enough bottle to direct his anger back at Roger.

"We were no different to you. How many countless lives have you taken?"

Roger suddenly grabbed Anthony's hair and lifted him up, once again slamming him back against the mirror.

"I was fighting for my country, you moron, protecting scum like you. There was no comparison."

"You weren't fighting for your country when you took the lives of my friends, were you?"

"No, sunshine, I was fighting back." Roger left Anthony and stepped away.

Anthony sniffed and wiped his nose on his sleeve. "What did you do to them?"

Roger's expression was one of confusion. "Why is that important?"

"They were my friends. You've wiped them all out."

Roger's expression grew even darker. "What's wrong with you? Jesus Christ, do you see no wrong in anything you've done? You killed my brother, you've cheated God knows how many people out of God knows how many millions of pounds, you've killed other people along the way, changed your identities, lied to the police. Is there a crime you haven't fucking committed?"

Anthony didn't answer. His head was a bigger mess now than when he'd walked in here. Considering everything Roger had done to the others, what in God's name did he have in store for him?

"What are you going to do to me?"

"He's not going to do anything to you, son," said a voice behind Roger. "That's down to me."

Chapter Sixty-four

Sean Reilly stepped into the battlefield. He was about to speak when he heard the sirens of more police cars and, hopefully, ambulances. As bad as he felt about leaving his partner, he had given Paul Benson and Patrick Edwards strict instructions to stay with him until help arrived, whilst he sorted out the mess inside the building once and for all – his way!

"Where's your partner, Sean?" asked Roger Hunter.

"Someone had the good grace to put a needle into him. Know anything about that, Roger?"

"I don't, but he will," he replied, pointing at Anthony.

Outside, the sirens stopped and doors slammed, and Reilly heard voices in the distance, asking for directions.

"One of you better had," said Reilly, pointing to Anthony Palmer, "I know he hates clowns, but what's with the mirrors?"

Roger glanced at Anthony. "He doesn't like them, either, or the music; absolutely shit-scared of it all. Has been since he was seven years old when he had an unfortunate incident in the hall of mirrors."

Reilly glanced around. "Hence the reason for all this shit. Sounds like you know more about him than you were letting on."

"Know thyne enemy, Reilly. Fail to prepare, and you prepare to fail."

Reilly was suddenly aware of Dave Rawson and Bob Anderson behind him. Four more operational support officers joined them.

"Oh, we've brought the cavalry, I see," said Roger, removing the pointed hat.

"In case it's escaped your attention," said Reilly, "my partner isn't with me. He's unconscious, possibly dying for all I know, so I want to know who stabbed him and what was in the syringe?"

"Like I said, it wasn't me," said Roger. "It was this lunatic here."

Reilly glanced at Anthony and then back at Roger. "But all of this was you," he said, spreading his arms and pointing to all the mirrors.

"Yes," said Roger, "this was my doing. I needed to draw him out, after everything he'd done."

"Killing your brother, you mean? I get that."

"And the others," Roger added.

"Others?"

"Yes, the rest of his team. He's killed them all."

Reilly still wasn't sure about that. He covered the short distance between them like a streak of lightning, grabbing hold of Anthony Palmer, pushing him back against the mirror. "What's in the syringe, sunshine?"

"I don't know," sobbed Anthony.

Reilly pinned him against the wall.

"Steady, Sean," said Anderson.

"Back off, Bob. I want an answer and one way or another he's going to give it to me." Reilly faced Anthony Palmer. "I'll ask you again, what was in the syringe?"

"I've told you, I don't know. It was all Zoe's idea."

"Zoe Harrison?"

"Yes. She contacted me yesterday, told me everything." Palmer stared at Roger Hunter. "Told me he was shit-scared of needles, like I am of clowns. She told me how to deal with him, and how and where to get what I needed. She set me up with a contact. Cost me a fortune."

"My heart bleeds for you. Who was your contact?"

"I don't know."

Reilly was losing his temper. He slammed Palmer back against the mirror, causing a splintering sound.

"My patience is wearing thin with you. If you don't give me information you're going to have a mirror where your face should be for the rest of your days. Where did you meet this contact?"

Anthony tried to cover his head with his hands. His knees buckled slightly. "I'm sorry. I'm sorry. I never saw the guy, never met him. I was told to go to an address in Beeston and collect a parcel in the shed. And I had to leave the money?"

"And you have no idea what was in it?"

"No… sorry."

"Have you completely lost your senses?" shouted Reilly, seething. "You might have killed my partner."

"It wasn't meant for your partner," screamed Anthony. "It was meant for him. That fucking nutter over there has killed everyone. I'm telling you now I did not kill my friends. He did."

Reilly glanced at Roger Hunter.

"He's lying, Reilly. He'll say anything to get out of the mess he's in."

"But he's been out of the country. How could he have killed his colleagues when he wasn't even here?"

"Don't be fooled by his pathetic appearance, the man is a cold-hearted killer. You know how good he is with computers. How do you know he's been out of the country? I'm telling you, he's done them all. He starved James, poisoned Michael, killed Zoe. Now it looks like he's tried to kill Gardener.

"Wake up and smell the coffee, Reilly." Roger backed away. "He set up the whole thing, murdered his colleagues because he wanted to keep everything for himself."

Reilly was going nowhere fast, and all the time his partner was in serious trouble.

"Enough," shouted Reilly. "I've heard enough of this shit and backbiting." He glanced at the operational support officers, and then toward Anthony Palmer.

Reilly removed his warrant card and waved it in Anthony's face. "Anthony Palmer, I'm arresting you for the murder of David and Ann Marie Hunter. You do not have to say anything, but it may harm your defence if you do not mention when questioned, something you later rely on in court. Anything you do say may be given in evidence."

He glanced at the operational support officers. "Take him down the station. He can explain everything when we have a lot more time."

The arrest was made swiftly and cleanly and the four officers dragged Anthony Palmer from the building.

"Well done," said Roger, "you've arrested the right man."

"For the murder of your brother, yes."

"And the others."

"Well that's where I have a problem, Roger, old son."

"Meaning what?"

"We know for a fact what killed Michael Foreman, a pretty lethal dose of nitrogen mustard. Now tell me, where would Anthony Palmer lay his hands on that stuff? We have your records, Roger, we know what you're capable of, where you work, and the fact that you were one of the people who developed HN-3. Need I go on?"

Roger remained silent, as was his right to do so.

"So," said Reilly, "easy way, or hard way?"

"No point doing things the hard way," replied Roger. "I've achieved what I set out to do. I'm just sorry that your partner got in the way. I hope he's okay, Reilly. I really do."

"That makes two of us." Reilly turned to Rawson and Anderson. "Another one for the station, boys."

Epilogue

Reilly arrived at the hospital and was shown to a side room. Gardener was in bed, wired up to a bank of machinery that was recording his every movement. But he was still unconscious.

Reilly sat down with a coffee and a doughnut. "Guess you'd have something to say about this shit I'm eating. But you'll have to let me off this time, I haven't eaten much today."

Reilly realised his partner was in the best place though he couldn't stand to see all the electronic machinery beeping away, but at least it wasn't a constant beep.

He was about to take a bite of the doughnut when a doctor entered the room, carrying a clipboard. He was thin, in his early twenties with short black hair, glasses, and a pock-marked complexion.

"Don't eat too many of those," he said to Reilly, "they're not good for you."

"I'll take my chances," said Reilly, glancing at his partner. "How's the boss man?"

"Stable."

"That's what you lot always say, when you're not saying 'we're doing the best we can.'"

The doctor smiled and wrote something on his clipboard.

"Did you find out what was in the syringe?"

"Yes. Secobarbital."

"That sounds Russian, which means it can't be any good for you."

"It's in a group of drugs we call barbiturates."

"What does it do and how dangerous is it?"

"It slows the activity of your brain and nervous system. Short-term it's used to treat insomnia, or as a sedative before surgery."

"And long term?"

"We don't use it for anything long term. Tell me, how is your friend's health in general?"

"He's about the fittest person we know." Reilly held up the doughnut. "Won't touch these things, or anything related to them."

"Okay. Has he been to see his doctor for anything recently?"

"Not that I know of. The last time he went to the surgery his doctor had retired and *he'd* dropped off the system. They usually have to send for him to see if he's still alive."

The doctor nodded, writing more stuff down. "What's that rash on his face?"

"I'm not entirely sure but I found a can of mace very close to where he was attacked."

Reilly thought he caught a sigh of relief from the doctor. He asked why.

"We thought it might have been an allergic reaction to the barbiturates. That can happen. But the pepper spray would explain things. Has he been subjected to anything else recently?"

Reilly thought about the crime scene with Michael Foreman and the nitrogen mustard. He had no choice but to mention what had happened and that he didn't think his friend had actually been exposed to it.

"That's for us to decide but thank you for telling me, Mr Reilly." The doctor lowered his clipboard, stepped over to the machinery, recording the readings.

He was about to leave the room.

"Just hold your horse there, Doc. Are you not even going to tell me how he is?"

The doctor glanced at Gardener. "He's stable, Mr Reilly."

"You're just full of clichés. Come on, son, give me a gut feeling here. Is he okay; he is going to live, isn't he?"

The doctor smiled and tapped Reilly's shoulder. "We're doing the best we can."

If you enjoyed this book, please let others know by leaving a quick review on Amazon. Also, if you spot anything untoward in the paperback, get in touch. We strive for the best quality and appreciate reader feedback.

editor@thebookfolks.com

www.thebookfolks.com

ALSO AVAILABLE

If you enjoyed **IMPOSTURE**, the sixth book, check out the others in the series:

IMPURITY – book 1
IMPERFECTION – book 2
IMPLANT – book 3
IMPRESSION – book 4
IMPOSITION – book 5
IMPASSIVE – book 7
IMPIOUS – book 8
IMPLICATION – book 9
IMPUNITY – book 10
IMPALED – book 11

All available from Amazon on Kindle and in paperback

Printed in Great Britain
by Amazon

39245162R00152